The Honorable Rogues® Books 1-3

A Historical Regency Romance Collection

COLLETTE CAMERON

Blue Rose Romance®

Sweet-to-Spicy Timeless Romance®

THE HONORABLE ROGUES® BOOKS 1-3
A Historical Regency Romance Collection
Copyright © 2020 Collette Cameron
Artwork by: Teresa Spreckelmeyer
Cover by: Sheri McGathy

A Kiss for a Rogue Copyright © 2014 by Collette Cameron
A Bride for a Rogue Copyright © 2015 by Collette Cameron
A Rogue's Scandalous Wish Copyright © 2016 by Collette Cameron

This book is a work of fiction. Names, characters, places, and incidents are the product of the author's imagination or are used fictitiously. Any resemblance to actual events, locales, or persons, living or dead, is coincidental.

All rights reserved under International and Pan-American Copyright Conventions. By downloading or purchasing a print copy of this book, you have been granted the *non*-exclusive, *non*-transferable right to access and read the text of this book. No part of this text may be reproduced, transmitted, downloaded, decompiled, reverse engineered, or stored in or introduced into any information storage and retrieval system, in any form or by any means, whether electronic or mechanical, now known or hereinafter invented without the express written permission of copyright owner.

Please Note
The reverse engineering, uploading, and/or distributing of this book via the internet or via any other means without the permission of the copyright owner is illegal and punishable by law. Please purchase only authorized electronic editions, and do not participate in or encourage electronic piracy of copyrighted materials. Your support of the author's rights is appreciated.

No part of this book may be reproduced or transmitted in any form or by any electronic or mechanical means, including photocopying, recording or by any information storage and retrieval system, without the written permission of the publisher, except where permitted by law. For permission requests, write to the publisher, addressed "Attention: Permissions Coordinator," at the address below.

Attn: Permissions Coordinator
Blue Rose Romance®
P.O. Box 167, Scappoose, OR 97056

eBook ISBN: 9781954307179
Paperback ISBN: 9781954307186

www.collettecameron.com

The Honorable Rogues®
A Kiss for a Rogue
A Bride for a Rogue
A Rogue's Scandalous Wish
To Capture a Rogue's Heart
The Rogue and the Wallflower
A Rose for a Rogue
'Twas the Rogue Before Christmas

Check out Collette's Other Series
Castle Brides
Heart of a Scot
Seductive Scoundrels
Daughters of Desire (Scandalous Ladies)
Highland Heather Romancing a Scot
The Blue Rose Regency Romances: The Culpepper Misses

Collections
Lords in Love
Heart of a Scot Books 1-3
The Honorable Rogues® Books 1-3
The Honorable Rogues® Books 4-6
Seductive Scoundrels Series Books 1-3
Seductive Scoundrels Series Books 4-6
The Blue Rose Regency Romances- The Culpepper Misses Series 1-2

Contents

A KISS FOR A ROGUE, Book One
A lonely wallflower. A future viscount. A second chance at love.

A BRIDE FOR A ROGUE, Book Two
She can't forget the past. He can't face the future.
Until fate intervenes one night.

A ROGUE'S SCANDALOUS WISH, Book Three
A marriage offered out of obligation…
…an acceptance compelled by desperation.

About the Author

A Kiss for a Rogue

Dedication

For the sweetest lady I know.

Friend, encourager, prayer warrior, and woman of God.

Acknowledgements

A Kiss for a Rogue is my first attempt at a novella, and my first trip down the self-publishing road. I wasn't even sure I could write a novella, but as always, my wonderful Regency critique partners said to go for it. And to the most amazing reader group ever, **Collette's Chéris**, who daily prove what generous, giving, and supportive people readers are.

Bless each and every one of you!

xoxo

Collette

A lady must never forget her manners nor lose her composure.

~A Lady's Guide to Proper Comportment

London, England
Late May, 1818

"This is a monumental mistake."

God's toenails. What were you thinking, Olivia Kingsley, agreeing to Auntie Muriel's addlepated scheme?

Why had she ever agreed to this farce?

Fingering the heavy ruby pendant hanging at the hollow of her neck, Olivia peeked out the window as the conveyance rounded the corner onto Berkeley Square. Good God. Carriage upon carriage, like great shiny beetles, lined the street beside an ostentatious manor. Her heart skipped a long beat, and she ducked out of sight.

Braving another glance from the window's corner, her stomach pitched worse than a ship amid a hurricane. The full moon's milky light, along with the mansion's rows of glowing diamond-shaped panes, illuminated the street. Dignified guests in their evening finery swarmed before the grand entrance and on the granite stairs as they waited their turn to enter Viscount and Viscountess Wimpleton's home.

The manor had acquired a new coat of paint since she had seen it last. She didn't care for the pale lead shade, preferring the previous color, a pleasant, welcoming bronze green. Why anyone living in Town would choose to wrap their home in such a chilly color was beyond her. With its enshrouding fog and perpetually overcast skies, London boasted every shade of gray already.

Three years in the tropics, surrounded by vibrant flowers, pristine powdery beaches, a turquoise sea, and balmy temperatures had rather spoiled her against London's grime and stench. How long before she grew accustomed to the dank again? The gloom? The smell?

Never.

Shivering, Olivia pulled her silk wrap snugger. Though late May, she'd been nigh on to freezing since the ship docked last week.

A few curious guests turned to peer in their carriage's direction. A lady swathed in gold silk and dripping diamonds, spoke into her companion's ear and pointed at the gleaming carriage. Did she suspect someone other than Aunt Muriel sat behind the distinctive Daventry crest?

Trepidation dried Olivia's mouth and tightened her chest. Would many of the *ton* remember her?

Stupid question, that. Of course she would be remembered.

Much like ivy—its vines clinging tenaciously to a tree—or a barnacle cemented to a rock, one couldn't easily be pried from the upper ten thousand's memory. But, more on point, would anyone recall her fascination with Allen Wimpleton?

Inevitably.

Coldness didn't cause the new shudder rippling from her shoulder to her waist.

Yes. Attending the ball was a featherbrained solicitation for disaster. No good could come of it. Flattening against the sky-blue and gold-trimmed velvet squab in the corner of her aunt's coach, Olivia vehemently shook her head.

"I cannot do it. I thought I could, but I positively cannot."

A curl came loose, plopping onto her forehead.

Bother.

The dratted, rebellious nuisance that passed for her hair escaped its confines more often than not. She shoved the annoying tendril beneath a pin, having no doubt the tress would work its way free again before evening's end. Patting the circlet of rubies adorning her hair, she assured herself the band remained secure. The treasure had belonged to Aunt Muriel's mother, a Prussian princess, and no harm must come to it.

Olivia's pulse beat an irregular staccato as she searched for a plausible excuse for refusing to attend the ball after all. She wouldn't lie outright, which ruled out her initial impulse to claim a *megrim*.

"I ... we—" She wiggled her white-gloved fingers at her brother, lounging on the opposite seat. "Were not invited."

Contented as their fat cat, Socrates, after lapping a saucer of fresh cream, Bradford settled his laughing gaze on her. "Yes, we mustn't do anything untoward."

Terribly vulgar, that. Arriving at a *haut ton* function, no invitation in hand. She and Bradford mightn't make it past the vigilant majordomo, and then what were they to do? Scuttle away like unwanted pests? Mortifying and prime tinder for the gossips.

"Whatever will people *think*?" Bradford thrived on upending Society. If permitted, he would dance naked as a robin just to see the reactions. He cocked a cinder-black brow, his gray-blue eyes holding a challenge.

Toad.

Olivia yearned to tell him to stop giving her that loftier look. Instead, she bit her tongue to keep from sticking it out at him like she had as a child. Irrationality warred with reason, until her common sense finally prevailed. "I wouldn't want to impose, is all I meant."

"Nonsense, darling. It's perfectly acceptable for you and Bradford to accompany me." The seat creaked as Aunt Muriel, the Duchess of Daventry, bent forward to scrutinize the crowd. She patted Olivia's knee. "Lady Wimpleton is one of my dearest friends. Why, we had our come-out together, and I'm positive had she known that you and Bradford had recently returned to England, she would have extended an invitation herself."

Olivia pursed her lips.

Not if she knew the volatile way her son and I parted company, she wouldn't have.

A powerful peeress, few risked offending Aunt Muriel, and she knew it well. She could haul a haberdasher or a milkmaid to the ball and everyone would paste artificial smiles on their faces and bid the duo a pleasant welcome. Reversely, if someone earned her scorn, they had best pack up and leave London permanently before doors began slamming in their faces. Her influence rivaled that of the Almack's patronesses.

Bradford shifted, presenting Olivia with his striking profile as he, too, took in the hubbub before the manor. "You will never be at peace—never be able to move on—unless you do this."

That morsel of knowledge hadn't escaped her, which was why she had agreed to the scheme to begin with. Nevertheless, that didn't make seeing Allen Wimpleton again any less nerve-wracking.

"You must go in, Livy," Bradford urged, his countenance now entirely brotherly concern.

She stopped plucking at her mantle and frowned. "Please don't call me that, Brady."

Once, a lifetime ago, Allen had affectionately called her Livy—until she had refused to succumb to his begging and run away to Scotland. Regret momentarily altered her heart rhythm.

Bradford hunched one of his broad shoulders and scratched his eyebrow. "What harm can come of it? We'll only stay as long as you like, and I promise, I shall remain by your side the entire time."

Their aunt's unladylike snort echoed throughout the carriage.

"And the moon only shines in the summer." Her voice dry as desert sand, and skepticism peaking her eyebrows high on her forehead, Aunt Muriel fussed with her gloves. "Nephew, I have never known you to forsake an opportunity to become, er …"

She slid Olivia a guarded glance. "Shall we say, become better acquainted with the ladies? This Season, there are several tempting beauties and a particularly large assortment of amiable young widows eager for a *distraction*."

Did Aunt Muriel truly believe Olivia don't know about Bradford's reputation with females? She was neither blind nor ignorant.

He turned and flashed their aunt one of his dazzling smiles, his deeply tanned face making it all the more brighter. "All pale in comparison to you two lovelies, no doubt."

Olivia made an impolite noise and, shaking her head, aimed her eyes heavenward in disbelief.

Doing it much too brown. Again.

Bradford was too charming by far—one reason the fairer sex were drawn to him like ants to molasses. She'd been just as doe-eyed and vulnerable when it came to Allen.

"Tish tosh, young scamp. Your compliments are wasted on me." Still, Aunt Muriel slanted her head, a pleased smile hovered on her lightly-painted mouth and pleating the corners of her eyes. "Besides, if you attach yourself to your sister, she won't have an opportunity to find herself alone with young Wimpleton."

Olivia managed to keep her jaw from unhinging as she gaped at her aunt. She snapped her slack mouth shut with an audible click. "Shouldn't you be cautioning me *not* to be alone with a gentleman?"

Aunt Muriel chuckled and patted Olivia's knee again. "That rather defeats the purpose in coming tonight then, doesn't it, dear?" Giving a naughty wink, she nudged Olivia. "I do hope Wimpleton kisses you. He's such a handsome young man. Quite the Corinthian too."

A hearty guffaw escaped Bradford, and he slapped his knee. "Aunt Muriel, I refuse to marry until I find a female as colorful as you. Life would never be dull."

"I should say not. Daventry and I had quite the adventurous life. It's in my blood, you know, and yours too, I suspect. Papa rode his stallion right into a church and actually snatched Mama onto his lap moments before she was forced to marry an abusive lecher. The scandal, they say, was utterly delicious." The duchess sniffed, a put-upon expression on her lined face. "Dull indeed. *Hmph.* Never. Why, I may have to be vexed with you the entire evening for even hinting such a preposterous thing."

"Grandpapa abducted Grandmamma? In church, no less?" Bradford dissolved into another round of hearty laughter, something he did often as evidenced by the lines near his eyes.

Unable to utter a single sensible rebuttal, Olivia swung her gaze between them. Her aunt and brother beamed, rather like two naughty imps, not at all abashed at having been caught with their mouth's full of stolen sweetmeats from the kitchen.

She wrinkled her nose and gave a dismissive flick of her wrist. "Bah. You two are completely hopeless where decorum is concerned."

"Don't mistake decorum for stodginess or pomposity, my dear." Her aunt gave a sage nod. "Neither permits a mite of fun and both make one a cantankerous boor."

Bradford snickered again, his hair, slightly too long for London, brushing his collar. "By God, if only there were more women like you."

Olivia itched to box his ears. Did he take nothing seriously?

No. Not since Philomena had died.

Olivia edged near the window once more and worried the flesh of her lower lip. Carriages continued to line up, two or three abreast. Had the entire *beau monde* turned out for the grand affair?

Botheration. Why must the Wimpletons be so well-received?

She caught site of her tense face reflected in the glass, and hastily turned away.

"And, Aunt Muriel, you're absolutely positive that Allen—that is, Mr. Wimpleton—remains unattached?"

Fiddling with her shawl's silk fringes, Olivia attempted a calming breath. No force on heaven or earth could compel her to enter the manor if Allen were betrothed or married to another. Her fragile heart, though finally mended after three years of painful healing, could bear no more anguish or regret.

If he were pledged to another, she would simply take the carriage back to Aunt Muriel's, pack her belongings, and make for Bromham Hall, Bradford's newly inherited country estate. Olivia would make a fine spinster; perhaps even take on the task of housekeeper in order to be of some use to her brother. She would never set foot in Town again.

She dashed her aunt an impatient, sidelong peek. Why didn't Aunt Muriel answer the question?

Head to the side and eyes brimming with compassion, Aunt Muriel regarded her.

"You're certain he's not courting anyone?" Olivia pressed for the truth. "There's no one he has paid marked attention to? You must tell me, mustn't fear for my sensibilities or that I'll make a scene."

She didn't make scenes.

The *A Lady's Guide to Proper Comportment* was most emphatic in that regard.

Only the most vulgar and lowly bred indulge in histrionics or emotional displays.

Aunt Muriel shook her turbaned head firmly. The bold ostrich feather topping the hair covering jolted violently, and her diamond and emerald cushion-shaped earrings swung with the force of her movement. She adjusted her gaudily-colored shawl.

"No. No one. Not from the lack of enthusiastic mamas, and an audacious papa or two, shoving their simpering daughters beneath his nose, I can tell you. Wimpleton's considered a brilliant catch, quite dashing, and a top-sawyer, to boot." She winked wickedly again. "Why, if I were only a score of years younger ..."

"Yes? What *would* you do, Aunt Muriel?" Rubbing his jaw, Bradford grinned.

Olivia flung him a flinty-eyed glare. "Hush. Do not encourage her."

Worse than children, the two of them.

Lips pursed, Aunt Muriel ceased fussing with her skewed pendant and tapped her fingers upon her plump thigh. "I would wager a year's worth of my favorite pastries that fast Rossington chit has set her cap for him, though. Has her feline claws dug in deep, too, I fear."

Displaying envy or jealousy reflects poor breeding; therefore,
a lady must exemplify graciousness at all times.
~*A Lady's Guide to Proper Comportment*

*D*uty.

An heir apparent must marry.

Allen snagged a flute of champagne from a passing servant.

Bloody well wish it were a bottle of Sethwick's whisky.

Part Scots, Viscount Sethwick boasted some of the finest whisky Allen had ever sampled. The champagne bubbles tickling his nose, he took a sip of the too sweet, sparkling wine and, over the crystal brim, canvassed the ballroom.

Which one of the ladies should he toss his handkerchief to and march down the aisle with?

A posturing debutante, beautiful and superficial?

A cynical widow, worldly-wise and free with her favors?

A shy chit past her prime but possessing a fat dowry?

Or perhaps a bluestocking or a suffragist who preferred reading books and carrying on discourses about women's oppression rather than marry? At least with the latter he could have intelligent conversation about something other than the weather and a bonnet's latest accoutrements.

He really didn't give a damn—didn't care a wit who he became leg-shackled to or who the next Viscountess Wimpleton would be. The only woman he'd loved had left England three years ago, and he hadn't heard from Olivia since. His gut contracted and shriveled up.

So much for forgiveness and love's enduring qualities.

Livy's gone and not coming back. You drove her away and now must pick another bride.

Familiar regret-laced pain jabbed Allen's ribs, and he clamped his jaw. He had been an immature arse, and the consequence would haunt him the remainder of his miserable, privileged life. Heaving a hefty breath, he forced his white-knuckled grip to relax before he snapped the flute's stem.

Mother, no doubt, was pleased as Punch at the crush attending his parents' annual ball. If too many more guests made an appearance, the house might burst. Devilishly hot, the ballroom teemed with overly-perfumed, sweaty—and the occasional unwashed—bodies.

God, what he wouldn't give for a more robust spirit than this tepid champagne. The weak beverage did little to bolster his patience or goodwill. At this rate, he would be a bitter curmudgeon by thirty. A drunkard, too. Given the brandy he'd imbibed prior to coming down stairs, he was half-way to bosky already.

After finishing the contents in a single gulp, he lifted the empty glass in acknowledgement of his mother's arched brow as she pointedly dipped her regally coiffed head toward Penelope Rossington.

He might not give a parson's prayer who he wed, but his parents did. She must be above reproach, and if Mother thought Miss Rossington suitable ...

Responsibility.

Allen had an heir to beget.

Miss Rossington was pretty enough, exquisite some might say, and generously curved too. Her physical attributes made her quite beddable. She was also dumb as a mushroom and shallow as a snowflake. He'd had more intelligent conversations with barmaids.

He cocked his head as she gave him a coquettish smile before murmuring something to her constant companions, the dowdy and turnip-shaped Dundercroft sisters. They giggled and turned an unbecoming, mottled shade of puce.

A practiced flirt, Miss Rossington had recently become possessive of him and exhibited an unflattering jealous streak. Still, she would do as well as any other, he supposed, since those behaviors seemed universally present in the *ton's* marriageable females.

Allen released a soft snort. He never used to be so judgmental and jaded.

Exchanging his empty flute for another full one—only his third this evening—he caught his mother's troubled expression. She pulled on Father's arm before lifting onto her toes and fervently whispering in his ear.

Father speared him a contemplative glance, and Allen raised his glass once more.

Cheers. Here's to a bloody miserable future.

His parents couldn't fathom his cynicism since theirs had been a love match.

Frowning, Father murmured something and patted Mother's hand resting atop his forearm.

Casting Allen a glance, equally parts contemplative and maternal, she nodded before smiling a welcome to Bretheridge and Faulkenhurst, two of Allen's university chums.

Steering his attention overhead, Allen contemplated the gold plasterwork ceiling and newly painted panels adorned with dancing nymphs and other mythical creatures. Mother had begun massive redecorating shortly after Olivia Kingsley had left. He'd always suspected she had done so to help erase Olivia's memory.

Bloody impossible, that.

Fully aware Olivia had ripped Allen's heart from his chest and hurled it into the irretrievable depths of the deepest ocean, his parents worried for him. They also fretted for the viscountcy's future if he didn't shake off his doldrums and get on with choosing a wife.

Propriety.

He'd always been the model of decorum.

Tedious, dull, snore-worthy respectability.

Except for a single time when he had rashly shoved aside good sense, Allen had always heeded his parents' and society's expectations. Never again would he indulge such an impulse. His position required he attend these damnable functions, dance with the ladies, and ensure the

Wimpleton name remained untarnished. Bothersome as attending the assemblies was, pretending to enjoy himself proved Herculean, though, he had become quite adept at the subterfuge.

Copious amounts of spirits helped substantially, but drowning self-recriminations in alcohol fell short of noble behavior, or so his Father had admonished on numerous occasions, most recently, this afternoon.

Finally acquiescing to his parents' gentle, yet persistent prodding, Allen had set his attention to acquiring, what would someday be, the next viscountess. Another blasted obligation. Those not borne into the aristocracy didn't know how fortunate they were, especially only sons.

However, once he had made his choice, he needn't feel obligated to attend as many social functions, and when he did appear, he could spend the evening in the card room, or better yet, escape to the study with a few coves and indulge in a dram or two.

Maybe he and his bride would retire to the country, at least until the title became his—not that he wished his father into an early grave or was overly eager to assume the viscountcy. Since seeing the magnificent horseflesh bred at Sethwick's castle, Craiglocky, Allen had considered entering into a cattle breeding venture of his own. Surely that would keep his mind occupied with something other than melancholy musings.

His wife would want for nothing except his affections. Those weren't his to give. A certain tall, fiery-haired goddess possessing sapphire eyes had laid claim to them, and his love would forever be entangled in her silky chestnut hair. But he would be a kind and faithful husband. He quite looked forward to dangling his children upon his knee, truth to tell.

An image of a chubby-cheeked imp with sea-blue eyes and wild cinnamon curls sprang to mind. On second thought, he did have one stipulation for his future wife. She could not have red hair.

Taking a sip of champagne, he rested a shoulder against a pillar.

Miss Rossington glided his way, a coy smile on her rouged lips, and if he wasn't mistaken, a bold invitation in her slanted eyes. Her dampened gown left little to his imagination, and though she wore virginal colors, he would bet the coat on his back, she'd long ago surrendered her maidenhead.

He quirked his mouth. Perhaps, she wouldn't do after all. Though he must wed, he didn't relish cuckoldom.

Barely suppressing an unladylike curse, Olivia gave her aunt the gimlet eye. Did she say a year's worth of pastries? Hound's teeth, then it was a given. Aunt Muriel took her pastries very seriously, as evidenced by her ample figure.

Olivia scowled then immediately smoothed her face into placid lines.

Ladies do not scowl, frown, or grimace.

Or so Mama had always insisted, quoting *A Lady's Guide to Proper Comportment* as regularly as the sun rose and set from the time Olivia was old enough to hold her own spoon.

She hadn't quite decided how to go about competing for Allen's affections, if any chance remained that he still cared for her. Perhaps she should ask Aunt Muriel for advice.

On second thought, that might prove disastrous. Her aunt had already suggested a clandestine kiss. No telling what scandalous, wholly inappropriate notion Aunt Muriel would recommend. Why, Olivia might find herself on the edge of ruin in a blink if she followed her aunt's advice.

Tonight, she would find out precisely where she stood with Allen, whether she dared still hope or should concede defeat and accept her heartbreak. Just what kind of woman was she up against, though? "No doubt this Rossington miss is excessively lovely."

If only Aunt Muriel would say she's homely as a toad with buggy eyes and rough, warty skin. Oh, and Miss Rossington was missing several teeth and had a perpetual case of offensive breath.

"Hmph. If you consider a heavy hand with cosmetics, dampened gowns, and bodices that nearly expose entire bosoms lovely, I suppose she is." Aunt Muriel resumed her preening.

Bradford's mouth crept into a devilish smile. "I quite like dampened gowns—"

"Brady!" Olivia kicked his shin. Sharp pain radiated from her slippered toe to her knee. *Bloody he—*

Proper ladies do not curse, Olivia Antoinette Cleopatra Kingsley! Mama's strident voice admonished in Olivia's mind.

"—and exposed bosoms." Brady risked finishing, nestled in the carriage's corner with his arms crossed and a mouth-splitting, unrepentant grin upon his face.

He enjoyed quizzing her, the incorrigible jackanape.

"Of course you do." Aunt Muriel lifted her graying eyebrows. The twitch of her lips and the humor lacing her voice belied any true censure. "My poor sister would perform one-handed somersaults in her grave if she knew what a rogue you have become, always up to your ears in devilry. Don't know where you got that bend. Your father was as stiff and exciting as a cold poker, and your mother never did anything remotely untoward, always quoting that annoying comportment rubbish."

Another rogue dominated Olivia's thoughts.

What if Allen dismisses or cuts me?

The possibility was quite real.

She had no reason to believe he might yet hold a *tendre* for her, but she most know for certain, no matter how devastating or humiliating. She feared her rehearsed speech would flit away the moment she opened her mouth, leaving her empty-headed and tongue-tied, and although she had attempted to prepare for a harsh rebuff, practicing imaginary responses couldn't truly ready her for his or the *ton's* rejection and scorn.

As the carriage lurched to a rumbling stop, she sent a silent prayer heavenward. No stars, dim from the new gas streetlamps before the mansion and the coal-laden clouds blanketing London shot across the sky for her to wish upon. It had been on a night very much like this that she'd been a young fool and crushed her and Allen's dreams of a future together. However, in her defense, she had only known him for a blissful fortnight before he proposed.

Already completely taken with Allen, she'd become teary-eyed during a waltz and shared her dismay. In a matter of days, her father intended to move the family to the Caribbean for a year. Father hadn't given them any notice or time to prepare, just announced, in his impulsive, eccentric way, that they were off to Barbados to oversee a sugar plantation. She had been full of girlish hopes and dreams, and Father's plans severed them at the root.

What maggot in his brain had possessed him to buy a plantation? He had known nothing of farming or harvesting, preferring fossils and rocks to humans and their usual activities. Even Olivia's Season could be ascribed to a deathbed vow Father had made to Mama; one he had repeatedly attempted to renege on until Bradford had intervened on Olivia's behalf.

She had long suspected Father never intended for her to marry, but to remain at his side as his companion, housekeeper, and nurse until his days ended.

Closing her eyes, she pictured that romantic dance three years ago.

Allen had held her closer than propriety dictated, but not so much as to be ruinous. After whisking her onto the veranda, he'd captured her hand, and they had sped to a garden alcove. Whether he'd planned to ask her, or had been caught up in the moment and spontaneously decided to, she would never know, but he had hurled convention to the wind, dropped to one knee, and after promising to love her for eternity, asked her to share the rest of his life.

She had loved him almost from the first moment she'd seen him standing across the ballroom, sable head thrown back and laughing unrestrained. Her chest welling with emotion, she had tossed aside her mother's constant harping on proper comportment as carelessly as used tea leaves, and said yes, even though Papa wouldn't have approved.

Olivia hadn't cared.

Especially when Allen had smiled, his countenance full of joy, and then had sealed their troth with a scorching kiss. Her nipples pebbled and a jolt of arousal heated her blood as recollection of their potent embrace produced a familiar response. A quick survey of her wrap assured her that her body's reaction remained a secret, and Aunt Muriel and Bradford hadn't a hint of her sensual musings.

That had been the happiest moment of her life, and the cherished memory elicited a tiny, secretive smile.

Then, Allen had revealed his intention to elope to Gretna Green.

That night.

Taken aback at his impetuous suggestion, uncertainty had niggled, its sharp barbs pricking and stirring her misgivings. Mother had died a year ago, and Father suffered from ill-humors. It might have been too much for his frail health if Olivia had eloped. She had thought to have a few weeks, months perhaps, before wedding Allen. Besides, a fortnight wasn't enough time to truly fall in love—not a deep, abiding, eternal love, was it?

More than enough time when your soul finds its other half.

She breathed out a silent, forlorn sigh. Her silly doubts had fueled her fear of making a hasty, impulsive decision. And so, regretfully, she'd said no to hieing off to Scotland, and instead, asked him to wait a year for her to return to England.

"We could write back and forth, truly get to know one another and plan for our future together. A year isn't so very long." She tried to persuade Allen to wait. "Many couples are betrothed for a lengthy period."

Setting her from his embrace, his answer had been an emphatic, "Like hell I shall. I love you and want to marry you now, not in a year, dammit. That's a bloody eternity."

"But, I cannot elope tonight." She touched his arm, trying to reclaim the happiness of a moment before but, shoulders and face stiff, he had turned away from her. "It's too sudden, Allen, and I'm worried what the shock would do to Papa."

Head bowed, his forearm braced against the arbor entrance, and his other hand resting on his narrow hip, Allen had spoken, his voice so raspy and quiet, she had strained to hear him.

"If you really loved me, you wouldn't want to wait to marry. You would be as eager as I am." Dropping his hands to his sides, he faced her, his voice acquiring a steely edge. "It seems I have misjudged your affection for me. Go to the Caribbean. I won't try to dissuade you again."

He had left her standing, crushed and weeping, in the arbor. Wounded at his callousness, after regaining her composure, she had made her way to the veranda where she'd encountered Allen's sister, Ivonne. Claiming to feel unwell, Olivia had asked her to find Father and Bradford and tell them to meet her at the entrance. Betrayal fueling her anger, she hadn't even bid her hosts farewell.

It wasn't until the ship was well out to sea did she realize, she hadn't ever told Allen she loved him. Not a day had passed since sailing that she hadn't lamented not eloping. Wisdom had arrived too late, and she had destroyed her greatest opportunity for love and happiness.

Maybe my only opportunity.

No doubt the torturous road to Hades was paved with a myriad of regrets, for life without him would surely be—*had been*—hell.

A white-gloved footman in hunter green livery opened the door. He set a low stool before the carriage and smiled. "Good evening, Your Grace."

"Good evening, Royce. My nephew will see us alighted." Aunt Muriel waved her hand at another carriage where a large woman teetered within the doorway. "Go help over there before Lady Tipples topples onto the pavers and cracks them." A grin threatened. "Tipples topples. Didn't plan that. Funny though."

"At once, Your Grace." After bowing, Royce dashed to the other conveyance. He and another footman managed to wrangle the squawking woman, swathed in layers of orange ruffles and bows, onto the pavement.

"Wouldn't mind her absence tonight, truth to tell." Jutting her chin toward the commotion, Aunt Muriel slipped her reticule around her wrist. "She always wants to bore me with the latest clap trap or her current revolting ailment. I heard more about gout and constipation last week than a body ever needs to know."

Chuckling, Bradford descended first then turned to hand Aunt Muriel down.

Hands clasped so tightly, her fingers tingled, Olivia remained rooted to her seat, her attention fixed on the entrance.

Allen is in there.

Bradford stuck his head inside the carriage. All signs of his former joviality gone, he regarded her for a long moment, kindness crinkling the corners of his eyes. He chucked her beneath her chin.

"Come along, Kitten. Put on a brave smile, and let's go meet the dragon. I dare say the past three years have been awful for you, always wondering if Wimpleton still cares. Who knows, mayhap tonight is providential. In any event, you'll have an answer, and you can get on with your life."

Bradford had suffered the loss of his first love, and his facade of a carefree, womanizing rake, hid a deeply injured man. If anyone understood her plight, it was he.

"I suppose that's true." Although her existence would be only a shadow of what life might have been with Allen.

Such a pity hindsight, rather than foresight, birthed wisdom.

Bradford extended his hand. "Let's be about it then."

Sighing, and resigned to whatever providence flung her way, Olivia placed her palm in his. "All right."

"That's my brave girl." He gave her fingers a gentle, encouraging squeeze.

Not brave. Wholly terrified. "So help me, Brady, you step more than two feet away from me, and I shall—"

"Never fear, Kitten. I shall forsake my romantic pursuits and act the part of a diligent protector for the entire evening. I but lack my sword to slay your fears."

Despite her rioting nerves, Olivia grinned. "How gallant of you, dear brother, and a monumental sacrifice, at that."

"Indeed. A selfless martyr." Sarcasm puckered Aunt Muriel's face as if she had sucked a lemon. "For certain he's deemed for sainthood now."

"Anything for you, Liv. You know that." He tucked Olivia's hand into the crook of one elbow while offering the other to their aunt before guiding the women up the wide steps. A few guests smiled and nodded in recognition as the trio entered the manor.

Olivia forced her stiff lips upward and reluctantly passed her wrap to the waiting footman. Had he detected her shaking hands? The scarlet silk mantle provided much more than protection from the spring chill; it shrouded her in security. Her stomach fluttered and leaped about worse than frogs on hot pavement, threatening to make her ill.

She ran her hands across her middle to smooth the champagne-colored gauze overlay of her new crimson ball gown Aunt Muriel had insisted on purchasing. The ruby jewelry she wore was her aunt's as well.

Though Bradford, now the newly titled Viscount Kingsley, had inherited a sizable fortune, Olivia had balked at acquiring a new wardrobe. "My gowns are perfectly fine. I'll simply wear a shawl or mantle until I become accustomed to England's clime once more."

Besides, if she didn't reconcile with Allen, she was leaving London, and a wardrobe bursting with the latest frilly fashions was a senseless waste of money as well as useless for country life.

"Chin up and smile, Livy. You look about to cast up your crumpets." Bradford clasped her elbow, as if lending her his strength.

Casting up her accounts was the least of her worries. Swallowing her panic, she offered him a grateful smile as they stood before the butler.

"Her Grace, the Duchess of Daventry, Lord Kingsley, and Miss Kingsley." The majordomo announced them in the same droning monotone he had the previous guests.

Behind Olivia, someone gasped.

Perfect.

A low murmur of hushed voices circled the room in less time than it took to curtsy as the three of them advanced into the ballroom. Perhaps Bradford's rise in status caused the undue interest. After all, he had been third in line to the viscountcy, and if their curmudgeon of an uncle and two cousins hadn't drowned in a boating accident, Brady would have been spared a title he disdained.

Combing the room from beneath her lashes, her stomach lurched.

Every eye was trained upon them. Her. At least it seemed that way from the brief glimpse she had braved.

This is a mistake.

Head lowered and her attention riveted on the polished marble floor, she prayed for strength. Where was the pluck Papa had praised her for, or the feistiness Bradford often teased her about? Or the spirit Allen had so admired?

She could do this. She must if she were ever to discover the truth. Otherwise, not knowing would badger and pester her, preventing her from ever finding the peace she craved.

Had Allen forgotten her? Did he love another now? That Miss Rossington?

There was only one way to find out.

Olivia forced her eyes upward. Inhaling, she squared her shoulders, commanded her lips to tilt pleasantly, and lifted her head.

Her gaze collided squarely with Allen's flabbergasted one.

A lady of gentle-breeding should never appear too eager to engage the attentions or affections of a gentleman.
~*A Lady's Guide to Proper Comportment*

3

What the hell is *she* doing here?

Allen damned near dumped his champagne down Miss Rossington's ample bosom upon hearing Olivia's name announced. Unprepared to see the woman he had once loved more than he had thought humanly possible standing in his home again, her presence had blindsided him.

Utterly lovely, staring at him, her eyes startled and huge, Olivia's beauty clobbered him with the same force as a horse's kick to the gut. Those huge, Scottish beasts Sethwick's sister raised with hooves the size of carriage wheels.

Vises clamped his heart and squeezed his lungs as whooshing echoed in his ears, wave after wave, in accompaniment to his frantic heartbeat. Perspiration broke out across his upper lip and beaded his forehead. He didn't need a looking glass to know he had gone white as new-fallen snow.

For one very real moment, he couldn't suck in an ounce of air and feared he would swoon. Wouldn't that give the quartet of chinwags standing by the potted ficus something to bandy about? Especially Lady Clutterbuck, the worst gossipmonger in Town.

Say, did you see Wimpleton? Keeled over like an ape-drunk sot.

That he had taken to imbibing freely for some time now would lend credence to the tattle.

Tiny blackish specks frolicked before his eyes, and the roaring in his ears became deafening.

Breathe, man.

Jaw rigid, he marshaled his composure and dragged in a painful, inadequate breath, then another. The blood thrumming in his ears lessoned a degree.

One more ragged breath and his vision cleared a mite.

Olivia's presence sent him hurtling back to the evening she had announced her father's intention to move her family to Barbados— *in two bloody days.*

Desperate not to lose her, and willing to endure censure and scandal, Allen had thrown his pride aside and implored her to flee to Scotland with him that very night. His one instance of selfish impulsiveness. Look how well that had turned out.

Now, she hovered, hesitant and anxious, at the ballroom's entrance, and a tidal wave of devastation and hurt crashed down upon him, drowning him in remorse. It took every ounce of self–control to regard her impersonally.

One hand pressed to her throat, Olivia looked positively wan—terrified even.

Hell's teeth. She better have a damned good reason for showing up on her aunt's coattails.

When had the Kingsleys returned to England? Why hadn't anyone told him? Warned him?

Likely because he had been absent from London the previous week, overseeing the delivery of some prime horseflesh to Wyndleyford House, their country estate. He'd only returned to London this morning.

The duchess, stately as any queen, perused the ballroom. Her regard lit on Allen for an extended moment, and she dipped her head, her mouth arcing before her scrutiny gravitated onward.

No blatant snub from her grace. Well, at least that was something.

Allen fought dual impulses. One, to turn on his heel, giving Olivia the cut direct, and the other, to charge across the room, sweep her into his embrace, and beg her forgiveness in front of everyone.

Only she had the ability to make him act recklessly, and the last time he'd done so hadn't gone all that well. No. Much wiser to keep his distance, pretend she hadn't once been his reason for living, and focus on his pursuit of an acceptable bride.

Miss Rossington clawed at his arm, her citrine eyes sparking with jealousy, and her ruby-tinted lips tightly pursed. She looked about to fly into one of her starts.

"Who is she? I don't recall seeing that creature before." She squinted, her tightly furrowed brows forming a vee between her eyes. "Egads, she's a longshanks, isn't she? Probably starves herself to stay that slender. And would you look at her hair? Colored, to be sure, just like a lady of the night."

Her almond-shaped eyes tapering to slits, she tittered with feline satisfaction. Haughtiness turned her striking features into an over-indulged, petulant child's.

What did she know of ladies of the night?

He took a half-step back and took her measure, as if finally seeing her for the first time.

Deuce take it.

Allen cupped the back of his neck where a pair of cannon balls seemed to have taken up residence. Was he addled? He had half-heartedly contemplated courting this hellcat. Large bosoms and a beautiful face didn't compensate for a narrow mind and spiteful shallowness.

"Men prefer a woman with curves, or so I've been told." She rubbed her breasts against his arm, fairly purring. This was no innocent miss, but a woman skilled in using her physical charms. Very experienced, or he missed his mark. "She's a bit long in the tooth, isn't she?"

Allen clamped his jaw, his nostrils flaring, as she hurled yet another insult at a woman she had never met. It said much about her character. ... Or lack, thereof.

His too, that he had slid to such depths, that he would have ever considered tainting the Wimpleton name, his family's heritage and exemplary standing, with a trollop like Penelope Rossington just so he could put the distasteful task of marriage behind him.

That had been before Olivia's unexpected return.

Now the notion of a making a match with Miss Rossington was as welcome as gargling hot coals. Allen contemplated his half-full champagne flute. More fine bubbles floated to the top and popped. Truthfully, a union with anyone except Olivia held as much appeal.

How could he still want her?

His treacherous eyes searched her out again, a brilliant scarlet bloom in a bouquet of pale pinks, creamy ivories, and chaste whites.

How could he not?

"Do you know who the gentleman with her is?" Miss Rossington practically licked her lips as she ogled Kingsley. "He seems far superior in breeding. Perhaps she's a poor relation—"

"He's her brother. Her name is Olivia Kingsley, and she's ..." He paused and looked at Miss Rossington.

She glared at Olivia, jealousy distorting her face.

My God, such a bratling.

"How old are you?" Odd, he'd never wondered at her age before.

Miss Rossington shifted her focus to him and elevated her chin. Her green eyes flashed with confidence, even as a seductress's smile bent her overly-rouged mouth. "Eighteen. Almost nineteen."

The same age as Livy when we met.

He tipped his lips at the edges. The termagant clutching his arm was about to receive a proper set down. "She only boasts three years on you, and I assure you, that *is* her natural hair color."

From the corner of his eye, he covertly scrutinized the crowd. Most of the guests had made a pretense of resuming their activity prior to the announcement of the Kingsleys' and duchess's arrival.

Olivia had drawn the consideration of nearly everyone present. Beauty such as hers commanded recognition, though she would be the first to decry the attention. Modest, she'd never seen the exquisiteness in her looking glass others did when gazing upon her. Maneuvering her way along the perimeter of the crowded ballroom, her brother and aunt, like alert sentinels, guarded her.

Rather, the Duchess of Daventry, much like a schooner, the wind filling its canvases, sailed forth, parting the seas before them. With furled brows and piercing gazes, she and Kinsley cowed the more brazen or insolent guests who dared to stare at Olivia outright.

Though her face held a placid expression, Olivia's stiff posture and the firm set of her shapely mouth revealed she was well-aware of the murmurs behind fans and hands directed her way. Her vibrant coppery hair and ruby jewelry shone beneath the glowing chandeliers, but Allen detected vulnerability in her sooty-lashed eyes.

His heart pinched painfully at her discomfort. Why he should care a whit about her feelings was beyond him, and that he yearned to comfort and protect her rankled him no end. A man should be able to control his deuced, capricious emotions, yet his disloyal heart—what was left of the mangled organ after she had shattered it to hell and back—ached for her.

Nodding at something Kingsley said, the bronze highlights in Olivia's cinnamon hair glinted like dark honey.

Allen had always adored her glorious hair. "The color of her hair is splendid, is it not?"

Miss Rossington released an irritated huff, her talon-like fingers tightening on his forearm. Clearly, she did not agree. "And how would you know about her dull hair? Rusty nails shine brighter. Assuredly that shade is not God-given." Accusation rang in her petulant voice, and his estimation of her dove lower. "Women of her ilk are quite skilled at artifice."

You ought to know.

Taking Miss Rossington's measure, he gave himself a violent mental shake. God spare him title-hungry viragos with the morals of a bitch in heat. She had become much too possessive of late, and her disparaging Olivia was beyond the mark.

Yes. It was far past time to put Penelope Rossington in her place and disabuse her of any notion she was viscountess-worthy, once and for all. If ever a woman was beneath the privilege, it as she.

Feeling far freer than he had in a long while, Allen took a deep breath and notching his chin, he caught site of his mother poised, statue-still, her focus riveted on Olivia.

Her eyes round as tea saucers, Mother's gaze traveled from Olivia, lingered on Miss Rossington for a fraction then drifted back to Olivia once more. She unfurled her fan, and Allen swore he saw her grin—a face-splitting show of white teeth—before she began frenetically waving the fan and bustled toward Father, shoving guests aside in her haste.

"Well, don't you intend to answer me, Allen?" Miss Rossington's voice rose shrilly with all the charm and appeal of someone chewing glass. "How do you know her?"

Allen handed his flute to a passing footman. "It isn't any of your concern, but I shall indulge you anyway."

And quite enjoy your reaction.

He peeled her claws from his arm, finger by finger, and once free, smoothed his wrinkled coat sleeve.

"Olivia Kingsley is the woman I almost married."

Other than her gloved hands, at no time should any part of a lady's form touch a gentleman's while dancing.

~*A Lady's Guide to Proper Comportment*

*A*llen.

Olivia's heart cried silently across the distance as she ravenously scoured every inch of him from his burnished hair to his gleaming shoes, before returning to his adored face. Their gazes locked, and time hung suspended for an intense, agonizing moment.

"Olivia, stop gawking. People will think you're fast or desperate." Speaking under her breath, Aunt Muriel nudged her. "Come along. Let's find a seat, shall we?"

Olivia dragged her gaze from Allen, and Bradford took her by the elbow. Skirting the guests, they wove their way through the crush toward the black Trafalgar chairs bordering one side of the ballroom.

Allen was exactly as she remembered—ruggedly handsome and wholly irresistible.

With an utterly exquisite young woman on his arm.

Using her brother as a shield, Olivia covertly eyed Allen, drinking him in with her gaze.

Attired in black, except for a scarlet and silver waistcoat, he exuded maleness. High cheekbones framed a nose too strong to be considered aristocratic, but his lips were perfectly sculpted.

She had tasted those delicious lips once. So long ago. She touched her mouth with her gloved fingertips in remembrance.

"Olivia!" Aunt Muriel hissed from the side of her mouth while smiling and inclining her head at acquaintances as she sailed forth, towing Olivia in her wake. She squeezed Olivia's elbow when she didn't respond immediately. "Put your hand down. Compose yourself at once. I'll not have you disparaged for acting the ninny."

Olivia pretended to scratch her upper lip—indelicate, but a far cry better than pressing her fingers to her mouth—then dropped her hand, her attention still locked on Allen. "But, Aunt Muriel, you said you wanted Allen to kiss me. Surely that's scandal-worthy."

"True, but an indiscretion in a secluded nook is a far cry from making a spectacle in full view of the *beau monde*. A lady can do exactly what a strumpet does, the difference being, she doesn't carry on in the street." Exchanging nods with a dour-faced peeress, Aunt Muriel steered Olivia forward and muttered an almost inaudible, "Lady Clutterbuck. A pedantic fussock, and the worst tattlemonger in all London."

Adopting a smile, Olivia spared the dame a glance, nearly recoiling at the disapproval lining the woman's close-set eyes and, pouting fish lips. No ally there.

A group of arrogant, young bucks swaggered toward a cluster of giggling debutants, and Olivia seized the opportunity to sneak another look at Allen. His thick, sable hair swept across a high brow, accented his heavy-lashed malachite eyes. He had the most arresting eyes she had ever seen on a man. An errant lock curled over his tanned forehead, giving him a rakish air. Even across the room, his unusual green eyes glinted with something powerful.

Umbrage? Anger? Outrage?

Her step faltered, and she swallowed, not at all positive that what glistened in the depths of his gaze was hospitable. For certain, the black look his lovely companion glared at Olivia radiated hostility.

Miss Rossington?

"Buck up, Kitten. The *ton* is watching, their pointed teeth bared and ready to attack anyone showing the least weakness." Bradford whispered the warning in her ear as he led her to a trio of empty seats along what had once been a peach and ivory silk-draped wall, now a sunny primrose yellow.

Lady Wimpleton had recently redecorated and refurbished the inside of the mansion too.

Everything was much the same, yet different as well. Rather like Olivia and Allen. She stole another glance at him. His dark visage offered her no quarter, and her legs gone weak, she sank thankfully onto a chair.

Yes, indeed, this was the worst possible idea. Rather like setting sail upon the ocean in a leaky skiff.

During a tempest.

Without provisions.

Naked and blind.

Perhaps she would seek out the ladies' retiring room and spend the next hour or two cloistered there.

"Ah, I see Lady Pinterfield." Aunt Muriel indicated a woman wearing copious layers of puce and black, almost as garishly attired as she. "I need to speak with her. Her chef concocts the most delicious ratafia cakes. I simply must acquire the recipe, though she's been impossibly difficult to persuade to part with it. I haven't given up yet, mind you. I shall invite her to tea to sample her very own recipe. She cannot refuse me then." Pulling a face, Aunt Muriel sighed. "I suppose I can be persuaded to endure her company for an hour in exchange for those delicacies."

With a fluttering wave, she all but bolted toward the unsuspecting woman.

Olivia gave a closed-lip smile as Aunt Muriel swooped in on her startled prey. Heaven help Lady Pinterfield if she still wasn't eager to share the recipe.

True to his word, Bradford, after snaring a flute of champagne from a cheerful footman, took a position beside an enormous, cage-shaped potted ficus to Olivia's left.

Several twittering damsels openly ogled him, lust in their not-so-innocent eyes.

He curved his lips into a knowing smile and gave them a roguish wink.

A chorus of thrilled giggles and blushes followed, and then a quiet buzz hummed as they bent their heads near and a flurry of whispering commenced with an occasional bold peek from below fluttering lashes.

Others—older, more experienced ladies—spoke behind their fans to one another or, with a seductive curving of their painted mouths, brazenly stared.

His grin widened as he leaned, ankles crossed, against the wall and perused the assembled female guests from beneath his hooded eyes. He quite enjoyed the reactions he garnered.

Incorrigible scapegrace.

At six and twenty, he ought to stop behaving recklessly, but to do so meant he had put Philomena's memory aside. That wasn't something Olivia was certain he would ever be able to do. He had been just shy of twenty when Philomena had died, but he'd truly loved her. Still did, for that matter.

Olivia and Bradford made quite the pair, both doomed to suffer for their lost loves, although a large portion of Olivia's misery could be attributed to her own making.

A young woman pointed at her and snickered.

Tendrils of heat snaked from Olivia's neck to her cheeks. Edging her chin up a degree, she whipped her fan open. Waving it briskly, she surreptitiously studied Allen and attempted to ignore the not-altogether-kind feminine tittering further along the neat row of chairs. Let them prattle. She didn't count any of them as friends. Groups had gathered in nearly every open space, and from one, several gentlemen scrutinized her, likely trying to decide whether to ask her to dance.

Please don't.

To discourage their attentions, she angled her back toward them. Not that she didn't enjoy dancing—she rather adored the pastime, especially the waltz. It had been three years since she'd attended any event with dancing as part of the entertainment, but tonight, she only cared to partner with one man.

Deliberately turning even farther away from their appraisal, she caught her breath.

No. It cannot be.

A woman bearing a striking resemblance to Philomena disappeared through the French windows.

Impossible. Utter piddle.

Olivia had become so flustered upon seeing Allen, she now imagined things. See what the man did to her?

Allen stood across the ballroom, his stance rigid and his countenance an unreadable mask. He didn't acknowledge Olivia's presence with as much as a blink or a nod.

That stung. More than she cared to admit. She had attempted to brace herself for this response but underestimated how painful the actual rejection would be.

She flapped her fan faster, her grip on the slender handle tight enough to snap the fragile wood. Well, what had she expected? That he had forgiven her and would charge across the ballroom, take her in his arms, and profess his undying love in full view of all?

Yes. Though unrealistic, far-fetched, and idealistic, that is what she'd hoped for.

It would have been wonderful—more than wonderful—an answer to three years' worth of desperate prayers. Instead, it appeared he intended to disregard her. To give her the cut. He had never been cruel before, which proved how much she'd wounded him.

Deeply. Irrevocably. Permanently

A crest of disappointment engulfed her, and a sob rose from her chest to her throat as stinging tears welled in her eyes.

I will not cry. I. Will. Not!

Not here. Not now.

She wouldn't give the gossips the satisfaction. Later, in her bedchamber, when no prying or gloating gazes could witness her heartache and mortification, she would indulge in a good cry. One final time. Then, she would dry her eyes, square her shoulders, and march, head held high, into her lonely future.

Like waves to the shore, Allen drew her perusal once more. He held a champagne glass in one hand, his other arm commandeered by that stunning, petite blonde.

Olivia quirked her lips into a cynical smile. At five feet ten inches, and with a head of unruly auburn hair, she was neither petite nor blonde. Nor nearly as curvaceous as the creature clinging to Allen, gazing at him with adoration, her full breasts crushed against his arm.

Ridiculously huge breasts, truth to tell.

Did she stuff her gown? How did her small frame support those monstrosities? With her nipples poking forth so, it was a wonder she didn't topple forward onto her face and crack the parquet flooring with them.

The blonde shifted away from Allen slightly, bringing Olivia's less than charitable musings to a screeching halt.

She blinked in disbelief.

Were those ...?

No. They couldn't be.

Olivia's jaw loosened, but she managed to prevent it from smacking against her chest.

She squinted at the girl's bosom.

Yes. They were.

Dual earth-toned circular shadows were clearly visible through the gown's light fabric.

Good God. Wasn't she wearing a chemise?

Parading about naked beneath one's gown, displaying one's ware like a Friday night harlot was beyond the pale.

The woman peered up at Allen, her countenance enraptured, and blister it, from where Olivia sat, he appeared as entranced as the young lady. Or maybe it was the blatant display of womanly attributes he found spellbinding.

Her bountiful bosoms certainly held numerous other gentlemen's rapt attention.

Dropping her gaze to her beaded, crimson slippers, jealousy nipped Olivia, sharp and deep. Scorching tears pricked behind her eyelids again, and hiding behind her fan's protection, she shut them

Too late. I'm too confounded late.

She drew in a shuddery breath, willing her eyes to stop pooling with moisture.

Well, that was that. Bradford could find their aunt while Olivia waited in the carriage. At least she knew Allen's feelings now, but the knowledge brought her no respite.

"Miss Kingsley, may I request the pleasure of a dance?"

Startled, Olivia eyes popped open, and she clutched her throat, her fan tumbling to the floor. Allen had approached, rapid and soundless. And oh, so very welcome.

Where had the female barnacle gotten to? The way she had clung to Allen, Olivia doubted the chit had been pried loose voluntarily and was likely vexed. Offering a poised, albeit timorous smile, she peered past his black-clad muscled form as he straightened from his bow.

Ah, there she was, attached to another attractive gentleman, so scandalously close a starving flea couldn't have squeezed between them if the insect held its breath. Her cat-eyes sparked with irritation as she took Olivia's measure before turning her back in an intentional snub.

Had she some claim to Allen? An informal promise? A secret betrothal?

Olivia's stomach and hope withered.

"Has another requested the next dance?" Allen's melodious baritone drew her ponderings back to him.

Olivia opened her mouth, but her mind went blank—empty as a beggar's purse, just as she had feared.

Then dear Bradford was there, picking up her brisé fan and saving her from her gaucheness. "No. No one has requested a dance with my sister as yet. You are the first."

Bradford!

He avoided looking at Olivia as he stood upright. "Of course she would be delighted to accept your offer."

She chastised him hotly with her gaze.

Just you wait, Brady, you traitorous toad.

After returning the accessory to her, he extended his hand to Allen. "Good to see you, Wimpleton."

Allen smiled and clasped her brother's palm. He seemed genuinely pleased to see Bradford. They had been good friends before the Kingsley's departure.

"Likewise, Kingsley. Are you finding London's temperature a mite cool after your time in the tropics? No doubt you're eager to return to the milder climate." Green fire burned in the gaze he slid Olivia as he uttered the last slightly clipped words.

His stinging innuendo met its mark, and she flinched inwardly but refused to let him see he had affected her. Rather amazed at her ability to appear composed, she met his cool regard.

"We're not returning, Mr. Wimpleton. After Papa died last year, Bradford sold the plantation."

Allen's forehead creased in momentary surprise, and then he swiftly schooled his expression. "I heard of your loss. Please accept my condolences."

"Thank you." She inclined her head and another bothersome curl flopped free.

Dratted hair.

Allen's lip twitched. He'd forever been tucking stray tendrils behind her ears or helping her re-pin errant strands. More than once, he had expressed the wish to see her hair down.

Bradford grinned, his attention directed across the room. "Olivia, since Wimpleton is partnering you for this dance, I've a mind to reacquaint myself with his sister and ask her to introduce me to that delectable creature standing beside her."

Olivia followed his regard.

A ravishing brunette wearing a stunning lavender-pink gown burst out laughing at something Ivonne said. The raven-haired beauty really ought to be warned, so she could flee before Bradford ensnared her. Poor dear. Once under his spell, women usually stuck fast, like ants in molasses, for a good while.

Until he broke their heart.

He didn't do it intentionally, but when they became too clinging, their sights set on marriage, he gently severed his association. Only, they didn't always willingly go their own way, and then he was forced to brusqueness.

"Behave yourself, Brady."

He chuckled wickedly and wagged his eyebrows. "Always, Kitten."

With a devilish wink and half-bow, he took his leave and sauntered away.

So much for gallant promises.

His expression somber, Allen extended his hand, palm upward. "The waltz is about to begin. Shall we?"

Olivia stared at his outstretched hand.

Did she dare? Wasn't this why she had come?

Now was as good a time as any to test the waters. Sink or swim. Unable to take a decent breath, she did feel she was drowning, especially when she gazed into his eyes. Intense emotion simmered there, and her pulse quickened in response. She inhaled, an inadequate, puny puff of air.

Mayhap her new French stays were to blame for her breathlessness.

Fustian rubbish.

Allen was to blame.

The musicians' first strains echoed loudly in the oddly quiet room. Perhaps he commanded all her senses, and everything else had faded into the background.

"Miss Kingsley? The waltz, if you please?" Allen's soft prompt steadied her nerves.

"Yes, of course." Summoning a tremulous smile, Olivia placed her equally shaky fingers in his hand and allowed him to assist her to her feet. His unique scent—crisp, spicy, yet woodsy—smacked her with the force of a cudgel.

She inhaled deeply, savoring his essence as he tucked her hand into the bend of his elbow and led her onto the sanded floor.

A path opened before them. Like the parting of the Red Sea, several other couples moved aside, allowing them to pass, a few speculating openly as she and Allen walked by.

She had anticipated the *ton's* long memory but found it discomfiting, nevertheless.

Prickles along her spine warned her that dozens of guests watched their progress, some not at all pleased with the turn of events. A quick glance over her shoulder confirmed Miss Rossington's pinched face and fuming gaze.

Precisely what was Allen's relationship with the woman?

Please God, don't let them be betrothed.

He bowed, and Olivia curtsied, somehow managing to keep from teetering over from nerves. The floor soon filled with other couples, many of whom craned their necks and rudely gawked in her and Allen's direction. She felt rather like a curiosity at Bullock's Museum; a peculiarity to be stared at and discussed.

Why couldn't they mind their own business? She conceded this public reunion might not have been the wisest course after all, but the bread had been put to rise and there was no unleavening it now.

Allen took her in his arms, his stance too near to be considered wholly respectable. Nonetheless, she melted into his arms, reveling in their familiarity and comfort, much like returning home after a lengthy journey, which ironically, she had just done.

Shoulders stiff and coolly silent, he began circling them about the room.

He's angry.

Olivia peeked up at him through her eyelashes.

He looked straight ahead, his jaw clenched and a scowl pulling his eyebrows together.

No. He's livid.

While she couldn't get enough of him, he barely tolerated touching her. Why had he asked her to dance when he obviously struggled as much with her proximity as she did his, though for entirely different reasons?

For appearances? To prove she meant nothing to him?

She should never have come to the ball.

Such utter foolishness to think something might be salvaged of their love. She would endure this dance with some semblance of dignity, and afterward, she would make short work of finding Bradford and Aunt

Muriel. They would bid their hosts a hasty farewell, and Olivia would leave her dreams of happiness and reconciliation behind forever.

Expertly guiding her between two couples, Allen's shoulder muscles stiffened even more when she clutched him during a complicated turn. Relaxing her grip, she tried to ease away, to put a bit of distance between them. He either ignored her effort or was so lost in his thoughts and discomfort, he didn't respond to her subtle attempts.

Like strangers forced to spend time together, silence loomed, awkward and heavy. She and Allen had never had trouble talking before. In fact, their ease at conversing is one of the first things that attracted her to him. Now a cavernous chasm, eroded by years of separation, misunderstanding, and hurt divided them.

Nibbling her lower lip, she strove for something sensible to say, but all coherent thought had vanished the instant he touched her. His hand upon her back branded her with possessive heat, and each time his thighs brushed her gown, her legs responded by going weak in the knees.

Ridiculous things.

Ridiculous her.

For pity's sake. Allen was just a man, not a god with divine powers capable of mesmerizing the fairer sex. True, he was the first man to hold her in his arms in years, and the only one she ever wanted to from now until eternity flashed to an end, but she reacted like a wanton.

She concentrated on counting in time to the waltz's lilting strains—*one, two, three, one, two, three*—in an attempt to keep her mind occupied, but her cluttered thoughts hurtled around, bouncing off each other, dissonant and jarring, like church bells clanging on Sunday morning.

How could she have been so naïve as to think they might put the last three years behind them? While she had remained trapped in the Caribbean, caring for her dying father, Allen had gone on with his life. A tiny sigh escaped Olivia at the injustice, but then fate never claimed to be a mistress of fairness.

The lulling music wound its way around her taut nerves until she became lost in the music and gradually began enjoying the dance. She truly did adore dancing. With him.

She closed her eyes, remembering another waltz, where she and Allen had danced indecently close. Cheeks heated by the recollection, she opened her eyes and searched Allen's dear face. Though tall herself, she had to look up to meet his eyes.

He still stared at some point beyond her, tension ticking in his jaw.

His slightly spicy scent wafted past her nostrils again, flooding her senses. She stifled the impulse to bury her nose in his neck and kiss his throat, but she couldn't help drawing in another deep breath and inhaling his essence, not only into her lungs, but into her spirit.

These last treasured moments, dancing with him, were all she would ever have, and she was determined to savor each one fully.

Did he hold the minutest trace of warm regard for her still, or had his disappointment and anger irrevocably hardened his heart? Did he remember that fateful evening—their dance and kiss too?

His focus lowered, lingering on her lips for a brief moment. His nostrils flared, and his molded mouth tightened.

Yes. He remembered.

His expression closed and unreadable, except for the amber shards sparking in his eyes, he met her gaze. "Why are you here? Did you think to take up where we left off?"

Infinite care and consideration should be given when a lady chooses her words and even more so when she elects to speak them.
~*A Lady's Guide to Proper Comportment*

Allen cursed inwardly for asking Olivia the confounded question. He'd sworn to himself he would ask her to dance, uncover her scheme, and send her on her way. Completely unaffected, he would then go about his life and she about hers.

What a colossal, stinking pile of horse manure.

"You humiliated me, Olivia, practically leaving me at the altar."

Holy hell, do stubble it.

She gasped and stumbled, and he tightened his embrace, steadying her.

Her azure gaze, huge and alarmed, flitted about the room, probably seeking a means of escape. The tip of her pink tongue darted out and touched the pillow of her lower lip. "That's not true. We hadn't told anyone of our plans to marry. You had just proposed. No one knew."

He ought to give her that, but his anger wouldn't allow any

concession.

The moment he'd seen her standing in the entry, he had sworn he wouldn't acknowledge, let alone speak to her. Olivia was none of his concern. She held no interest any longer. He didn't want anything more to do with her. When she had chosen her father over him and left to go gallivanting off in the tropics, he'd slammed that door closed and drove the bolt home.

Ballocks, you unmitigated liar. You love her every bit as much as you did the night you rejected her.

His tongue, fueled by offended pride, paid his conscience no heed. "There were wagers on White's books, betting we would wed by summer's end. The entire *bon ton* recognized me as a besotted fool."

Maybe not the entire *ton*, but a sizable number had.

Olivia's beautiful eyes widened in wounded shock, and her lower lip quivered the tiniest bit before she dropped her thick-lashed gaze to stare at his shoulder.

The pulse in her throat beat erratically, and she trembled. "I beg your pardon. This dance was a mistake. Please return me to my aunt or brother."

"Like hell I will." He grated the words out beneath his breath, his voice a harsh rasp.

She stiffened and looked about, half panicked.

Dragging in a juddery lungful, he hauled his attention back to his surroundings. At the end of the opulent, overheated ballroom, his parents stood beside the Duchess of Daventry, concern etched upon their countenances.

They feared he would make a scene.

He feared he would make a bloody scene.

Allen had never been this out of control before. Olivia' presence had damned near knocked him head over arse, and he still hadn't completely recovered his composure.

Drawing in another fortifying gulp of air, he forced a smile to his taut lips and nodded at the gawkers stretching their necks to see what transpired between Olivia and him.

Bloody ballroom full of giraffes and ostriches.

Allen would've loved to tell the lot to bugger off.

Instead, he elevated a brow and leveled them a civil, yet quelling look.

Dancing nearby, Miss Rossington jerked her attention away with such abruptness she mashed her partner's foot. Tripping, the man muttered an oath and bumped into another couple. They too, faltered before regaining their balance.

An amusing vision of the dancers tumbling over like stacked cards, one after the other, and ending in a writhing pile of arms and legs upon the floor flashed before Allen. The corner of his lips skewed upward. It would give the guests something to blather about other than him and Olivia.

"Mr. Wimpleton, I demand you release me at once." Her face constrained, Olivia attempted to pull away. She gave his shoulder a small shove. "Let go."

She had tried that earlier, too, but he held her fast, craving her nearness. Desperately, dammit.

"Cease." He bent his neck, his mouth near her small ear. Another inch and he could trace the delicate shell with his tongue. How would she react if he did? He drew in an extended breath. God, she smelled divine. Warm, and flowery with the faintest hint of citrus. The creamy column of her neck beckoned, as did the silky spot just below her ear, and the velvety hollow at the juncture of her throat.

He swallowed, lest he give into the urge to trail his lips from one, to the other, to the other. "We shall finish this waltz, and you shall smile and pretend to enjoy the dance. I'll not intentionally give the gossipmongers a single morsel to toss about at my expense ever again."

Casting the dancers a sidelong glance, she stopped trying to escape. Her lips ribbon thin, she shook her head. A russet tendril sprang loose, toppling onto her ear. "Too late for that, I'm afraid. My being here has stirred that unpleasant pot into a bubbling froth. I never should have come. It was foolish of me."

"Why did you?"

"I ..." Her shoulders slumped, and she tucked her chin to her chest. "I wanted to see you."

He had to strain to hear her whispered words.

Her head sank lower. "Just one more time."

As simple as that. No pretense. No expectations or demands.

Was it possible Olivia had missed him as much as he had missed her? Despite his reservations, his treacherous heart rejoiced. Words were beyond him at the moment, and swallowing, he canvassed the room.

Mother poked Father with her fan and sent the duchess a sly, knowing smile at something her grace said.

The Duchess of Daventry looked much too pleased.

By thunder. Did she just wink at him? Had she orchestrated this?

Given her reputation for being unconventional and high-handed, he shouldn't be the least surprised. Befuddled, he wasn't sure whether to thank or curse her.

Allen edged Olivia even closer, until the crown of her head almost touched his chin. Despite insisting he release her a moment ago, she didn't resist.

Her light perfume tormented him, shooting a blast of sensation to his loins and sending his lust soaring. Hound's teeth, as if his manhood bulging in his breeches wouldn't cause more whispers and titters. And trying to dance with a stiffened rod bumping against one's leg presented an uncomfortable challenge.

Women didn't realize their good fortune in wearing skirts, for their arousal didn't tent their trousers—bloody apparent for the world to see.

Sixty seconds in his arms and Olivia had him at sixes and sevens.

And hard as marble.

Only she had this power over him. Even after an extended absence from her, he responded like a wet-behind-the-ears pup with his first woman.

Well done, old man. Your self-control is pitiable.

He dismissed his musing. All that mattered was this moment and holding her in his arms. Caressing the curve of her rib, Allen guided her through another difficult turn, made more so by the blatant eavesdroppers pressing near.

A slight smile edging her mouth, she unerringly followed his lead.

They had always been superb dance partners, and he hadn't a doubt she would have been unequaled as a bedmate. He'd been eager to introduce her to passion's promises once she became his wife.

His already-stirred member jerked, yanking his attention back to the present. He scrutinized Olivia through half-closed eyes.

She had grown even more beautiful.

Her gorgeous red hair, untamed and wild, like her, was streaked with gold, no doubt from exposure to the tropical sun. A jeweled ruby band peaked between artfully arranged curls—curls every bit as silky as they appeared.

Her eyes, the clearest ocean blue he'd ever seen, stayed riveted on his neckcloth. Her unique gown—cherry-red with an overlay somewhere between ivory and light gold—enhanced her glowing skin, giving her an almost ethereal appearance. Few red-heads dared wear crimson tones, but she managed to look exquisite in the becoming gown. A slight pout marred her pretty lips, slightly damp and pinkened from being nibbled, and vexation creased her usually smooth brow.

She possessed a woman's figure now. Her breasts were fuller, the creamy mounds surging above the neckline of her gown hinting at the treasures hidden beneath the fabric. Treasures he longed to sample. No, was desperate to taste and touch.

Fiend seize it, he had thought himself over her, and truth to tell, feared ever again experiencing the pain her betrayal caused him. He'd drowned himself in drink and staggered about half-foxed for a month after her departure. If he was honest, he taken to drinking too much since, as well.

The waltz's steps brought them near the French window at one end of the ballroom. The terrace doors stood wide open, summoning him. Before his conscience had a chance to raise an objection or dared to spout good sense, Allen whirled Olivia out the opening, just like he had that fateful night.

She stopped dancing at once and pulled from his embrace, glowering at him.

Not the same as three years ago.

"This is most improper." She attempted to step past him and reenter the house, but he blocked her path. Her color high, she glared at him. "I must return inside immediately or my reputation will be compromised."

"Not until I've spoken my piece." Allen grasped her elbow, preventing her escape. Intent on seeking a private bower, he glanced swiftly around before releasing her elbow only to clasp her hand.

"Allen, let me go." Eyes narrowed, she wriggled her fingers. "You cannot go about dragging ladies here and there willy-nilly at your pleasure."

His pleasure? Not by a long shot.

"Don't kick up a fuss. I simply want to talk without a score of ears listening to my every word." He steered her down the narrow flagstone steps and onto the lawn. Lanterns dotted the landscape, bathing the flowers and shrubberies in a warm glow, and where the lanterns couldn't penetrate the darkness, the moon's silvery beams provided a subtle half-light to all but the remotest recesses.

A woman's giggle echoed from somewhere within the garden. Seemed he wasn't the only one intent on bit of air and privacy. Her laughter sounded again, likely from the arbor further along the curving path that split the lawn as neatly as parted hair. A few stolen kisses might be had there away from the sharp eyes of the dowagers and watchful mamas.

"What are you doing?" Olivia tugged at her hand clamped within his. "Are you trying to ruin me? You just said you didn't want any more gossip. You don't think this," she gave another yank and bobbed her head toward the veranda, "won't signal the rumormongers that something's afoot?"

That halted Allen in his tracks. Standing in the center of the manicured garden, he scanned the area. They were fully visible to the few guests taking the air on the terrace, but far enough away that no one could easily overhear their conversation. Her reputation would remain intact, and he could say what he had burned to say since she stepped into the ballroom.

"I'm sorry I came tonight. It's evident my presence has upset you. That was never my intent." Olivia released a jerky breath, misery etched upon her lovely face. "Please let me return to the house, and I shall leave at once and not bother you with my presence again."

"Not yet." He shook his head and straightened his waistcoat before slanting her a wry glance. "I must confess, I am grateful I didn't wait the year you asked for, Livy." He leaned closer, holding up three fingers. "Since it has taken three for you to reappear on the London scene."

Gasping, she flinched as if struck. Her gaze faltered, but not before raw pain darkened her eyes, and she took a reflexive step back.

He released her hand. Hell, he was an unmitigated, chuckleheaded ass.

"I didn't think you wanted me to return." She lifted her chin a notch, her incredible blue eyes lancing him with accusation. "I remember your words from that night quite clearly, Allen."

God, he remembered, too, every grating, cold syllable spewing from his lips. Guilt and shame kicked him in the ribs, pulverizing his pride.

She stared at a point beyond his shoulder, her eyes swimming with tears. She blinked several times, and swallowed audibly, obviously attempting to control her emotions. Her voice hoarse, she repeated his hateful words.

"'Don't expect me to wait for you, Olivia. If you choose your father over me, we're finished.'"

A lady of refined breeding will, at all times, avoid raising her voice or engaging in public displays of histrionics.
~*A Lady's Guide to Proper Comportment*

6

"Olivia, I ..."

Allen reached for her once more. He mustn't cause her more anguish, must make amends for his cruelty. In that moment, he hated himself, hated what love had turned him into.

Olivia lurched away, hiding her hands behind her back.

Did she fear him? A knife, jagged and rusty, twisted in his bowels.

Poised to flee, distrust lurked in her gaze—her gorgeous eyes that had once sparkled with adoration.

He had done this to her, yet he had suffered equally. "Not one letter in three years. I assumed you had stopped loving me."

"You made no attempt to contact me either, Allen. You're the one who said we were finished. Surely, you knew the Duchess of Daventry had our address. For all I knew, you had married by now." The sorrow in her voice ripped at his gut.

"There's never been anyone else, Livy."

Never would be, either. He cast a swift glance over his shoulder. No one seemed to pay them any heed, unless ... He squinted. Unless that was Mother hiding amongst the draperies beside the French Windows. No. The figure was larger than Mother. Her Grace? He suppressed a chuckle. The woman knew no bounds.

Perhaps he could convince Olivia to join him in the library or Father's study to finish this conversation. Who knew who might be loitering in the shrubberies, eavesdropping on their every word? This discussion was too private to have bandied about by a loose-tongued tattlemonger.

"What about Miss Rossington?" Lips pursed, Olivia darted a telling glance toward the manor. "She seemed quite attached to you. I didn't imagine the darkling glowers she showered upon me."

He shook his head again, noting Olivia's high color. Was she jealous? The notion gave him a jot of hope. A disinterested woman didn't harbor envy.

"Her father and mine attended Oxford together. She's a guest of my parents, that's all, no more important than the bevy of other woman they have invited tonight."

Close enough to the truth, for Allen had never entertained any serious intentions regarding the chit. A drunkard's ale lasted longer than his brief foray into insanity when he had fleetingly considered courting her. She had proved an amusing diversion—a way to keep his parents content that he dutifully searched for a wife—that is, until Miss Rossington's true nature emerged. She'd fully exposed herself this evening, and her revelation had relegated her to an unsuitable.

"Oh." Olivia fiddled with the elaborate pendant nestled above her décolletage.

Envy seized him. He would like to take the pendant's hallowed place.

The matching ruby bracelet on her wrist sparkled in the muted light when she waved her hand. "And I suppose, as their son, you must do your *duty?*"

He hid a delighted smile.

Yes. Jealousy most definitely tinged her husky voice, though she attempted to disguise it with sarcasm. He quite enjoyed the notion she was jealous. It meant she still cared.

Rolling his head, he nodded once and grinned. "I like to think I'm a very dutiful son."

Actually, except for a couple years before meeting Olivia when he had sowed his wild oats, he had been the epitome of propriety. Not only did his parents insist upon it, he'd found he wasn't cut out to be a man about town. The drinking, whoring, gambling—all favorite pastimes of many of the *ton's* privileged—held little appeal for him. Though hopelessly unpopular with the elite set, he rather favored a quiet life with one woman in his bed. Olivia.

She cocked her head, one earring swinging with the action. "Ah, yet you expected me to forsake my duty as an obedient daughter and leave my father?"

Her words ripped apart Allen's attempt at lightheartedness. Damn, this wasn't the path he'd intended their conversation to take. Olivia had neatly turned the tables on him.

"Did it ever occur to you that demanding we elope at once scared and unnerved me?" She pressed her palm to her chest, her features taut. "Every bit as much as Father announcing we were off to the Caribbean in two days' time? Both situations frightened the living daylights out of me."

Her revelation rendered Allen mute. Her situation had been wholly impossible, made worse by his juvenile ultimatum.

"Papa's health had deteriorated since Mama died." Tucking a loose tendril behind her ear, Olivia inhaled deeply, as if struggling for control. She sent a furtive look to the terrace, no doubt worried about her reputation. "Defying Papa might have killed him. How could I have lived with myself then?"

Her eyes glistened suspiciously once more.

Whirling away, she wandered to a row of rosebushes edging another neat path. "You hadn't even asked Papa for my hand yet. He knew nothing of your intentions."

"We had only known each other a fortnight, Livy." Allen rubbed his nape before folding his arms. "I doubt your father would have received my request with any enthusiasm."

You could have made the effort, dolt.

"I'm not sure it would have made a difference in any event." She shrugged and offered a rueful tilt of her plump lips as she removed one glove. "My father was impetuous and disinclined to think about how his impromptu decisions might affect others. I've always suspected he didn't want me to ever wed."

Allen canted his head again. "And you truly knew nothing of his intentions? To pack you off to the Caribbean with no warning?" He gestured in the air. "I'm sure you can understand why I might find that hard to believe."

"Allen, you come from a stable home. You know nothing of living with a parent who acted on the slightest whim. It wasn't unusual for Papa to pack us up and cart the family off to some absurd location when he became obsessed with another peculiar notion. Bradford was spared somewhat when he went off to university. I've often wondered if the only reason he came back home when he finished was to act as a buffer and protect me."

Olivia bent and sniffed a creamy rose then released a small cry of pain. Thrusting her finger into her mouth, she sucked the scarlet droplet from the tip where a thorn had scratched her.

At the sensual sight, Allen's throat went dry as a more erotic image leaped to mind.

Egads, she's hurt, and I'm envisioning lewd acts.

After a moment, Olivia regained her composure. After tugging on her glove once more, she continued her hesitant exploration of the flowers.

"Why Papa kept the news of our departure a secret is anyone's guess. He was always been a bit eccentric and reclusive. After Mama's death, he became more so. And at times—I'm ashamed to admit—quite addlebrained, especially as he aged."

Another wave of guilt hammered Allen. Her father was ailing and, apparently, dicked in the nob, to boot. "I had no idea."

Stroking a velvety petal, she lifted a shoulder. "No one did. One doesn't discuss such delicate matters. It wasn't until after we'd arrived in Barbados that Papa confessed his physician had recommended a change of climate in order to extend his life. The milder tropical weather was supposed to improve both his health and his doldrums."

Remorse crushed Allen's chest. He hadn't known any of this, though it didn't excuse his brash behavior. He'd wager his inheritance that after his harsh ultimatum, Olivia's pride had kept her from telling him. Tarring and feathering was too merciful for him. His handling of the whole affair bordered on—no, *was* completely—despicable.

Striving for control, Allen tilted his head skyward and sucked in a steadying breath. "How long have you been in England?"

He lowered his eyes, unable to keep his gaze from feasting on her in the soft light. He needed to soothe her pain, to make amends for the hurt he'd caused. He yearned to hold her in his arms, as he had ached to do every day while she had been away.

"Just over a week." Head bowed, she folded her hands before her. "Bradford and I are staying with the duchess until other arrangements can be made. Our uncle let the Mayfair house and Bradford's never been fond of it so we're seeking accommodations elsewhere."

She's been back a week and made no effort to contact me?

"Three years, Olivia. You asked me to wait one, but you've been gone three years." Allen winced at the pain he heard in his voice.

Her gaze collided with his. Regret and something else flashed in the azure depths.

"I intended to return after a year. We all did, but Papa had apoplexy four months after we arrived. He never fully recovered, and the physician advised us travel was out of the question." Her eyes shone glassy with tears. "He said it would kill Papa."

"You never wrote." Allen wandered to the flower beds to stand beside her. She was so close, only a handbreadth away, yet a yawning abyss of unbridgeable misunderstanding lay between them.

Olivia touched another rose. "And what would I have said? You made your position very clear. You also said you wouldn't wait for me."

Each bitter truth impaled him. "You might have told me of your father's ill health."

"To what purpose?" She cast him a sidelong look.

He snapped a rose's stem then offered it to her.

"I would have known why you didn't return." *To me,* he ached to add.

"I thought you had come to hate me, Allen."

Intelligence, wit, and a polite smile are a lady's greatest weapons.
~*A Lady's Guide to Proper Comportment*

Accepting the scarlet rose, Olivia solemnly faced Allen. Even in the dim light, with only moonbeams and the glow from the house's windows, she glimpsed a trace of vulnerability in his turned down mouth and hooded gaze.

She had never been able to hide her emotions from him. What did she have to lose by being completely candid now? Not a blasted thing. After tonight, she would likely never see him again. She lifted the flower to her nose. Shutting her eyes, she sniffed deeply.

He'd given her a red rose. Did he know they symbolized love? Likely not. Purely chance he had selected that color of bloom. Foolish of her to wish the gesture meant more.

"I was so young—having just seen my eighteenth birthday the month before—and when you suggested we run away to marry that night, I panicked." She waved her hand back and forth. "Everything happened so fast between us."

He scowled, kicking at a stone lying on the grass. "Our love was real. Don't tell me it wasn't."

Olivia nodded, and another curl slid free to tease her ear. Why bother to put her hair up at all?

"Yes, I know it is ... was." She stumbled over her words, but recovered, her voice softening. "I've never doubted it for a moment."

He fingered a fragile petal. "Then why did you leave?"

"Why did you let me go?" She peered into his unfathomable eyes.

If he had only made some sort of effort, had come to her house or the ship, done anything to prevent her from leaving, her resolve would have melted as rapidly as sugar in hot tea.

The Lady's Guide to Proper Comportment says a lady never complains or criticizes—

Do hush, Mama.

Rubbing his thumb and forefinger together, Allen gazed off into space for an extended moment. The quiet hum of the guests on the terrace, the faint strains of the orchestra, and an occasional cricket's rasping song interrupted his weighty silence.

"My devilish pride," he finally murmured, splaying his fingers through his hair, leaving several tufts standing straight up. If his valet saw his destroyed handiwork, he would gnaw Allen's hairbrush to a nub. "I've always been too prideful. Arrogant some might say. Definitely privileged, and I seldom don't get what I want."

Allen's honest confession startled her, and Olivia dared to harbor the tiniest bit of optimism.

Grinning sheepishly, he rolled a shoulder. "I couldn't credit that you would leave me, that you expected me to wait a year for your return. I desired you then, and I acted the part of an intractable bratling."

"You broke my heart." Utterly shattered it was more apt.

He hadn't indicated he still cared for her, only that he had been as hurt as she. A breeze wafted past, and she crossed her arms, suddenly chilled. She must return inside soon, else Aunt Muriel and Bradford would become worried, not to mention the gossip Olivia and Allen's extended stay outdoors would ignite. "Fearing your scorn, I didn't dare reach out to you afterward. I have my pride too."

"I know, and I'm remorseful beyond words."

Stepping nearer, he took her hand in his. With his other, he lifted her chin until their eyes met. "Can you forgive me? Please? Might we begin again and take our time this go round?" He playfully tugged on of the escaped curls then caressed her cheek with his forefinger. "I promise not to be demanding and to always consider your feelings and needs. I beg you, give me another chance."

Blinking back tears of joy, Olivia swallowed the lump of emotion choking her. Even when the carriage had rattled to a stop before the mansion, she couldn't have imagined this most welcome turn of events. She nodded as one tear spilled from the corner of her eye.

Allen caught it with his forefinger. "I never want to make you cry again, Livy. A least not from sorrow I caused. Happiness or passion, yes, but never ... never tears of unhappiness again."

He kissed her forehead before resting his against hers.

They were probably being observed, and the tattlemongers would be flapping their tongues until next Season, but she didn't care. In fact,

Olivia wouldn't be surprised if Aunt Muriel—silently cheering, and clapping, and congratulating herself soundly for contriving this whole wonderful evening—wasn't lurking somewhere nearby, perhaps in those bushes just there, watching everything that transpired between Allen and her.

"I never stopped loving you." He kissed Olivia's nose. "Not for a single moment. When you left, the light went out of my life. I never wanted to smile again, and I cursed the sun for rising each day. I knew my selfishness and inconsideration had cost me the one thing that mattered most. You."

"Oh, Allen." She traced his jaw with her fingertips. "If only we had talked this through, this misunderstanding wouldn't have kept us apart all this time. Promise me we'll always be able to tell the other anything, and that we'll listen before ever jumping to conclusions or acting rashly again."

"Always." He grasped her hand and pressed a hot kiss into her palm. The heat of his lips burned through the fabric of her glove, sending delicious frissons spiraling outward. "Tell me you love me still, Livy. That there's a morsel of hope for us."

"Yes." She grinned and nodded. More curls sprang free. She didn't care. "I do love you."

He released a long breath, as if he had been afraid of her response. "Will you marry me? Not right away. We can wait if you wish. I won't rush you. I know I asked you before, but I want to go about it properly this time."

"Of course I will." She toyed with his jacket's lapel, giving him a coy smile. "Then you'll ask Bradford—?"

"Ask Bradford what?"

She whipped around to see her brother standing behind them. So caught up in the magical moment with Allen, she hadn't heard him approach. From the nonplussed expression on Allen's face, he hadn't either.

"Ask me what?" Bradford repeated, curiosity glinting in his eyes as he came nearer.

Allen stood taller and met his gaze straight on. "For your sister's hand in marriage."

Bradford's face broke into an immense grin, and he clapped his hands.

"Thank God. I had no idea what I was going to do with her if you two didn't reconcile." He planted his hands on his hips. "She has been in the doldrums for months and months, a regular Friday face, I tell you, scarcely cracking a smile during her fit of the blue devils and—"

Olivia whacked his arm with her fan. "That's enough, Brady. Say another word, and I shall not invite you to the wedding."

Revealing his perfect white teeth, Allen returned Bradford's silly grin. "Then we have your approval?"

"I'll say." Bradford chuckled heartily while pumping Allen's hand "My approval, consent, permission, blessing—"

"Bradford," Olivia warned. Must he carry on so? She hadn't been so awful, had she?

His eyes widened. "By George, I'll even pay for a special license, and we can have the deed done tomorrow."

"Not so fast, brother dear, else I may take offense at your eagerness to be rid of me." Olivia swung her amused gaze to Allen. "I should like a short courtship, but I would also like a wedding. Aunt Muriel will insist upon it, in any case."

Allen raised her hand to his lips. "Whatever you wish, sweetheart. I'm eager to make you my bride, but won't rush you. I'm just as certain my mother will want an elaborate showing too." He winked. "I think it may be dangerous to allow the duchess and my mother to put their heads together. We might very well end up with the wedding of the decade."

Olivia laughed. "Yes, Aunt Muriel is a force to contend with."

"There you are, Allen, my dear." Miss Rossington glided across the lawn.

Allen?

Only intimate acquaintances addressed one another by their first names, and unless betrothed to a gentleman, a young lady never did so in public. And she most certainly did not call him her dear.

A Lady's Guide to Proper Comportment, page thirty-six.

Her fine brow puckered in puzzlement, Miss Rossington looked between Allen and Olivia then turned her attention to Bradford, eyeing him like a delicious pastry she would like to savor. Or gobble up, rather. She batted her eyelashes and licked her lips provocatively.

Brazen as an east end bit of muslin.

"Whatever is going on?" She lowered her voice to a sultry whisper, her wanton wiles in full play.

Wasted on Bradford. He might like dampened gowns and appreciate a beautiful face and form, but he couldn't abide fast women, and Miss

Rossington would make it round the racetrack swifter than The Derby's prime blood.

Olivia couldn't suppress her pleased smile as Allen wrapped a muscled arm about her waist and tucked her to his side, even if his actions were outside of acceptable.

"Miss Kingsley has just done me the greatest honor by consenting to become my wife."

"What?" Miss Rossington, sounding is if she had gargled gravel, blanched and clutched her throat. "Your ... your *wife?*"

"Indeed. I told you she was the woman I almost married." He gave Olivia's waist a squeeze. "Well, now I'm beyond blessed to say that dream will at last come to pass."

Miss Rossington stomped toward Allen, her countenance contorted in rage. "You damned churl, toying with my affections. Do you know how many men's address I refused?"

Allen lifted a brow. "We both know that's utter gammon. An alley cat has more discretion."

The blonde sputtered and choked, daggers shooting from her eyes. She whipped her arm back as if to strike Allen. "Why you—"

Bradford swiftly stepped forward and snared her hand.

"I wouldn't. Do you truly want those denizens witnessing you acting the part of a shrew?" He thrust his chin toward the terrace. "I assure you, a dead codfish, green and rotting, has a greater chance of finding a husband amongst the *haute ton* than you do if you strike the son of a peer."

Yanking her hand from his, Miss Rossington turned on Allen. "You bloody bastard."

The curl of his lips simultaneously expressed his scorn and amusement.

Teeth clenched and seething with rage, she glared at Bradford then Olivia. "Damn you all to the ninth circle of hell."

Hiking her gown to mid-calf, Miss Rossington spun on her satin slippered heel. She proceeded to stomp her way back to the house, muttering additional foul oaths a woman of gentle breeding should never have let pass her lips.

Page nineteen, paragraph two.

A form separated from the shadows on one side of the French windows.

Olivia blinked in disbelief as Aunt Muriel emerged from behind the drapes. Olivia would wager the Prussian jewels she wore, her aunt had been watching the whole while.

Aunt Muriel lifted her nose and pulled her skirts aside as Miss Rossington tramped into the house. Then with a little wave at Olivia, Aunt Muriel bolted out of site. Likely to apprise the Wimpletons of what she had witnessed.

The adorable sneak.

"It seems we've drawn a crowd." Chagrin heated Olivia's cheeks as she canted her head slightly in the terrace's direction. At least a score of guests mingled about the porch, their rapt attention focused on the trio left standing on the grass.

Dash it all. Allen hadn't wanted additional fodder for le bon ton's gossipmongers.

A roguish glint entered his eyes. "Let's make it worth their while, shall we, darling?"

A lady never participates in public shows of affection.

Olivia cast a glance heavenward.

Then I guess I'm not a lady, Mama.

She didn't resist when Allen drew her into his embrace, although she cast her brother a hesitant look.

Bradford winked. "Please do, Wimpleton. Give the chinwags something to babble about. Make it something quite spectacular, will you? Something scandalous to keep their forked tongues flapping for a good long while."

With a smart salute, he turned his back on them and, whistling a jaunty tune, strolled along the path wending into the garden's depths.

Bradford was proving to be every bit as indecorous as their aunt.

Olivia inclined her head and eyed Allen. "Well? What outrageousness do you have in mind?"

"A kiss, perhaps?" He ran his thumb across her lower lip.

Olivia quite liked this rakish side of him. "Oh, yes."

Allen took another step closer, and his thighs pressed against hers, their chests colliding.

Winding her arms around his neck, she raised her mouth in invitation.

A scandalized voice carried across the expanse. "Do you see that? They're kissing. Right there on the lawn. In full view of all."

"Yes. It's utterly lovely, isn't it?" Aunt Muriel's delighted laugh filled the night air.

Allen dipped his dark head until their lips were a hair's breadth apart. "A kiss for Miss Kingsley?"

"Perfect." Olivia smiled as his mouth claimed hers.

Epilogue

Wyndleyford House
September 1818

"Do finish up, Olivia darling. We'll be late."

Allen lounged against the bedpost, looking irresistibly dashing as he watched Olivia's last-minute fussing. His pristine cravat was tied in another new, complicated knot, and his waistcoat matched his green eyes to perfection. However, it was the gleam of male satisfaction in his jungle gaze that sent her pulse cavorting again.

"It's not my fault you decided to exercise your husbandly rights just as I exited my bath."

Olivia gave him a playful pout as she deliberately applied perfume to her cleavage. That quite drove him mad. She touched the emeralds at her throat. He had placed them there just before they'd spent a blissful half an hour abed. "My *toilette* would have been completed long ago."

"I didn't hear you complaining overly much." Allen straightened and after adjusting his jacket sleeves, crossed the room, his long-legged strides covering the distance in short order. He bent and kissed her bare shoulder. "I knew the Wimpleton emeralds would look exquisite on you."

"They are stunning. Thank you." She turned her head up for a kiss. The scorching meeting of their mouths had her considering an even tardier arrival to her new in-laws' anniversary celebration. "I'm honored to wear them to the festivities tonight."

"It's our anniversary too, love. One month today, Mrs. Wimpleton. Slowest three months of my life, waiting to make you my bride."

She grinned. "I told you it was dangerous to let my aunt and your mother help plan our wedding. I about tripped over my dress when I saw Prinny sitting in a front pew."

"You and I both. I'd never seen a man attired completely in that shade of pink before. Looked rather like an enormous, glittery salmon." Allen withdrew a bracelet from his pocket then lifted her hand.

"More?" Olivia shook her head. "It's magnificent but, you know, I'm not a woman who requires jewels. I have all I ever wanted."

He settled it around her wrist and set the clasp. "Would you deny me my pleasure?"

Quirking her brow, she gave him an impish smile. "When have I *ever* denied you your pleasure?"

With a mock growl, he pulled her to her feet. Swinging her into his embrace, he plundered her mouth.

A scratching at the door interrupted the kiss. "Sir, madam, everyone has arrived."

"I suppose we must put in an appearance." Allen sighed and leaned away, acting put-upon.

Giggling, Olivia collected her shawl and fan. "Of course we must. Your sister and my brother are below with their spouses. Your parents must host more balls. Three weddings came about as a result of that one in May."

"I do believe that rout set a record." He chuckled and scratched his nose. At the door he caught her arm. "Have I told you that I love you today, Mrs. Wimpleton?"

She touched his face. "Yes, but I shall never tire of hearing it."

He dropped a kiss onto her forehead. "And I promise I shall never tire of saying it."

Dearest Reader,

A Kiss for a Rogue was inspired by a scene in *Triumph and Treasure* that mentions the Wimpletons' ball. I had so much fun writing the story, I decided to create a new novella series featuring waltzes and rogues. Hence, The Honorable Rogues™ series was born.

Readers said they wanted more time with Olivia and Allen, and that's why I expanded their story in this second edition. I'm truly delighted you chose to read *A Kiss for a Rogue*, and I hope it capitated you enough to take a peek at the other books in the series.

Please consider telling other readers why you enjoyed the book by reviewing it. Not only do I truly want to hear your thoughts, reviews are crucial for an author to succeed. **Even if you only leave a line or two, I'd very much appreciate it.**

So, with that I'll leave you.

Here's wishing you many happy hours of reading, more happily ever afters than you can possibly enjoy in a lifetime, and abundant blessings to you and your loved-ones.

A Bride for a Rogue

A Bride for a Rogue is for you, Grandma Cameron.

I only wished you'd lived to read my books.

Who knew I had so many stories waiting to be told?

Acknowledgements

As always, I owe a huge thanks to my critique partners and beta readers. Your honesty, insight, and suggestions have been invaluable to me.

To my cover artist, Darlene Albert, editor, Danielle Fine, and virtual assistant, Cindy Jackson, mega hugs!

And to my wonderful VIP reader group, Collette's Chéris. Thank you, darlings, for all you do!

xoxo

Collette

1

London, England
Late May, 1818

"There you are, Miss Wimpleton."

Ivonne Wimpleton whipped her gaze to Captain Melvin Kirkpatrick. Groaning in frustration, she snapped her fan closed, prepared to use the frilly accessory to give him a good poke or two, if necessary.

Fiend seize it. What is he doing here?

He must have arrived after she ventured outdoors.

She'd specifically asked Mother not to invite him tonight. Somehow, the boor had finagled an invitation to accompany another guest. Ivonne had hoped he'd finally sailed for Africa and wouldn't impose his unwelcome presence on her for six blessed months or more.

He staggered toward her secluded bench on the side terrace, a drunken smile skewing his mouth.

She shot to her feet, searching for a means to avoid him. The only possibility lay in the narrow stairway descending to the manicured garden where an occasional colored lantern glowed. Ivonne strode toward her salvation at a near run.

Captain Kirkpatrick caught her arm and pinned her against the balustrade with his great weight. Her fan fell, clattering to the flagstone.

Straining against him, Ivonne fought to breathe and gagged. Did the man ever bathe?

"What audacity. Unhand me, sir!"

He shook his head. Excitement glimmered in his glassy eyes. "I think not. You've played the reluctant miss long enough. It's time you tasted what our married life will be like."

"Are you dicked in the nob?" Though no match for his strength, Ivonne still fought to break free. As she struggled, her hair pins came loose and scattered onto the stones. "I. Am. Not. Marrying. You."

He tightened his clasp, and she winced as he held her arms in a bruising grip.

"I prefer blondes with blue eyes, but I cannot complain about your curves." Leering at her bosom, Captain Kirkpatrick licked his lips. He pawed her breast with one beefy hand as his other gripped her head in an attempt to steal a kiss.

His foul breath assailed Ivonne, sending her stomach pitching at the stench of strong spirits and onions. Intent on screaming like a banshee, she opened her mouth and sucked in a huge breath.

A chortling foursome of gentlemen burst through the French windows onto the other side of the terrace. Their sudden appearance rescued her from the captain's lewd groping. Panting heavily, his bushy red eyebrows scrunched together, he released her and scowled at her brother, Allen, Lords Sethwick and Luxmoore, and the Duke of Harcourt.

A pity the new arrivals weren't her twin cousins, Edwina and Edward. They would come to her aid and not breathe a word of the untoward situation. However, if Allen spied her in Captain Kirkpatrick's company, there would be the devil to pay.

Ivonne tried to blend into the manor's shadow, but the sea captain's stout form obstructed her. Her brother had warned the widower away from her once already. If he suspected the captain dared lay a hand on her, Allen would call him out. A dab hand at pistols—all firearms, for that matter—Captain Kirkpatrick might wound, or, heaven forbid, kill dear Allen.

She shuddered. It must not come to that. She peeked at the captain from beneath her lashes. More than a trifle disguised, his drunken focus remained on the other men. Ivonne seized the moment. Without hesitation, she kneed him in the ballocks with her good leg and gave him a mighty shove.

Bent double and growling in fury, he stumbled backward, clutching his groin.

Ignoring his gasps of pain and vile curses, she edged away. With one eye on the laughing quartet, she crept down the stairs. Once out of their view, she flew across the lawn as rapidly as her injured leg would allow. She'd broken the limb in two places in a riding accident three years ago. The leg pained her on occasion, and she endured a permanent, though slight, limp made worse by overexertion.

She darted behind a tall rose-covered trellis. In her haste, the ball gown's black net overskirt caught on a thorn-laden cane. Breathing labored and leg throbbing, she halted just inside the alcove and gave the skirt a gentle tug.

Dash it all. Stuck fast.

She sent a frantic glance along the footpath.

A twig snapped. Had Captain Kirkpatrick followed her?

A jolt of fright raised the hairs on her arms and stole her breath. Did she dare step outside the arbor and release the material? Would he see her if she did? She couldn't move farther into the enclosure, though if she remained here, she risked almost certain discovery.

A sleepy dove cooed from somewhere in the garden's trees. The night's festivities had no doubt disturbed its slumber.

Ivonne peered through the lattice slats.

Where was he?

With her forefinger, she nudged a couple of leaves aside. Her white gloves stood out, a stark contrast against the plants. Oh, to have the mythical mantel of Arthur in Cornwall and be invisible.

A soft wind wafted through her hiding place and rustled the leaves overhead. Several spun lazily to the ground. Guests' laughter and the lilting strains of the orchestra floated through the beveled French windows and carried to her on the mild breeze.

What possessed her to give into the impulse to venture outside alone and catch some air?

Because you dislike balls, gentlemen treating you as if you're beneath their touch, and all the pretentious nastiness that's generally present when the denizens of High Society gather.

Though only May, the crush of the crowd inside the mansion caused the temperature to rise uncomfortably. The heat, mixed with cloying perfumes, less-than-fresh clothing, the aroma of dozens of beeswax candles, and the occasional unbathed body, made her head ache and stomach queasy.

She'd sought a secluded niche on the side terrace to recover. Unfortunately, Captain Kirkpatrick, deep in his cups, found her there. Much like the shaggy bull he resembled, he'd stalked her at every social gathering.

A more off-putting man she'd never met.

Ivonne turned sideways and hoped the vines' thick cover concealed her. If fear had a scent, the captain's bulbous nose would lead him straight to her. Heavy footfalls crunched upon the gravel not more than a yard away. She closed her eyes as her heart lurched to her throat. Thank God she hadn't tried to detach her gown. He'd have been on her like dense winter fog on the River Thames.

"Miss Wimpleton, you saucy minx, where are you?"

A low, suggestive chuckle followed. "I do like a spirited gel in my bed. I do, indeed."

Ivonne's eyes popped open. Captain Kirkpatrick's gloating singsong whisper sent a shiver of loathing the length of her spine. She bit her lower lip, afraid to exhale lest he detect her presence.

He advanced another foot, pausing before the lattice.

She clenched her jaw and shut her eyes.

He stood so close, the noxious mixture of his dinner, pungent cologne, and sweat assaulted her nose. Hot bile rose to her throat, and she swallowed against the burning. Her nose twitched. Flaring her nostrils, she fought to suppress a sneeze.

If he discovered her hidden within the nook, there'd be no escaping the man's amorous attentions. He might claim to prefer blondes, but he'd become bolder each time she encountered him. Given the opportunity, God alone knew what the foxed knave might try in this private bower. Look what he'd attempted on the veranda in full view of anyone who might have come along.

Holding her breath, she pursed her lips.

Do not sneeze.

The captain planted his hands on his ample hips and scanned the shrubberies. He turned in a slow circle. The straining gold buttons of his black tailcoat gleamed in the moonbeams bathing the path. He withdrew a silver flask from his pocket, and after a furtive glance around, took a couple of healthy gulps.

"Where are you? Come out, my sweet." He belched and returned the flask to his pocket. "No need to be coy. I have something of importance to ask you."

Precisely why Ivonne huddled like a timid mouse amongst the foliage outside her parents' mansion. In the past two months, he'd asked the same question thrice before. Her firm "No" each time hadn't deterred him in the least. In fact, her reluctance appeared to make the stocky widower more determined to win her hand.

Grimacing and cautious to keep her gown from rustling, she shifted her weight to her good leg.

Ah, much better.

Wisteria and salmon-colored climbing roses concealed the garden nook. Her favorite hideaway, normally, she would have relished the fragrant air surrounding her. Tonight, however, she could only be grateful the roses' scent masked her perfume and hadn't produced a fit of sneezing.

Ivonne swallowed against the tickle teasing her throat. If only she dared pinch her nostrils. She mustn't. Her gloves against the verdant leaves might give her away. Yearning to slip into one of the nook's inky corners, she yanked her skirt again. The fabric didn't budge.

Captain Kirkpatrick swung his dark gaze to the trellis.

2

Petrified, Ivonne mouthed a silent prayer.

Dear God, don't let him find me.

The distant glow pouring from the manor's open doors bathed the captain in muted light. Kirkpatrick turned his head from side to side, a perplexed frown on his broad face.

"Where'd the chit get to?"

She nearly wept with relief. He hadn't discovered her after all.

Muttering a vulgar curse, he scowled at the couple strolling along the path in his direction.

Bless, Edmund and Edwina. Their presence in the garden wasn't accidental. They must have been looking for her and followed Captain Kirkpatrick. They wouldn't leave her to his mercy.

"Mr. Linville. Miss Linville." He offered the briefest of bows.

Edwina favored him with a tight-lipped smile. "It's a splendid evening for a turn about the gardens. The honeysuckle there," she pointed in the opposite direction of the alcove, "smells divine, does it not, Captain?"

"Er, indeed." He didn't spare the fragrant vine a glimpse. He peered behind them. "You haven't seen Miss Wimpleton, have you?"

Edmund canted his blond head. "Why no, not since I asked her to dance."

"She danced with you? She told me she doesn't dance." Scowling, Captain Kirkpatrick scratched his buttocks.

Staring pointedly at his indecorous behavior, Edwina raised a fair eyebrow.

"No, she doesn't dance anymore, but I still like to make the offer." Edmund flashed one of his engaging smiles. "Ivonne wanted to try her hand at cards tonight. Claimed she felt lucky."

Cards bored Ivonne as much as French lessons or gossip of Prinny, yet she would play the entire night if she didn't have to dance. Never nimble on her feet, with a lame leg, she'd become even less so. A blindfolded elephant in half-boots possessed more grace than she.

Creating a spectacle before two hundred guests again was unthinkable. She had done so once before and found herself plopped upon her derriere, her gown mid-thigh, exposing her legs for all to see. She no longer danced, and gentlemen rarely asked her to. Nonetheless, Edmund always made a token request at those gatherings that included dancing as part of the evening's entertainment.

Her nostrils tingled in warning. Eyes watering, she pressed her teeth together.

Don't sneeze. Don't sneeze.

Do. Not. Sneeze, Ivonne Georgina Augusta Wimpleton.

"Cards, eh?" Captain Kirkpatrick rubbed his chins. "She was taking the air on the terrace a few minutes ago. I'm positive I saw her wandering along this path."

Lying buffoon.

"Oh, I'm sure you're mistaken, Captain." Edwina's voice acquired a harsh edge. "Ivonne might be set upon by an uncouth, *inebriated* lout if she strolled about alone. Lord and Lady Wimpleton would be most displeased if such a thing befell their daughter."

Brava, Edwina.

"Why don't you accompany us inside?" Edmund turned his sister in the direction of the house. "We'll look for Ivonne together."

Ivonne smiled. Her cousins would have the widower examining every unused, cobwebby cranny in the manor. She held her breath against another potential sneeze. Something else must be in bloom. Roses didn't cause her this distress.

The captain shook his oversized, red-haired head. "I'll be along in a moment or two. It's too hot in the house, and I need a few moments more to cool off."

He removed his handkerchief from his coat pocket.

In the faint light, Ivonne detected thick beads of sweat glistening on his mottled features. He did rather resemble a great lathered ox. Truth to tell, everything about the man shouted brutish beast, from his thick-set build, bullish shoulders, and wide face, to his bulging round brown eyes, clomping walk, and gruff, deep-toned voice.

After wiping his damp face, he returned the sopped cloth to his pocket.

Ivonne swore Edwina slid a sidelong glance in the trellis's direction. No surprise there. Her dearest friends, the twins had spent many hours sequestered in this sanctuary with her.

Another sneeze threatened. Ivonne wriggled her nose and twisted her lips, fighting the urge. Was there anything as annoying as trying *not* to sneeze?

Oh, do go along, Captain, will you?

How much longer could she keep stifling her sneezes?

"Captain, I do believe Lady Wimpleton has a delicious iced punch for the gentlemen. A cup or two of the bracing beverage ought to refresh you." Edwina linked her arm with Captain Kirkpatrick's.

Bold as brass was Edwina. Given the man's malodorous form, she was stoic as an undertaker, as well.

"S'pose it would at that." He allowed himself to be led away. Before rounding the footpath's bend, he glanced over his shoulder. His intense gaze lingered on Ivonne's hiding place.

Could he see her?

She retreated and gave her gown a fierce yank. The fabric tore free. The force rattled the lattice, bathing her in a lush shower of petals and leaves. Mouth closed, she sneezed into her hand. A strangled snort emerged.

"What was that?" Captain Kirkpatrick spun around. His gait unsteady, he pounded toward the arbor.

Edwina and Edmund tore along behind him.

Ivonne stepped backward.

Once. Twice. Three times. And bumped into a figure obscured at the rear of the arbor. She shrieked and lunged to flee the alcove.

Firm arms encircled her.

"Hello, Ivy," a familiar male voice whispered in her ear.

3

Chancey Faulkenhurst inhaled Ivy's perfume, relishing the unexpected gift of holding her in his arms. He wanted to kiss her, drink in her essence, water his parched soul with her sweetness.

God, he'd missed her.

"Falcon?" Wonder in her voice, she turned and touched his face. "Is it really you?"

He released a low chuckle. "Indeed, Ivy, it is."

Her nickname slipped from his tongue as if, instead of six long years, he'd seen her yesterday. He'd dubbed her Ivy a score ago—whenever he and Allen came up from school on holiday, she'd clung to them as tenaciously as an ivy vine—and the pet name stuck.

She'd been infuriated and began calling him Falcon instead of Chance as his friends did. He'd rather liked the nickname until her brother started tossing it about. Now, most of Chance's intimate friends addressed him as Falcon.

He wished he could see her features clearly. The fragmented moonbeams revealed little more than ivory skin, dark plum lips, and shiny eyes.

Ivy's gaze sank to his cheek. Her glorious eyes widened, and her breath caught. She brushed a hesitant finger across the scar. "What's this? You've been hurt? Why did no one tell me?"

The puckered inch-long streak was the least of his wounds. Nonetheless, her concern warmed his cynical heart. A heart he'd long ago given to her, though she mustn't know.

He wasn't free to woo her.

"Shh. It's naught." Chance caught her hand with his good one. He pressed her palm to his chest, the only affection he dared show. "I take it you're hiding from that half-sprung brute?"

He tilted his head in the direction of the approaching footsteps. Ivy probably couldn't see the movement. "That obnoxious fellow. Has he been both—"

Kirkpatrick plowed into the arbor, sending another cascade of leaves and petals down upon them. Wheezing, he swung his head back and forth like an enraged bull.

"What goes on here?" he bellowed, sounding much like the creature he resembled.

The fair-haired duo plunged into the bower's other side.

Stifling a snicker, Chance grinned. They reminded him of a pair of fierce pugs ready to take on a bull mastiff. Kirkpatrick didn't stand a tick's chance in hot oil against Ivy's two determined protectors.

The captain drew himself up, his large frame blocking what light managed to penetrate the slats. "Miss Wimpleton, as my future wife, I demand to know. What are you doing in the arms of this man?"

Chest heaving, he flicked his thick fingers contemptuously at Chance.

"Your future wife?" Ivy stiffened and whirled to face the captain. "Have you taken leave of your senses?"

She trembled. In outrage or fear? Both, perhaps.

Ivy made no attempt to step away from Chance, and he allowed himself a pleased smile.

Kirkpatrick scowled and narrowed his eyes to infuriated slits when Chance didn't release her.

He firmed his embrace a fraction, silently challenging the ox.

The other pair stared at his arms encircling her. As one, they raised questioning gazes to his.

Were they prone to nattering? Best not to give them more juicy tidbits to spread about. He reluctantly withdrew his arms, but rested one hand on the small of Ivy's back, as much to satisfy his need to touch her after all this time as to lend her comfort and support.

She wrapped her arms around her middle and edged a step closer to him. Odd, she'd never been one to retreat from a challenge. She did fear the man. That warranted further investigation.

Chance leveled the captain a furious glare.

Voice raspy, she said, "Captain Kirkpatrick, I have told you three times already. I *do not* want to marry you. I *shall not* marry you."

"Three times? Persistent bloke, isn't he?" Chance made no attempt to keep the mockery from his voice.

The twins—Edwina and Edmund Linville, if Chance recalled correctly—laughed.

Giggling, Miss Linville managed, "And those were just the formal proposals. There were at least another half dozen written ones."

"Along with some ... ah ... *creative* poetry scribbled on the reverse of calling cards jammed into bouquets." Edmund offered those morsels, seemingly unaffected by the hostile glower Kirkpatrick leveled at him. In fact, brazen as a doxy on a Saturday night, the plucky fellow winked at the captain. "Delivered every Monday and Thursday, I believe."

Chance took the captain's measure. "You don't say. Perhaps persistent is the wrong word. I'd suggest obsessed might be more apt."

Ivy nodded, the silky hairs on her crown, tickling his chin.

A good portion of the russet strands tumbled about her shoulders. How had her hair come to be in such disarray? Had that sot dared to touch her? Through a haze of ire, Chance tamped down his desire to rearrange the seaman's beefy features. Instead, he concentrated on Ivy's rounded behind pressing into his groin. All sorts of distracting images soared forth as his manhood twitched in approval.

"What say you, Ivy? Have the captain's attentions become bothersome?" Chance pressed her spine gently.

Her focus on Kirkpatrick, she tilted her head. "Yes, Mr. Faulkenhurst, though I've asked him to leave off several times."

She smelled divine, a mixture of spring rain and iris. Chance enjoyed a pleasant view of the valley between the creamy bosoms swelling above her gown's neckline. She made no attempt to put a respectable distance between them.

Then again, she regarded him as a harmless older brother. One of the reasons, at three and twenty, he'd petitioned for a transfer to India to support the East India troops. A harmless older brother didn't harbor the sensual fantasies she elicited in him or want to step closer to enjoy her womanly curves more fully.

Though a commissioned lieutenant in His Majesty's Regiments, as a second son of an earl, he had nothing to offer a viscount's daughter except a hundred or so sheep and a long-neglected estate in Cheshire his mother bequeathed him. Did Foxbrooke Cottage even remain standing? When he'd last heard, the rundown house wasn't fit for habitants other than vermin and insects.

He couldn't claim an officer's income anymore either. Naturally, he'd sell his commission, but at less than twelve hundred pounds, the monies wouldn't begin to restore Foxbrooke, let alone support Ivy in the manner she was accustomed to.

He could seek a position as a steward or a secretary with one of his titled friends. However, with a hand short two fingers, writing presented a challenge. Would offers of employment be prompted by pity rather than genuine need? Heaven forbid. He continued to practice writing with his right hand but made slower progress than he wished. And truth to tell, even if gainfully employed, he'd not be worthy of Ivy.

The damnable agreement Father contrived with his crony, Lord Lambert, while Chance fought in India, presented a rather troublesome complication too. For a hefty marriage settlement, his sire pledged Chance would marry Lambert's widowed daughter, Cornelia Washburn, when he returned to England.

Eight years his senior, if Chance's memory served correctly, she possessed a termagant's temperament and had one eye that was wont to look off sideways.

He adjusted his injured arm, and white pain vibrated to his shoulder. The wound hadn't completely healed. The optimistic surgeon who'd repaired the limb assured Chance he'd get *most* of the use of his arm back, though the same couldn't be guaranteed of his hand.

Astute fellow. One could assume the man of medicine had never known a human to regrow fingers.

The twins advanced further into the arbor, their hostile gazes raking the fuming captain.

Linville brushed a strand of hair off his forehead and met Chance's gaze. "Allen told the captain to desist in his addresses, yet he continues to pursue Ivonne."

"I've given him no cause whatsoever to encourage his attentions." Ivy glanced at Chance, desperation in her eyes. "I've taken to avoiding him at every turn."

She held her head high, although he detected the tremor in her voice. Kirkpatrick terrified her. Chance reached for his sword, but his hand met air. The blade no longer hung by his side. He'd like nothing better than to run the captain—in his cups or not—through for tormenting Ivy.

"Why don't you leave off? Miss Wimpleton has made it clear she doesn't return your regard." Chance turned his blandest stare on the seaman.

Kirkpatrick grunted and waved his hand. "It's not like she has a multitude of other offers. I'm the only man of means who's shown any interest in her this season."

Bloody bastard.

Ivy drew in a swift breath and stiffened. "My offers are none of your concern."

"Have you set your sights on one of those pretty pocket-to-let milksops whose only interest in you is your sizable settlement?" He wiped his mouth with the back of his hand and blundered on. "Once wed, they'll retire you to a countryside hovel and not look upon you again."

She snorted. "Don't pretend you're not as interested in my portion, Captain. Though we both know it's Garnkirk House you covet."

"Garnkirk House?" Chance wasn't familiar with the place.

She gave a sharp nod. "An estate—mine upon my marriage—near the Scottish border."

Kirkpatrick puffed out his barrel chest. "I, at least, am prepared to overlook your limp—"

Limp? What limp?

"—and unremarkable appearance to keep you at my side." A self-satisfied smile bent the captain's mouth. He ogled Ivy's breasts, clearly finding her far more appealing than he admitted.

Damn him to hell.

Fury gripped Chance. He didn't care if excess drink had emboldened Kirkpatrick, the churl deserved a sound throttling.

Was the lackwit blind? Ivy was exquisite. At least the woman-child Chance had left behind had been.

The light in the arbor only hinted at her current loveliness, though he had no doubt she'd developed into a rare beauty. Nothing ostentatious like a diamond or ruby, but rather a pearl or opal, stunning in its innocent simplicity. The delightful creature he'd held in his arms moments ago had been perfectly rounded in the right places too. The recollection sparked a predictable and uncomfortable response from his manhood.

Chance itched to plant Kirkpatrick a facer. Breaking the knuckles of his remaining decent hand would be worth it. Only years of soldiering lent him the self-control he required to warn the captain with words rather than pummel the bounder with fists.

Sometimes, being a gentleman was a blasted bore.

"You step beyond the mark, Captain. Way beyond." Chance curved his fingers around Ivy's slender waist.

She shivered and scooted nearer to him.

Muted voices sounded outside. He cocked his head. Allen and his chums? Chance smiled to himself. Yes. This ought to get very interesting.

He scratched his nose. "Pray tell me, Kirkpatrick, why, in all that's holy, would Miss Wimpleton marry you after you've publically insulted her?"

Let the seadog rant on. He wouldn't be allowed anywhere near the upper salons or *haut ton* gatherings once Harcourt and the others gave the captain the cut direct.

Kirkpatrick pointed a stubby finger at her. "She ought to be grateful I'd consider wedding a chit almost on the shelf."

Ivy and Miss Linville gasped in mutual indignation.

"You misbegotten cur!" Hands fisted, Linville made to confront the captain.

Chance's hand to the young buck's shoulder stayed him. "Don't. The sot's burying himself, good and deep. He's neck high in horse manure. A couple more words and the dolt will be choking on the filth."

Captain Kirkpatrick narrowed his eyes, scowling at Ivy.

"Don't tell me you intend to accept decrepit Lord Walsingham or doddering Lord Craythorn? Both are sixty if they're a day." He lifted his nose and raked her from toe to top, his censure obvious. "You told me you adored children. Neither of those codgers could get a child on you a decade ago, let alone now."

More gasps followed his crass statement.

God rot the bloody bugger.

Smirking, Kirkpatrick patted his chest. "I assure you, I'd have you expecting in a blink."

Ivy made an inarticulate sound and swayed.

Chance steadied her, clenching his jaw against the oaths surging to his tongue. He ached to call the oaf out. Wisdom warned him that to do so meant certain death. His fighting arm was useless. Frustration and impotent rage seized him. He couldn't protect Ivy the way she deserved.

Through half-closed eyes, he observed her.

Profile to Chance, she stared at Kirkpatrick. An almost undiscernible curling of her upper lip hinted at the repugnance she attempted to conceal. Her rapidly rising and falling breasts revealed her agitation.

Did she think Chance a coward for not confronting the captain? The idea stung sharper than his wounded arm. By God, he'd die to protect her, but he wasn't a dullard. Cunning and shrewdness must be his weapons of choice.

Kirkpatrick, wrapped in his own self-importance, seemed oblivious to her contempt. "Why, I have five strapping boys already."

"Ill-mannered bratlings you mean." Miss Linville jutted her chin skyward and glared at him. "Horrid little fat beasts."

"Indeed they are." By way of explanation, Edmund added, "We came upon them in Green Park last week. The older two chased a terrified dog, the middle two threw pebbles at passersby, and the toddler had dropped his drawers in full view of everyone to relieve himself on a tree."

Chance choked on a guffaw.

God's toenails.

Ivy *must* be spared such horror.

She stalked to Captain Kirkpatrick and slanted her head to meet his gaze square on.

There was the feisty girl Chance remembered.

"You pretentious buffoon. You think I'm so desperate to avoid spinsterhood, I'd accept the likes of you?" Her voice quivered and raised an octave with her last few clipped words.

Spinsterhood?

Ivy couldn't be more than, what? One or two and twenty? Hardly old maid material.

Three tall forms shadowed the trellis outside. Ah, the reinforcements had arrived.

Chance stepped beside Ivy. "If you have a lick of sense, Kirkpatrick, you'll leave now."

The captain swaggered further into the bower. "Or what? You'll make me? Ivonne is all but betrothed to me. Her father has as much as promised me her hand."

"No. He has not." Ivy clasped a hand across her mouth, backing away and shaking her head. "He wouldn't."

"That's a brazen lie!"

"How dare you address her by her first name?"

The Linville twins' voices rang out in unison.

Chance allowed a slow grin to tilt his lips. "Impossible."

Ivy peered at him, curiosity in her gaze.

He took her quaking hand in his, careful to keep his disfigured fingers tucked inside his coat. "You see, Kirkpatrick, Ivy is already promised to ... another."

4

*P*romised?

Ivonne angled her head. She'd misheard. Her nerves and this hullabaloo with Captain Kirkpatrick had her hearing ridiculous things.

Silly goosecap.

Falcon hadn't announced she was pledged to another. Had he?

She tried to read his expression in the muted light. What was he about? Trying to protect her? He almost sounded jealous.

The notion sent a delicious spark to her middle, and the warmth spread to other unmentionable parts in a most curious fashion. She shifted to alleviate the peculiar sensation.

He didn't know that Captain Kirkpatrick wouldn't rest until he unearthed her phantom intended. The widower wanted Garnkirk House. The one hundred eighty acre estate boasted prime hunting and fishing lands. The captain's obsession with his hobbies bordered on unhealthy.

Falcon's long absence from the *ton* had kept him ignorant of Kirkpatrick's reputation. The wealthy ship captain's questionable business association with several powerful peers permitted him the luxury of hovering on *le beau monde's* outer fringes.

The widower would place a few prying questions in the right ears and the truth would out. Then where would she be? She expelled a controlled breath. As long as the captain turned his interest elsewhere, she didn't care what *on dit* the chinwags bandied about. She was made of sterner stuff than that.

Or so she told herself.

A disturbance outside the arbor reined in her musings. The Earl of Luxmoore, the Duke of Harcourt, and Allen crowded into the already overfull bower. A herring-packed tin allowed more room for movement. She wrinkled her nose. And possibly smelled better too.

She sneezed then sneezed again.

"Bless you." Edwina produced a lacy scrap of cloth. "Have you need of a handkerchief?"

"Yes, thank you." Ivonne accepted the linen and pressed it to her nose. The cloth offered some relief from Captain Kirkpatrick's reeking person.

The cozy nook meant for two or three, now teemed with eight bodies, six of whom were muscular males, and one of those rivaled a gorilla in size, smell, and mannerisms.

Ivonne's leg ached, and all of a sudden, she felt somewhat faint. The confined quarters, Falcon's startling announcement, and the captain's belligerent presence, along with her empty stomach, contributed to her light-headedness.

She attempted, without success, to shift away from the mass of bodies.

Captain Kirkpatrick's intimidating form lurked before her.

No reprieve there.

Edmund stood mashed against her on the right. The arbor's wall hindered movement to her immediate left. Both prevented her from easing away from Falcon's solid form pressing into her from behind.

The latter she didn't mind too much, truth to tell. In fact, the most outlandish urge to lean into him and wiggle her bum plagued her.

How would he react if I did?

The stale air and lack of food must have addled her senses.

Giving herself a mental shake, she peered at the new arrivals. She could scarcely make out who was who within the gloomy interior.

His countenance grim, Allen faced Captain Kirkpatrick. "I've asked you before, as has my father, to direct your attentions elsewhere. My sister is not now, nor will she ever be, available to consider your suit."

The widower's eyes widened before narrowing in suspicion. "Because she's promised to another? Who?"

"I'd say that's a private family matter." Luxmoore flicked something from his shoulder.

A leaf?

A spider?

Were the nasty devils burrowing into her tresses? Ivonne swept her hand across the top of her head, and then through the tangled mass at her nape a couple of times. She'd be hard-pressed to say which she reviled more. ... The captain or the spiders?

"If she's not on the Marriage Mart, why haven't I heard mention of the fact before?" Captain Kirkpatrick crossed his arms and glared round the nook. "Something here is too smoky by far, and I mean to find out what it is."

On second thought, spiders are adorable creatures compared to Kirkpatrick.

"Why don't you do that?" Lord Luxmoore stepped forward. "Elsewhere."

"Yes, a splendid idea." The duke joined Luxmoore beside the widower. "I'm sure there are a multitude of eager gossips within the house willing to assist you with your intrusive meddling."

Each placed a hand on one of the sea captain's arms.

Snarling, he jerked from their holds. He loomed before Ivonne.

Lifting her chin a notch, she forced herself to meet his angry eyes as he towered above her. Marriage to this man was unthinkable. He would terrorize her every day he remained ashore.

"I mean to get to the bottom of this, Miss Wimpleton. I delayed sailing and wasted months courting you with the intention of making you a mother to my sons. I won't be made a fool of."

"Did that by yourself, seems to me," Edmund muttered.

Beside him, Edwina clapped and giggled. "Brilliant, Eddy."

Captain Kirkpatrick rounded on Edmund. "Stubble it, young pup, before I thrash you soundly."

"Do come along, Kirkpatrick." An exaggerated sigh echoed from near the exit, and His Grace beckoned. "I've had quite enough of your Drury Lane theatrics for one evening. ... Unless we need to notify Lord Wimpleton we require a dozen strapping footmen to haul you from the premises."

"You sure a dozen will suffice?" Falcon's jeer resulted in another round of snickers.

"Bloody arses." Spinning on his heel, the captain stomped from the nook.

The duke and earl swung their attention to her brother.

Allen waved them away. "We'll see you inside. Keep an eye on Kirkpatrick, will you?"

With a nod and a half-bow to the ladies, Harcourt and Luxmoore trailed after the grumbling seaman.

"We'll also be going." Edwina's curious gaze swung between Ivonne and Falcon. "I'm sure you've much to discuss."

She didn't move an inch but instead, head angled and finger on her chin, continued to study Ivonne and Falcon. Edwina was too astute by far. "Ivonne, do you—"

"Um, yes," Edmund seized his sister's arm. "We'll let Aunt Mary and Uncle Walter know where you are. Come along, Winnie."

After a cocky salute, he dragged Edwina from the enclosure.

They broke into furious whispers the moment their feet hit the gravel path. What were those two conjuring now?

Ivonne eyed the exit longingly.

This evening had the makings of a Cheltenham Tragedy. She'd been accosted, made an inglorious spectacle of, rescued by the only man who'd ever sent her heart palpitating and nether regions tingling, and she would bet her pin money that within fifteen minutes, her name would buzz about the ballroom thicker than bees on honey.

She wanted nothing more than to sneak in the house's side entrance and flee to her room where she could hide under her bed until next December.

Maybe her parents could be persuaded to depart for Addington Hall early. The social whirl ended in a few weeks in any event. Unless God performed a miracle, she stood no more chance of snaring herself a husband this go round than she had the previous Seasons. She had become an object of scorn and pity.

She would simply refuse to attend another. After all, five stints in Town had quite proved the *bon ton* deemed her an undesirable. Only fortune hunters sought her out, and even they treated her with barely concealed disdain. Allen could contrive some drivel about her phantom intended crying off.

He had eloped with an actress, entered a monastery, had been sat upon by a blind hippopotamus ...

The reason didn't much matter.

Ivonne had long since accepted her fate. Some women were destined to live life alone. Her shoulders slumped. Weariness born more from emotional turmoil than physical fatigue encompassed her.

"If you'll excuse me, I need to repair my appearance." She offered Falcon a brave smile. He would never know how much it cost her to pretend indifference when what she longed to do was throw her arms around his neck, kiss those gorgeous lips of his, and tell him she loved him.

Stop it, goosecap.

He'd made no effort to contact her in six years, and that stung something fierce. No, his indifference had left a deep wound and no small amount of distrust.

"It was wonderful to see you again, Mr. Faulkenhurst."

Should she suggest he call?

No. Likely Allen had already extended an invitation of some sort, which explained Falcon's presence here tonight. Let her brother be the one to issue another. She would only appear desperate to see Falcon again.

Because I am. But to what point?

Waterworks threatened, and Ivonne blinked rapidly. She would not shed another tear for him.

She would not.

"Ivy ...?" He reached for her hand, concern shading his voice.

A single tear trickled a scalding path from the outer corner of her eye. She spun away. Lifting her skirts, she tore from the alcove.

5

Ivy wept.

Chance was certain, although his gut told him her tears couldn't be attributed solely to the captain's boorish behavior.

Allen stared after his sister's fleeing form before facing Chance, a question in his hooded eyes. "I say, what was that about?"

"I'm sure I have no idea why she pelted off in such haste." Raising a brow, Chance met Allen's shuttered scrutiny.

He did, but the niggling thought was scarcely more than a heartbeat. Her response to him hadn't been that of a sister. He needed time to reflect on the notion. He must tread carefully if he had any hope, no matter how remote or seemingly impossible, of making her his.

Staring at the now empty pathway, Chance rubbed the side of his nose. "Perhaps Ivy feared someone would see her in disarray."

"No, not her abrupt departure. I meant telling Kirkpatrick my sister is promised to someone else." Allen eyed him, expectancy written on his features.

Damn, Allen wouldn't let that falsehood go unaccounted for.

"Ah, that." Chance offered a weak chuckle. "Not one of my cleverer moments, I'll confess."

He traced the scar on his cheek, recalling Ivy's gentle touch. She hadn't seemed the least repulsed by the jagged mark.

"I said the one thing I thought would make the boor leave off pursuing her." He didn't elaborate how he'd bitten his tongue to keep from saying, "Promised to *me*."

If only he'd dared to. What would have happened?

Mrs. Washburn's freckled face, immediately followed by his sire's disproving countenance, flashed to mind. Hell, with that ridiculous millstone about his neck, Chance must proceed with the greatest of caution.

He rubbed his arm then his hand. He might indulge in a bit of laudanum tonight—to take the edge off the pain. More on point, the drug would numb his mind and the tormenting thoughts of Ivy, which guaranteed another sleepless night.

Allen drew in a gusty breath and ran his hand through his dark hair. "I'm heartily sick of the captain, I can tell you. I don't trust the sod one whit. He'll not let this fabricated affiancing story die a quiet death. Of that I'm positive."

"Why is he here tonight if you and Ivy find him so offensive?" Chance's arm throbbed. He needed to say his farewells soon. "Did your mother invite him?"

Allen snorted. "Absolutely not. Mother cannot abide Kirkpatrick, either. The bugger hangs on the coat sleeves of others. I'm sure he wrangled an invitation to accompany one of his business cronies."

Allen exited the bower ahead of Chance.

"I'll speak to Mother. I'm thinking she needs to further refine her guest list."

"Indeed." Chance followed him outside, grateful for the fresh air filling his lungs. He'd guess no part of Kirkpatrick had seen the inside of a tub in a good while. Imagining Ivy with the man set Chance's teeth on edge once again.

"So, this is where you got off to." Grinning, Allen gestured toward the alcove. "Thought you were in the library, but when I checked, you'd disappeared. I wondered where you'd sequestered yourself."

He threw an arm across Chance's shoulders. "No need to hide, Faulkenhurst."

Chance winced as pain speared his arm and hand. "I wasn't hiding. I wanted to reacquaint myself with the grounds, and you have to admit, the air within the house is intolerable."

Not nearly as intolerable as the arbor.

Truth to tell, he had been avoiding the throng inside the manor.

He'd arrived this evening, terrified he'd encounter Ivy and equally desperate to do so. He hadn't expected her to dash into the bower while he lurked there. Rather awkward to be caught skulking in the garden alcove. He'd opened his mouth to tell her he stood behind her when the sea crab appeared.

Her fear of the man tangible, Ivy had needed safeguarding. So, Chance remained silent and, in some measure, grateful he had a legitimate reason not to return to the ball.

Pasting a fake smile on his face and pretending nonchalance about his crippling injuries took a greater toll than he'd imagined they would. He'd endured more pitying glances and ignored more horrified gasps and looks of revulsion than anyone ought to in a single night.

Wonder what long-toothed Mrs. Washburn and her father will think of my condition?

Didn't matter what they thought. Chance had no intention of honoring his father's ludicrous proposal. Although the blame for the bumblebroth lay at Father's feet, the delicate situation needed discrete handling.

Excusing himself from the ball early on, Chance had drifted to the library. Reading had proved futile. Laying the book aside, he'd wandered to the French windows and stared blankly at the night. The lure of the arbor called him.

He'd been unable to resist a visit to another time, when he'd dreamed Ivy might be his. She'd dwelled in his thoughts, and though he'd been no monk, he'd never desired another as much as her.

When a man gave his heart to a woman, other females might temporarily satiate his physical desire, but his soul continued to yearn for its mate, seeking the wholeness no other could offer.

Yesterday, when Allen insisted he join him at his table at White's, Chance had posed several subtle questions regarding the family's health, business ventures, and finally, he'd dared to inquire about Ivy.

Allen had smiled knowingly, as if he'd expected the conversation to shift to a discussion about his sister. Peculiar that. Chance had never confided in his long-time friend, never hinted he held Ivy in any special regard. He couldn't contain his broad smile or the joy that had swept him upon learning she remained unmarried.

"There's no shortage of damsels inside eager for dance partners." His arm about Chance's shoulders, Allen set their course toward the bustling mansion. "Unless you forgot how to perform *Mr. Beveridge's Maggot* in the wilds of India."

Chance didn't want to dance with those ladies. A sable-haired, hazel-eyed sprite with a beauty mark beside her left nostril was the only woman he ever wanted to hold in his arms. And if he'd heard correctly in the arbor, she didn't dance anymore.

"I'll tell you, I could use a stiff swallow of French brandy after that nonsense with Kirkpatrick." Allen withdrew his arm and quickened his pace.

Their shoes clicked on the limestone pavers as they neared the house.

"I'd not say no to a nip of cognac," Chance admitted.

"Let's find you a dance partner, and I'll make sure the Jack Nasty Face took his leave." Allen tossed Chance a familiar teasing grin. "Then we'll both indulge in a finger's worth or two."

The drink sounded wonderful.

The dance Chance would pass on. Dancing required the touching of hands.

Allen's grin widened. "I do believe that scar on your cheek improves your devilish good looks. Makes you seem mysterious and debonair. Second son or not, the ladies will be vying for your attention."

Chance stopped and yanked off his modified glove. He raised his disfigured hand. "Even with this? I think you over-estimate my attraction, my friend."

"Does it pain you still?" Brow creased, Allen stared at the two nubs where Chance's middle and forefinger used to be.

A long, jagged scar disappeared into the wristband of his coat sleeve.

"Some. It's been less than six months." He tugged the glove on, not without some difficulty. Thank God Allen didn't offer to help. Chance crooked his lips upward.

"You should see the scar on my forearm. Nearly lost the thing. I imagine I look a bit like that creature in that new novel. What's it called?"

He sent a contemplative glance skyward.

"Ah, I remember." Chance lowered his voice to an eerie growl. *"Frankenstein."*

Allen's expression grew serious. "Don't be absurd. Mangled arm and minus two fingers, you're more of a man than ninety percent of the coves here tonight."

"Only ninety?" Chance quipped to hide the emotion Allen's kind words aroused.

Lost in thought, Chance ascended the terrace steps. The veranda swarmed with guests, no doubt seeking fresh air.

Allen stopped on the top riser and gave him a broad grin. "I've missed you, Falcon. We all have."

"There you are, Allen, Faulkenhurst." Lord Wimpleton, his usually jovial countenance severe, strode in their direction. Upon reaching them, he gave a cursory glance around.

No one paid them any mind.

His brow furrowed, the viscount dropped his voice. "Please explain to me if either of you have the slightest idea why, in the last ten minutes,

I've had several guests offer me congratulations on my daughter's betrothal."

6

Edging the library's terrace door open a crack, Ivonne peered inside. No one.

A single lamp burned low atop the mantle. A leather volume lay open on the dark puce and ebony settee. Odd. Who would have been in here tonight? One didn't attend a ball with the intention of seeking a spot to read.

Someone chose to avoid the gathering. Why?

She slipped inside, closing the door behind her. The latch sank home with a soft click. She still clutched Edwina's wadded handkerchief. Ivonne smiled wryly and tucked the cloth inside her bodice. Rushing to the other entrance, her emerald satin slippers scuffed atop the Axminster carpet.

Her gaze fell on her reflection in the oval mirror positioned above a mahogany drum table, and she faltered to a sudden stop. Gads, her appearance bordered on indecent. Without much stretch of the imagination, guests might ponder if she'd indulged in a dalliance in the garden.

Ivonne raised a hand to the hair trailing down her spine and over her left shoulder and plucked two small leaves from the tendrils. Glancing down, she sighed. A torn piece of black netting dangled above her hemline. Bending, she inspected the tear.

Not awful. A few artful stitches ought to repair the rip.

Should she seek her chamber on the third floor or the lady's retiring room just down the hall? The retiring room seemed the more logical choice to set herself aright. Except ... what if other ladies occupied the chamber? How would she explain her unkempt appearance? The gossip coffers already overflowed on her behalf tonight.

She shrugged. So be it.

She would tell any ladies in the room that she took a spill into the shrubberies. Given her penchant for tripping and stumbling, no one ought to question the taradiddle.

Ivonne cracked open the door and took a furtive peek up and down the hall.

All clear.

She hurried the few yards to the retiring room. Taking a deep breath, she pasted a smile on her face and pressed the lever down. The door swung open.

Empty, thank goodness. Not even a maid.

Where was Barrett? It wasn't like the servant to leave her post.

Grateful for the reprieve Ivonne stepped inside and closed her eyes for a long moment. She took a steadying breath—the first relaxed one she'd enjoyed since tearing from the terrace.

Chancey Faulkenhurst.

Falcon.

His handsome face forced its way to the forefront of her mind. After all this time, he'd returned. Her imprudent heart beat faster. Why did he have to return now, when she'd finally put him behind her? When she was crippled and considered past her prime? When he could never be hers?

Ivonne opened her eyes and shook her head. A rose petal floated to the floor. His homecoming changed nothing.

Locating a table with mirrors, assorted fripperies, hair pins, and such, she took a seat. After yanking off her gloves, she set them aside and went about haphazardly repinning her mass of hair.

Falcon had spent many hours in the garden nook with her—until he'd left for India. She had pleaded with her parents for two weeks straight before they finally relented and gave her permission to correspond with him, as long as they read every letter first.

A flush of chagrin heated her face. What they must have thought. She'd been such a fawning, green girl.

She'd not heard from Falcon once during his absence. Not a single page, though she'd written to him every week the first year. At sixteen, she'd believed her heart would never recover when she finally accepted he wasn't going to answer her letters. She'd brooded about in a fit of the blue devils for months.

If he'd cared an iota for her, he would have written. Not a single line in six years sent an indisputable message. He wasn't interested. She was no featherbrain. She'd misinterpreted his kindness and thoughtfulness for something more.

Something which would never be.

Ivonne had come to realize her childish dream of marrying him had been just that: a silly, unattainable fantasy. Somehow, the knowledge alleviated her girlish infatuation, although over the years, she hadn't become enamored of anyone else. Nor had she encouraged other suitors' attentions either—not that there'd been a horde of them to begin with.

Nonetheless, a part of her heart would always belong to Falcon. She had resolutely tucked that piece away and refused to extract the fragment from its snug resting place. The remainder of her heart she kept guarded, not willing to suffer such torment again. Once in a lifetime was quite enough, thank you.

As much as she once adored him, years' worth of callous indifference had created a chasm between them. She would never trust her emotions again, especially not love.

She supposed that's why she'd been accused of being unapproachable and standoffish.

On one occasion, she overheard a group of gentlemen suggest that the swan ice sculpture their hosts commissioned for the Yuletide gala possessed more personality and warmth than she. One dandy had mockingly called her Icy Ivonne. The others sniggered in obvious agreement.

Truth to tell, she compared every man to Falcon, and all came up wanting.

She paused and stared at her reflection in the mirror.

The woman peering back at her wasn't disagreeable nor was she particularly noteworthy. Clear hazel eyes, more oval than round and almost green in the candlelight, were her best feature besides her alabaster skin. A rather square chin, pert mouth with too full lips, and straight dark hair of a nondescript shade of brown completed her inventory.

No, a diamond of the first water she wasn't. Falcon possessed the beauty she lacked. Men weren't supposed to be beautiful, but to describe him otherwise, didn't do him justice.

No other male possessed eyes quite the same gray-blue as he, like the sea after a mighty winter tempest. A hint of humor and kindness always glimmered in their thick-lashed depths. High cheekbones and a straight aristocratic nose, combined with those sculpted lips and his dark blond hair streaked with gold ... she released a long, shuddering breath.

He was as close to Adonis in the flesh as she'd ever seen. She'd been paraded before young dandies and bucks aplenty, and although handsome, some profoundly so, all paled in comparison to Falcon.

Ivonne frowned.

He bore a fresh scar on his cheek. In the arbor's muted light, the mark barely showed. His hair had gleamed gold, more than she remembered, though his eyes seemed darker.

Cooler. Distant.

Icy Ivonne she might be, but Falcon's smile possessed the ability to transform her into a mass of melted flummery. Only, now, she neared her third and twentieth birthday and no longer wore her emotions on her sleeve like a flighty girl.

He'd never learn how he affected her.

Securing the last pin, she scrutinized her attempt to repair her coiffure. She patted the back of her head, unable to tell if all her hair was in place. True, the style wasn't the elaborate coiled knot Dawson created earlier this evening, but at least her locks weren't tumbling down her back in shocking disarray.

Ivonne twisted to examine the chamber. Where were the sewing supplies?

The door flew open and several women filed in.

Lydia Farnsworth smiled kindly before disappearing behind a screen.

The Dundercroft sisters, Francine and Lyselle, tripped to a stop, as did their constant companion, Penelope Rossington.

Perfect.

Three of London's worst rumormongers with scarcely a speck of common sense amongst them.

Barrett scooted past the ladies. She dipped a curtsy.

"Oh, Miss Wimpleton, please excuse my absence. I had to fetch more towels." She lifted the stack of snowy cloths she held. "The ladies have suffered dreadfully from the heat this evening."

Ivonne smiled. "It's quite all right. I need to mend my gown. It sustained a minor tear when I was in the garden."

A petite, shapely blonde, Miss Rossington glided further into the room. Uncommonly attractive, she knew it well.

Ivonne stifled a gasp. Had Miss Rossington dampened her gown?

That's what came of having no mother, an overindulgent father, and the morals of a barnyard cat.

Ivonne's modest endowments appeared childlike next to such curvaceousness. Of course, if she puffed her chest out in the same manner, she'd appear more buxom too. Walking about aiming one's bosoms skyward must cause a fierce backache and wreak havoc on one's balance.

Not worth the discomfort or danger.

She prayed the attention Allen directed toward Miss Rossington was driven by politeness and not any intent on his part to court the wench. A slight shudder shook her. A worse sister-in-law she couldn't imagine.

"Whatever were you doing that you tore your gown, Miss Wimpleton?" Miss Rossington's gaze focused on the mirror behind Ivonne. Her citrine eyes—the exact same shade as Ivonne's ancient cat, Sir Pounce—rounded. A smirk curved Miss Rossington's ruby-tinted lips.

Captain Kirkpatrick. Blast him to Hades.

The freckled Dundercroft misses tittered behind their pudgy hands.

Ivonne stared at the trio, a chill causing the flesh on her arms to pucker.

What Banbury Tales had the captain concocted when he'd come inside? Alarm and shame engulfed her. What would she say to her parents? How could she explain this bumblebroth away without partially blaming Falcon for claiming she was promised?

"Is it true?" Miss Rossington advanced another few mincing steps. She cast her cohorts a secretive smile. "You've managed to get yourself affianced at *long* last?"

Heaven help me.

"I ..." Ivonne swallowed, dread drying her mouth. She loathed lying.

"Who is he?" Envy twisted the corners of the elder Miss Dundercroft's thin lips.

"Yes, do tell." Miss Lyselle fairly danced in anticipation. Her plump bosoms and curls bounced with her excitement. She clapped her hands together. "Do we know him? Is he here tonight?"

"Is that why you've shrubbery in your mussed hair and your dress is torn?" Miss Rossington swept her hand across her perfectly styled flaxen hair. Her diamond and sapphire bracelet shimmered in the candlelight. She smiled, a malicious glint in her feline eyes.

She tittered unkindly. "Your hair looks like an owl in an ivy bush ... *a-la-blowze.*"

Poufy? Still?

Ivonne touched her hair and peered into the mirror over her shoulder.

Miss Rossington snuck up behind her. In one deft move, she plucked something from Ivonne's hair. She displayed the coral petal for the others to see.

A fresh round of giggles erupted from the Dundercrofts. Glee pinkened their already ruddy complexions. Bright red blotches covered their faces, chests, and arms.

Miss Kingsley appeared behind them.

Ivonne's breath caught. She was in attendance tonight? Did Allen know? When had she arrived?

An exquisite redhead, the woman had been in the Caribbean with her brother and father for the past three years. At one time, Ivonne had thought Allen enamored of the beauty.

"Really, *girls.*" Miss Kingsley emphasized the word, indicating what she thought of them and staring pointedly at Miss Rossington. "I'm certain if Lord and Lady Wimpleton wanted their guests to know Miss Wimpleton's joyous news, they'd make an announcement this evening."

No condemnation in her gaze, she flashed Ivonne a brilliant smile. "Sometimes, people prefer to keep the arrangements to themselves for a time. A promise to marry is, after all, a very special occurrence, and one to cherish, not toss about like a shuttlecock during a game."

Miss Rossington's face flamed, and she scowled at Miss Kingsley.

"Don't you agree, Miss Rossington?" Miss Kingsley tilted her head, a secretive smile curving her lips.

Miss Rossington suddenly became fixated with her bracelet.

Ivonne couldn't recall a time when the chit didn't have some sort of sharp retort on the tip of her tongue.

Lydia Farnsworth emerged from behind the screen. "Miss Wimpleton, if you'll permit me, you've a few leaves and rose petals in your hair."

She pointed to Ivonne's head. "Just there, below your crown."

Ivonne braved a smile. No doubt they considered her a promiscuous tart now that she was supposedly betrothed. She couldn't refute a word of it. She nodded and turned to face the mirror once more. "If you would be so kind."

After giving Ivonne a reassuring smile and skimming her gaze over Miss Rossington, who glared daggers, Miss Kingsley took her turn behind the painted screen.

Through lowered lashes, Ivonne observed Miss Rossington in the mirror's reflection. She sank gracefully into a chair before another mirror at the same table where Ivonne sat. The Dundercrofts huddled on either side like dumpy sentinels.

Two other tables and she must choose to sit at this one?

A smug smile stretched Miss Rossington's lips, exposing her perfect teeth.

What, no feline incisors? No claws hidden inside her gloves or tail twitching beneath her skirt? No hissing or scratching? No gagging and choking on an enormous, hairball, more's the pity?

"Mr. Faulkenhurst is in attendance this evening," Miss Rossington fairly purred as she removed her gloves and sent a sideways glance toward the screen.

Ah, baring our claws now, are we?

Her cat eyes narrowed. "Newly arrived from India, I believe."

"Oh, he's a handsome one." Miss Lyselle sighed, a dreamy expression on her chubby face.

"No, dear, he won't do at all." Miss Dundercroft admonished her younger sister with a stern stare. "Not only is he a penniless second son," disgust pinched her mouth, "the man's disfigured."

How dare she?

Ivonne straightened her spine, prepared to give the haughty chit a proper set down. "He most certain—"

"They say," Miss Rossington ran her fingers along her fan's carved ivory guard, her sultry gaze affixed on Ivonne, "he lost his *manhood* to those barbarians."

7

The Wimpletons' mahogany longcase clock chimed the early morning hour of two. Legs stretched before him and his ankles crossed, Chance settled further into the leather wingback chair before the library's blazing hearth. He took a long pull from the glass he held, welcoming the brandy's heat sluicing to his gut.

In the silence of the slumbering household, he'd grown chilled.

The house proved drafty, and London's temperatures were far cooler than those he'd become accustomed to in India. He'd forgotten how penetrating the damp could be. After asking a footman to light the logs arranged in the Rumford fireplace, Chance had spent the last hour staring into the soothing, hypnotic flames.

Yesterday, he'd gratefully accepted Allen's invitation to stay with the Wimpletons until he became settled in England. Chance boasted no residence of his own in London, and although he could open his brother's house in Mayfair, that seemed more bother than necessary. Especially since Chance didn't know how long he'd be in Town. He had several business dealings to attend to before he trotted off to Suttoncliffe Hall and surprised his family.

He hadn't written to inform them of his return or that he'd been injured. They had worries enough of their own. Thad, his brother, and Thad's wife expected their first child any day, and Chance's sister, Annabel, had her hands full with her scapegrace of a husband.

The rhythmic *tick-tocking* of the clock beckoned sleep, yet slumber eluded Chance as it often had these past months. When he drifted into a fitful rest, nightmares awakened him. Drenched in sweat, his heart pounding with the force of a blacksmith's hammer against an anvil, he'd stare into the darkness until the horrific visions faded into the shadows of his mind.

Concentrating on Ivy's serene features, sweet smile, and the dimple in her right cheek banished the memories until sleep seduced him once more.

A greater concern this night was the damage Kirkpatrick's jealousy and flapping tongue had caused. Not only had he stretched Chance's suggestion that Ivy was promised to another into a full-fledged contracted betrothal, the blackguard had suggested the wedding would take place within a month or two.

As Chance came in from the terrace, he overheard the captain speaking to a small crowd

"Lord Wimpleton insists the announcement will be forthcoming any day," Kirkpatrick said.

Lying cawker.

At Chance's behest, Sethwick questioned the captain. "How is it you are privy to such intimate information?"

Kirkpatrick told Sethwick, in addition to several other guests, "Lord Wimpleton requested an audience with me the moment I reentered the ballroom."

What drivel.

According to Captain Kirkpatrick, Lord Wimpleton apologized for his daughter's fast behavior as well as leading the poor widower on.

"My daughter knows full well I negotiated a settlement with another gentleman long before either she or I made your acquaintance, Captain Kirkpatrick. Please accept my humblest apologies, and rest assured, if she were not already spoken for, I would be most happy to consider your offer."

Blatant lies, according to Allen and his father.

Recalling the conversation, Chance scowled.

If Kirkpatrick couldn't have Ivy, he was determined no one else should either. He'd backed Lord Wimpleton and her into a corner. Either they produce her intended or henceforth be labeled liars.

And the fault was Chance's.

Intent on protecting her, he'd lost control for one brief moment.

God Almighty, he'd only made matters worse, bloody fool. Guilt and remorse gnawed at him. He examined every angle of the situation, trying to arrive at an amenable solution. If only he were unencumbered ... *and wealthy.*

He shut his eyes against the remorse. Ivy's features immediately floated before him.

She had blossomed into a rare beauty. He'd known she would.

Her hair, the richest sable, had been as silky beneath his chin as he'd imagined. Her pearly skin, smoother than a rose petal, begged to be touched. Her thick-lashed eyes, stormy-sky gray one minute and sage green with silvery flecks the next, reflected the peace of the deepest forest. And her lips, full and luscious, would have tempted Adam in the Garden of Eden.

Not the typical *haut ton* measure of loveliness, no, his Ivy was something far more exceptional. An unpretentious dove amongst strutting peacocks and brazen parrots.

Opening his eyes, Chance twisted his mouth into a smirk. Drink had him waxing poetic.

He swirled the glass of cognac. The fire's glow lightened the brandy's umber hue to mellow amber. He'd indulged more than he ought, but he'd changed his mind about taking a dose of laudanum.

While abroad, he'd seen too many opium addicts and detested using the tincture. A dram or two of strong spirits proved a better choice to induce sleep. His lips curled into a self-deprecatory smile. The three prior glasses of brandy he'd imbibed could hardly be considered medicinal.

He uncrossed his ankles and laid his head against the chair's high back, watching the fire's shadows dance and stretch across the ceiling.

The boring-as-stale-bread novel he'd attempted to read earlier lay unopened on the table beside him. Chance drummed his fingers on the chair's arm. He ached to play the piano in the drawing room. A consummate pianist in his youth, these past six years there'd been few opportunities to indulge in the pleasurable pastime.

Despite his father's adamant disapproval of Chance's *womanish obsession*, his mother had encouraged his playing. Then Mother died, and

Father began pressuring him to find a suitable wife.

One with a nice, fat purse.

He didn't want to wed any woman except Ivy. Right before he'd left for India, he'd approached Lord Wimpleton and asked for her hand.

The man had laughed, though not unkindly. "My daughter's much too young for me to consider any talk of marriage. Return when she's older and you have something besides a besotted heart to offer her. Then, I'll consider your suit."

Offer her? What?

A fortune.

How?

India.

More than a few nabobs had purchased a seat in Parliament and risen to the *ton's* top tiers after acquiring a fortune via trade with India. Chance possessed no interest in Parliament or government, but he had hoped to become modestly prosperous. Enough that Lord Wimpleton would consider granting him his daughter's hand in marriage.

Unfortunately, his duties for the East India Company Troops allowed minimal time for business ventures. Aside from a single investment he'd made with a British businessman, Clement Robinson, when Chance first arrived in Madras, no further opportunities to pursue that avenue had arisen.

Not long after meeting Robinson, Chance had been transferred to Calcutta and then moved to four other provinces, each remoter than the last. He'd eventually arrived in Maratha Territory, where he'd been gravely wounded.

Although he'd attempted to reach Robinson several times, after two years without success, Chance gave up. He'd been made a May Game of, and the paltry inheritance Mother left him had been stolen by an unscrupulous scoundrel.

So, Chance had stayed in India. His aspirations of marrying Ivy shriveled into crumbs of crushed hope, and the arid desert winds scattered them into oblivion. If he couldn't make her his wife, he wouldn't wed at all.

An unpleasant notion burst into his thoughts.

Bloody hell.

What if Lambert or Mrs. Washburn had yammered about the proposed union between Chance and her? He would have written and told his father he refused the match, except the postal service in the remote provinces wasn't to be relied upon.

Due to the frequent movement of East India Troops, mail delivery was delayed or, oftentimes, didn't reach the person intended at all. In fact, Chance hadn't received the first of Ivy's correspondences until after he'd lost what meager monies he had possessed. He had nothing to offer her and did what he believed best: ignored her letters, telling himself she would soon find someone to give her heart to.

Except she hasn't give her heart to anyone in all this time. Why?

Splaying the fingers of his ruined hand, he stared at the empty space where the digits ought to be. Peculiarly, but he felt them at times. They itched, ached, twitched—not in actuality, of course, but phantom sensations of what once was. At times, he even tried to pick up items with the missing appendages.

Losing himself in the magic of music had been his singular passion, other than Ivy. Now, both were lost to him.

Sighing, he set aside the brandy. Brooding served no purpose. After shoving to his feet, he banked the fire before circling the room and blowing out the candles, except one three-branched candelabrum. A final glance at the fireplace assured him the meshed brass guard prevented embers from escaping.

Determined to put the day behind him, he snatched the candelabrum and exited the room. Across the hall, the drawing room door stood open. Lid closed, the grand piano washed in the moon's silvery glow beckoned him. He stood in the doorway for several long minutes, his emotions vacillating.

A scan of the corridor confirmed Chance alone remained below at this ungodly hour. He advanced into the room, standing unsure for a moment. He placed the candles atop the piano and ran a hand along the carved mahogany. A truly grand instrument.

After shrugging out of his coat, he tossed the cutaway on a needlepoint parlor chair. Before he sat, he unbuttoned his shirtsleeves and rolled them to his elbows. The ivory keys gleamed in the soft light. He rested a tentative hand upon their surface, relishing their familiar cool presence beneath his fingertips.

His useless left hand lay on his thigh. He ran his right fingertips across the keys and, pressing the quiet pedal with his foot, played a familiar melody, one-handed.

"Falcon?" Ivy whispered his name, her voice a blend of curiosity and wonder.

8

Ivonne tossed the bedcovers off and sat up.

What was the time?

After lighting a candle, she examined the bedside clock. Past two.

Releasing a beleaguered sigh, she flopped onto her back. She would be a sleep-deprived disaster in the morning. Maybe she would stay in bed the entire day and wallow in her doldrums.

Miss Rossington's shocking revelation about Falcon had made sleep impossible. Ivonne hadn't been capable of returning to the ball either. She feared the moment she laid eyes on him, she would burst into tears. Learning of his shattering injury from Miss Rossington—of all people—was beyond the pale. Feigning a headache, Ivonne had bolted to her bedchamber.

She eyed the clock again.

A trip below stairs was in order. Father possessed a number of yawn-inspiring books. She would select the most boring tome on philosophy the library had to offer—Descartes or Hume would do nicely—and be asleep within fifteen minutes.

Common sense halted her halfway out the bedchamber door. She wore nothing but her lacy nightgown. Gads. That wouldn't do. Snatching her robe from the foot of the bed, she paused. What if someone else prowled about below? Not likely at this hour.

It mattered not. She required a tedious book to put her to sleep.

Ivonne shoved her arms into the sleeves. Silver candleholder in hand, she made for the library. Halting piano music lured her into the drawing room.

Falcon sat before the instrument, utter defeat in his hunched shoulders and dejected profile.

Lonely, lost soul.

Her heart wrenched.

"Falcon?"

He stopped playing the instant she uttered his name. Turning his head, he faced her. Vulnerability tinged with embarrassment lingered in his gaze. His beautiful eyes searched hers.

What did he seek?

Pity? Compassion? Sympathy?

Each overwhelmed her, but he didn't need those emotions at present.

He required hope. Acceptance. Strength. *Love.*

Falcon's keen focus sank to her attire then to her bare toes. His lips twitched, and warmth swept her cheeks.

At least she'd thought to throw on her robe. Appearing before a gentleman in her nightwear with her unruly hair billowing about her shoulders was most improper. Truth to tell, at the moment, she didn't care. The lavender silk nightgown and robe swished around her ankles and calves as she hurried to him. Her cold feet sank into the lush carpet.

Ivonne placed her candlestick next to the other candleholder atop the piano. Ignoring wisdom, she sank onto the bench beside him. The heat of his solid thigh wedged against hers sent a strange shock along her nerves.

Neither of them made an effort to put a suitable distance between them. But then, nothing about being here in the middle of the night clothed in a diaphanous nightgown and robe, unchaperoned to boot, could be considered remotely acceptable.

If caught, she would be ruined.

She gave a mental shrug. That didn't matter. Everything in her ached to be with Falcon, to seize whatever precious moments destiny afforded her. Ivonne's need to be with him at this moment shoved aside the sting of his prior disinterest.

Drinking in his features, her focus hovered on the fresh scar marring his handsome face. She longed to kiss the pinkish mark, to somehow convey that she found knowing he'd suffered excruciating to bear.

God above, she'd missed him.

Her eyes misting with tears, she directed her attention to his hands lest she cause him more discomfit. She gasped, barely suppressing the cry surging to her throat.

His poor hand.

Falcon made no attempt to hide it.

Ivonne blinked away burning tears.

Two fingers. Gone. Falcon, a gifted pianist, would make music no more.

Lifting her gaze to his, she forced a facade of composure.

He returned her regard, his gaze guarded and appraising. This was not the carefree, jovial individual she'd known most of her life. He'd suffered, and suffered greatly. What happened in India to change him thus?

"How ...?" She cleared her throat, determined to show the same fortitude he did. She deliberately didn't return her scrutiny to his hand. No doubt, he was self-conscious enough already. "How did you come by your injury?"

Lifting the limb, he allowed her to see the vicious scar disfiguring his arm from hand to elbow.

She reached to touch the puckered flesh, but hesitated. He didn't pull away. Ever-so-gently, she trailed her fingers along the rough skin.

Dear God, the agony he must have endured.

Fresh tears sprang to her eyes. She swallowed them away. "Does it hurt terribly?"

Falcon shrugged, his broad shoulders bunching beneath the light linen shirt.

"Sometimes more than others." He flexed his remaining fingers. "My movement improves daily."

He lost his manhood.

Miss Rossington's acrimonious words echoed in Ivonne's mind.

"Do you have ... other wounds?" She practically ground her teeth in vexation.

Curse her wagging tongue. Of course he does, dimwit. Do you expect him to blurt the God-awful truth about his ... his ... maleness?

He turned his arm over so she could see the other side. The wound wrapped around his forearm, a reddish-purple serpent of mutilated flesh. "I've a few others, mostly on my ribs and back."

"What happened?" Ivonne didn't want him to tell her what trauma he'd undergone. Her heart could barely tolerate seeing these scars. Somehow, she sensed he needed to talk of the experience in order to put the ordeal behind him. To heal in his soul as well as his body.

"My commander ordered us to surround and invade the Pindaris." Falcon sighed and gave her a sideways look. His handsome mouth twisted into a wry grimace. "I tried to save a woman and her four children trapped inside their burning home. Two Pindari attacked me before I could get the last boy out."

His eyes darkened to midnight, and grief hardened his features. "The Pindaris' homes were destroyed. Burned to the ground, every one."

The muscles in his jaw taut, he closed his eyes for a lengthy moment.

"Not a day passes that I don't regret requesting a transfer to India. The devastation some British have inflicted on those unfortunate people, caused by insatiable greed for land and resources ..."

"It sounds absolutely horrid." Ivonne laid her hand on his arm, the flesh warm and rough beneath her palm. "You couldn't have known what to expect."

Why had he asked to go to India in the first place? He'd never told her. Never said how long he'd be gone. Or if he planned on returning. Ever. Every day, she'd prayed for his safety, forcing away her feelings of betrayal and despondency.

A thought struck Ivonne, the absolute certainty of the epiphany penetrating to her soul. The knowledge left her flabbergasted, and the air hitched in her lungs, all the more proof she had hit upon the truth. She caressed his beautiful face with her gaze.

She'd waited for him, secretly hopeful he'd return someday. And that maybe, by some miracle of providence or God's grace, he'd missed her as much as she'd missed him. That was why she hadn't entertained the attentions of other beaus.

She'd been waiting for Falcon's homecoming.

His eyes hooded, a slow, sensual smile curved his mouth.

Did he know? Had he guessed? How could he have?

She dropped her attention to the piano, afraid he'd read the truth in her eyes.

Men as handsome as he didn't settle for spinsterish misses like her. No, they drew diamonds of the first water to them as naturally and uncontrollably as the moon's irresistible draw upon the tide. Beauty sought beauty. Each to their own kind.

The injustice of that reality didn't escape her.

"May I ask you something?" Falcon brushed a lock of hair off her cheek.

Oh, to have the right to turn her face into his hand and press her lips to his palm.

"Of course." In the faint candlelight, he was even more striking than she'd remembered. "What is it you wish to know?

"In the arbor, Kirkpatrick spoke of your limp. What happened?"

Ivonne gathered her hair and twisted the mass into a thick rope before draping it across her shoulder.

"I broke my leg in two places, the result of a riding accident." She toyed with the ends of her hair. "One break didn't heal properly."

Falcon inclined his head in the direction she'd come from moments before. "I didn't notice a limp just now."

"It's less noticeable on soft surfaces and if my leg is rested."

Enough talk about her. She wanted to learn what his plans were. More specifically, where would he make his home? Would he take a wife?

The notion, as unsavory as tainted fish, coiled in her stomach.

She absently played a couple of chords with her left hand and then began fingering the bass line of a favorite sonata. "What will you do now?"

9

"Do you have any plans?"

Ivonne asked the question burning on her lips since she'd bumped into Falcon in the garden. Why hadn't he traveled straight to his family estate, Suttoncliffe Hall, instead of choosing to stay in London? After all, he hadn't seen his family in over half a decade.

He tapped out the right hand accompaniment to her chord progression.

A nascent smile bent her mouth. They played rather well together.

His playing became stronger as he slid her a sideways glance. "I'm not altogether certain what I'll do. It depends on several things."

Falcon stopped playing. His stare intense, he stroked her cheek with the back of his good hand, and his attention sank to her mouth.

She sighed and closed her eyes, angling her face into his palm. His touch never failed to send her senses reeling.

"Such as?" My, she was brazen tonight.

"You."

Ivonne's eyes fluttered open. She played a part in what he intended to do?

Dear God, please let him feel something more than friendship toward me.

"Me?" Was that husky voice hers? She couldn't tear her gaze from his parted mouth.

He traced her lips with his rough thumb.

"Why me?" she managed to whisper, fighting the urge to touch his thumb with her tongue.

He didn't answer. Instead, he lowered his head, bit by bit, as she angled her chin upward. Cupping her nape with one hand, he wrapped the other in her long tresses, trapping her.

He was so close. She smelled brandy on his breath and the faint remains of his woodsy cologne. Every nerve tingled in anticipation.

"Ivy?"

She trembled at the husky timbre of Falcon's voice. Heat suffused her, a delicious, heady warmth spreading from her middle outward, hardening her nipples and causing a curious ache between her legs.

"Yes?" She clutched his solid biceps to keep from melting onto the floor. Did the man have a soft spot anywhere?

"I want to kiss you."

Not more than an inch separated their lips.

"Yes." She dared not breathe, having waited for this moment for so long. Nothing must disturb the magic.

"You're sure?" His nostrils flared, and his hot gaze fastened on her lips. Ever the gentleman, Falcon paused and lifted heavy-lidded eyes to hers. He brushed her lower lip with his thumb again. "You want me to continue?"

Woman's intuition told her he asked for much more than a kiss or two. Ivonne smiled, past caring if he discovered the secret she'd long nurtured in her soul. "I've waited a lifetime to kiss you."

The smile he gave her set her pulse careening. His lips met hers, firm yet gentle at the same time. He shifted his arms, encircling her and lifting her closer.

She entwined her arms around his neck, snuggling against his chest, her aching breasts mashed flat.

He kissed each corner of her mouth then nudged her lips apart with his tongue.

A contented sigh escaped her.

No other suitors' fumbling attempts to kiss her had prepared her for Falcon's seductive assault on her untried senses. Light-headed, swept away on unfamiliar sensation, she parted her lips, granting him access. She was his to do with as he pleased.

He cupped one breast, gently twisting the nipple between his thumb and forefinger as he swept her mouth with his tongue.

She groaned, arching into his hand and meeting his thrusting tongue with her own. Coherent thought flew in the face of her passion. This was all that mattered. Being here with Falcon, finally experiencing what she'd dreamed of for years.

He bent his neck, feathering her throat with scorching kisses before nudging aside the satin of her gown and settling his lips around a swollen nipple.

Head thrown back, Ivonne clung to him, savoring the experience and storing away precious memories. The tender exploration of her breast with his mouth and tongue undid her. When he abandoned her breast, she almost cried out in protest. Then he nuzzled her neck, trailing delicate kisses across her jaw and cheek.

This wonderful, tender man would never be a father.

Joy mingled with sharp sorrow ravaged her emotions. Scalding tears slid from her eyes.

"You're crying?" Falcon stiffened and leaned away, examining her. A shuttered expression settled on his face. "I apologize. I oughtn't to have kissed you."

He shifted, preparing to stand.

"No, Falcon. I wanted you to."

With a volition of its own, her gaze skimmed his wounds. "It's just that you ..."

She couldn't explain her heartache to him. For him. That she grieved because he'd returned from India a partial man. To do so would cause him more pain and humiliation.

He stood, his face an impassive mask.

"I believe I understand perfectly, Miss Wimpleton. Once I satisfied your schoolgirl curiosity about kissing me," he lifted his arm, mockery dripping from his voice, "my disfigurement repulsed you."

Ivonne surged to her feet.

How can he think that?

She shook her head, her hair swirling about her shoulders and back. "No, you have it wrong. I'm not disgusted. I would never—"

"Spare me your feeble excuses." He laughed, a cynical bark of amusement. "I'm well aware of how females react to my wounds, and your expression says much."

His hostile gaze cut a wide swath across her vulnerable heart and sliced it open, leaving a gaping wound. Hands lifted palm upward in entreaty, she moved toward him.

He took a single step backward. Detached regard replaced the heated glimmer his eyes had held moments before.

The look froze her in place.

He despises me.

The knife twisted deeper into her bleeding heart.

Somehow, she must make him understand. "My tears are for what you've lost, Falcon, for what you'll never have."

He gathered his coat and then draped it across his unmarred arm.

"Or," with bored nonchalance, he yawned behind his misshapen hand, "do you weep for what *you'll* never have?"

She jerked her head as if he'd slapped her.

"You've proved yourself wholly disappointing." After sketching a mocking bow, Falcon presented his back and strode from the room.

Ivonne stared at the vacant doorway. The pre-dawn chill roused her from her stupor as the library clock tolled the hour of three. She blinked several times in an attempt to gather her scattered wits. The agony of her shattered heart hurt far worse than the breaks in her legs ever had. Shivering, she hugged her shoulders.

Had Falcon kissed her to determine if she would measure up? And found her wanting?

Ivonne furrowed her brow. No, he wouldn't do that. Would he?

She cast a glance toward the room's entrance.

Perhaps the old Falcon wouldn't have, but this new one ...?

Ivonne didn't know what him capable of anymore. She took a shaky breath, fearing he had toyed with her. The notion sickened her. He'd become callous. His words, though softly spoken, lanced deeper than a short sword. She'd been ten times a fool to harbor any hope he regarded her with anything more than ... what?

Not brotherly affection, for certain. Their kiss proved that beyond measure. Inexperienced she might be, but he'd been every bit as engaged as she.

Or perhaps not.

Retying the sash at her waist, she curled her toes against the numbing cold permeating her feet and rising to her calves.

Rogues faked ardor and affection.

Mother had warned her of that very thing when, motivated by lust for her sizable settlement, particularly unsavory gentlemen had begun to pay Ivonne uncommon attention. Her heart rebelled at likening Falcon to that lot, yet he had refused to even listen to her explanation.

He called me wholly disappointing.

One at a time, Ivonne blew out Falcon's candelabrum's tapers. In the increasing gloom, doubt niggled. Had his wounds and the savagery of warfare made him angry and bitter? It appeared he'd changed much.

What was the exact nature of the damage to his male parts? She wasn't supposed to know of such things, but as she matured, ladies became less cautious about what they whispered in her presence. She'd had quite an education these past two Seasons about men's *Man Thomas's* and *whirligigs.*

Nonetheless, she could claim more ignorance than knowledge.

Did men feel desire and have urges if that region was impaired? There wasn't anyone she could ask. Mother would faint dead away, and Dawson, Ivonne's aged abigail, would expire from apoplexy. To ask Father or Allen was unthinkable.

I say, Allen, Father, would you please explain to me precisely what losing one's manhood entails? Don't concern yourself with my delicate sensibilities. I assure you, I want to know every last detail.

She almost giggled, imagining their appalled reactions.

Perhaps Falcon had only lost the ability to father children. Was he intact?

Did it matter?

Her gaze drifted to the piano bench, where moments before she'd experienced her greatest joy.

No, it didn't matter. Not to her.

Yes, she desired children, desperately. However, she wanted Falcon more. Besides, she'd already determined before he returned that spinsterhood was her fate. There'd be no brood of chubby-cheeked toddlers hanging on her skirts.

Ivonne smiled sadly and retrieved her candleholder.

She loved Falcon—deeply, gut-wrenchingly, beyond everything loved him. Loved him enough that she would marry him despite his disfigurement.

If he'd have her. Though truthfully, she stood a greater chance of weeping tears of gold.

A lifetime without him would be far bleaker than one deprived of children. Besides, waifs and orphans aplenty wandered London's streets, desperate for a good home.

She released a hefty sigh. It mattered not.

Such imaginations were the stuff of nonsensical fairy-tales. She inhaled a tremulous breath. Hadn't his reaction, his harsh words, proved his position?

He found her lacking.

Tears coursed down her cheeks. Ivonne made no attempt to wipe her face as she plodded toward her bedchamber.

This time, she did weep for what she would never have.

Her tears were short-lived, however. Before she reached the top riser of the curved stairway, her sorrow transformed to ire. Fury like none she had ever known burgeoned within her.

Enough of men acting like I am beneath their touch.

Falcon wasn't that different from Captain Kirkpatrick and the other gentlemen in that regard. He ... they believed her drab, undesirable, *disappointing.*

Well, this dowdy mouse was about to make a bold transformation.

Newfound determination in her step, Ivonne marched to her chamber No more being made sport of and pitied for her ordinary appearance. She was about to set London on its ear.

"Just you wait, gentlemen."

10

"Miss Ivonne, wake up." Dawson prodded Ivonne's shoulder with a bony finger.

Ivonne groaned and forced her eyelids open. She raised a hand to her forehead and blinked away the grittiness in her eyes from too much crying and not enough sleep. Memories of last night and Falcon descended, the burden of their dual yoke weighing heavily upon her.

Seizing the jonquil velvet bed curtains, the maid swept them to either bedpost. "His lordship and her ladyship wish you to meet them in the study."

Plucking at the embroidered counterpane topping her bed, Ivonne sighed. She longed to crawl beneath the silk coverlet and ignore her parents' summons. She could claim to be indisposed. Truth to tell, she did feel rather awful. ... Until she remembered the plan she concocted last night. She barely refrained from an unladylike snicker and rubbing her hands together in glee.

Moments later, Dawson threw open the heavy draperies. Sunlight blazed into the chamber, revealing a breakfast tray atop a dainty table situated before the balcony. A chemise, stockings, and a mint green morning dress trimmed in ecru lace lay draped across a rosewood fainting couch.

"I let you sleep as long as I could." Dawson grinned, revealing her slightly crooked front teeth. "You didn't stir a jot, even when I cleaned the grate."

Ivonne yawned and sat up. She attempted to smooth her tangled hair. She ought to have plaited the mane before retiring. "I couldn't sleep last night. The hour was after five when I finally dozed off."

She gestured in the direction of the tray and gown. "I see you've been busy this morning."

"Morning?" Dawson chuckled, deep wrinkles etching her face. She pointed to the boudoir clock. "Not for an hour."

"It's after one?" Ivonne stared in disbelief. She leaped from the bed, and then winced, laying a hand to her head. Pain thrummed behind her eyes. "I never sleep this late. What time am I to meet my parents?"

"Two o'clock. Sharp." Dawson tucked a stray grayish-blonde strand of hair into her cap. "The master's exact words."

After a hasty washing and slightly less swift toilette, Ivonne gulped down two bites of toast and a swallow of tepid tea. She shot the clock a hurried glance. Three minutes to make the study. Though normally good-natured, Father didn't abide tardiness.

So much for putting the scheme she'd hatched into action today, dash it all. With a little wave to Dawson, Ivonne hustled from her bedchamber. On second thought, this was better. It gave her more time to plot.

The first item on the agenda?

A secret meeting with her notorious second cousin, Emilia Leighton. A well-known demirep, Emmy seemed the perfect person to help Ivonne accomplish the task she'd set herself: transforming into an alluring creature no man could resist, least of all a golden-haired Greek god.

Not that I would have him after last night.

A wave of trepidation swept Ivonne. God help her if caught with Emmy. Turning a corner, Ivonne lifted her skirt and picked up her pace. Emmy wasn't received by anyone in the family these days. Although if the *on dit* could be believed, she was most popular with the demimonde and gaming hell set.

Ivonne had frequently heard Emmy's name whispered at elite gatherings. Usually spiteful remarks made behind fans by matrons long past their prime or on-the-shelf ladies, their voices shrill with envy.

Breathless from rushing down two corridors and the flight of stairs, Ivonne paused outside Father's study. The black walnut door stood closed.

People murmured within, their voices a muted drone through the thick wood.

Taking a deep breath, she smoothed her skirt and squared her shoulders. With newfound resolve, she rapped twice. The carved door swung open before she lowered her hand. The study smelled of leather, tobacco, and Father's cologne. She breathed in the familiar, comforting essence.

"Hullo, Sleeping Beauty. I've never known you to slumber this late." Allen grinned and leaned down to peck her cheek. Stepping back, he examined her. "I must say, the rest did you good. You look exquisite today, sister."

Pleased as Punch by the compliment, Ivonne placed her hand on his arm.

From his contrived messy hairstyle to his pristine knotted cravat and gleaming Hessians, Allen epitomized current fashion. Even the tobacco brown jacket he wore matched his hair to perfection and deepened his eyes to malachite. The next Viscount Wimpleton could claim exceptional looks, as could Mother and Father.

Ivonne, alone, possessed a sparrow's drab plumage.

She smiled inwardly. Not for long although she'd held no aspirations of ever nearing Mother's beauty. Raven haired and possessing the same unusual green eyes as Allen, Mother—at five and forty—outshone most women half her age. Today, the soft coral and peach gown complemented her flawless skin's youthful glow.

Father cut quite a handsome figure as well. Tall and slender, he boasted a full head of chestnut hair sprinkled with gray at the sideburns. At two and fifty, his striking, almost foreign features garnered much attention from moon-eyed females. He claimed a notorious sheik lurked in the family tree several generations back.

Now that would be a tale worth hearing.

After closing the heavy door, Allen guided Ivonne further into the room. "What, were you prowling about last night instead of sleeping? Or did sweet dreams of handsome beaus keep you abed?"

Her heart lurched for a panicked instant, and she searched his humor-filled eyes. He couldn't possibly know about her pre-dawn encounter with Falcon.

Allen winked.

She smiled as much in relief as at his teasing banter. No, he didn't know.

"I assumed you'd be hard-pressed to sleep, too, brother dearest." She grinned and whispered, "I saw the charming Miss Kingsley last night."

A guarded expression entered Allen's eyes, although his smile didn't falter. "As did I, minx. I shall see her today too. She agreed to become my wife last night."

Miss Rossington was out of the picture, thank God.

Ivonne's smile widened, and she hugged him. "Now that is most welcome news."

Miss Rossington must have caught wind of the betrothal.

I wish I'd been present to witness that.

It explained her peevish behavior toward Miss Kingsley in the retiring room.

"Come along, you two." Father pocketed his watch. "Allen and I have a four o'clock appointment at White's. One I'm not looking forward to, I might add."

Ivonne considered him. He appeared a trifle tense, and his attention repeatedly fell to the papers scattered atop his desk. Most irregular. Father typically kept his desk neat and tidy.

Mother, seated on a cherry-red damask sofa, smiled and held out her arms. "Darling, that gown does remarkable things to your skin, and your eyes are a spectacular shade of green today."

Ivonne breathed an iota easier.

She'd been afraid her mother would detect traces of last night's waterworks. Cosmetics hid the evidence quite nicely, and Ivonne also credited them for the improvement in her appearance. The transformation the light touch of rice power and lip rouge achieved proved remarkable, the boost in her self-assurance, nothing short of astonishing.

Mother twisted to catch Father's attention. "Don't you agree, Walter?"

Father glanced to his wife then squinted at Ivonne.

"Yes, you're quite right, my dear." He smiled, his eyes crinkling at the corners. "Ivonne, you do look exceptionally lovely this afternoon."

She couldn't contain her wide grin.

Precisely what she'd hoped for. Emmy could advise her on what other artifices Ivonne should purchase. She quite liked feeling attractive. She intended to utilize the cosmetics, and anything else her cousin recommended, on a daily basis.

She launched a silent prayer heavenward.

Let the gentlemen find my appearance pleasing as well.

Particularly one gentleman she sought to make jealous.

Now, if only I could learn to flirt.

After embracing her mother, Ivonne took a seat on the sofa.

Allen lounged against the desk, his countenance gone somber. He toed the edge of the Oriental carpet, seemingly distracted.

Ivonne met everyone's gazes in turn. Shifting on the settee, she faced her mother. "You wished to see me?"

"Dear, an upset occurred last night." Mother gave her a brittle smile.

Drat, drat, drat.

Ivonne dug her fingernails into the sofa's piping.

Here we go.

What had Captain Kirkpatrick said? She itched to box his ears, the smelly tattlemonger.

Mother paused and looked to Father. A pinched expression wrinkled her forehead.

He inclined his head.

"To do with Luxmoore's father," Mother said.

Ivonne relaxed her grip. This wasn't about the captain. Or the events in the arbor or on the terrace. "Nothing serious, I pray. Is everything well today?"

"No, no, not at all, I'm afraid." Father sighed and tapped his pipe. He fingered the bowl. "His father died ... er ... unexpectedly last night. Poor Luxmoore learned of the tragedy while at our ball."

"That's awful." Ivonne's eyes welled with tears. Lord Luxmoore had always been unfailingly kind to her, and he had a delightful sense of humor.

Allen straightened and rubbed his forehead. "I've given my word we'll not discuss the misfortune with anyone outside of this house except Faulkenhurst."

Falcon? Where was he today, anyway? Had he departed for Suttoncliffe already? A surge of hurt seized her. She shrugged inwardly. So much the better for her plan to succeed. What he did was of no importance to her.

Liar.

Ivonne's stomach growled and then rumbled again, much louder. She pressed a hand to her complaining middle. Except for those bites of cold toast in her room earlier, she'd eaten nothing since snaring two Shrewsbury biscuits from the kitchen yesterday afternoon.

"I shall certainly keep Luxmoore's confidence." She rose partway. "If that's all, I am rather famished."

Cook usually had a tasty treat or two, fresh from the oven. Ivonne could almost taste the warm seedcake, or maybe there'd be fresh maid of honor tarts.

Father raised his hand. "No, my dear, that's not all."

"Oh." Ivonne dropped fully onto the sofa once more. What else was there? She searched her parents' faces before settling on Allen's.

His focus remained riveted on the carpet as he tormented the fringed edge with his boot.

"There's something else?" She reluctantly forced the question past her lips.

An uncomfortable, pregnant pause followed. Her family looked at each other before their troubled gazes settled on her.

Dash it all.

So much for avoiding the Captain Kirkpatrick bumblebroth. Best to get it done with.

Ivonne stared at her hands clenched atop her lap. Her fingertips gleamed white.

"I'm sorry I ventured onto the terrace alone." She scanned their strained faces again. "I wouldn't have had I known Captain Kirkpatrick had arrived. He wasn't invited, and I didn't expect him to be so brazen as to come with—"

Father shushed her with a casual wave of his hand. "That wasn't wise of you, but that's not the issue we need to address."

"Walter, must we? There's no other recourse? You're sure?" Mother's eyes glimmered with tears, and her chin quivered.

Alarm seared Ivonne.

Mother didn't cry in front of others.

Ivonne threw Allen a desperate look.

He stared at the floor, his mouth pressed into a grim ribbon.

Whatever was wrong?

Giving one curt nod, Father set down his pipe. "Ivonne, everyone at the ball last night—and by now, half of London—believes you are newly betrothed."

"Is that what this is about?" She released a relieved laugh. "Well, I'm not. We'll just have to refute that ludicrous chitchat."

Chuckling, she flattened her palms on her knees, easing the stiffness from her numb fingers. "*Le bon ton* does love to make a hullabaloo out of nothing."

"It's not as simple as that, Ivy." Allen crouched before her. He took her hands in his, giving them a squeeze. "You see, not only did Captain Kirkpatrick fuel that preposterous rumor, word of your *good news* reached Prinny."

Her breath left her in a rush, and Ivonne gaped at her brother. "Prinny? The Prince Regent?"

Who else, goosecap?

She swallowed, not liking the direction this conversation headed. "What has he to do with this farce?"

Allen squeezed her hands again. "Seems he's a particular friend of the Duke of Petheringstone, and that stinking lickspittle is as tight as a tick on a hog's arse with Kirkpatrick."

"Mind your tongue, Allen." Mother dabbed at her eyes with an embroidered handkerchief. She wrinkled her nose the merest bit. "Though it's true, Petheringstone has no more fondness for cleanliness than the captain."

Why are they blathering on about bathing habits?

Ivonne slanted her head to meet Father's gaze. "I don't understand how or why the prince is involved."

Father lifted an elaborate gold-trimmed, beribboned document clearly bearing the Regent's insignia. "The prince has demanded an introduction to the groom, and Prinny's announced he'll attend the wedding."

"Pardon?" Ivonne yanked her hands from Allen's. "You cannot be serious. The Regent hasn't spoken more than a dozen words to me since I was presented at court."

All pretense of calmness splintered to pieces. Pressing her fingers to her temples, she tried to lessen the sudden pounding in her head. She darted a frantic glance to her father. "And I don't recall Father being a particular favorite of his either."

Unable to sit a moment longer, Ivonne surged to her feet.

"Why would he insist on attending my wedding?" She pointed at her chest before flapping her hand in the air. "An imaginary wedding at that?"

Tears pricked her eyelids and clogged her throat.

Father came round from behind his desk. Wrapping her in his embrace, he held her head against his chest and awkwardly patted her back.

"I'm afraid Petheringstone is an old enemy. I believe he suspects there's no groom and hopes to get us—your mother and I—deep in suds with His Highness."

Mother stood and touched Ivonne's shoulder. "Petheringstone never forgave your father for winning my hand in marriage."

"That's true." Father's voice rumbled deep in his chest as if he struggled with his emotions. "But more on point, he never forgave me for besting him in the duel we fought over you."

"Duel?" Allen and Ivonne chimed as one.

Father sighed before kissing the top of Ivonne's head. "Yes. He fired before the count finished. By the grace of God, he only nicked my shoulder."

"A drunken one-eyed goat herder has better aim than Petheringstone." Mother gazed at Father with admiration.

"True, the man's always been a wretched shot, though his skill with a blade is far worse." Father took a step away from Ivonne. "I had no desire to kill the blackguard, so I shot him in the foot, thinking the leather of his boot offered him some protection. He's been lame since."

"Some jealous cawker gets to dictate my future?" Ivonne couldn't keep the scorn from her voice.

Mother grasped Ivonne's shoulder, turning her until she faced her mother. "I'm sorry, darling. There's no help for it. The duke, much like Captain Kirkpatrick, is a man obsessed."

Cupping Ivonne's face, her mother attempted a brave smile that better resembled a watery grimace.

"Petheringstone has the prince's ear and his favor. The Regent won't be dissuaded. That," Mother pointed to the oval desk where the document lay, "is, in effect, a royal decree."

"This is utterly ridiculous," Ivonne protested. "Who does he think he is, meddling in our private affairs? This is 1818, for pity's sake."

Allen slapped his thigh, his expression fierce. "Once he gets a notion in his pickled head, there's no changing his mind. His disfavor isn't something anyone wants to be at the receiving end of, I assure you."

He met Father's troubled gaze. "I'm certain you recollect what happened to Lord Forester when he ignored His Highness's *suggestion* that the baron ought to wed Mrs. Ellington."

"Mrs. Ellington?" Ivonne didn't recall her. And, come to think of it, she hadn't seen the baron at all this Season. "Who is Mrs. Ellington?"

Allen fumbled in pouring himself a glass of sherry and splashed a few droplets on the rosewood cabinet. "One of Prinny's ... ah ..."

"Mistresses who found herself in the family way." Pink tinted Mother's high cheekbones.

Ivonne fought the urge to roll her eyes skyward. For heaven's sake, they acted like she had no idea such indiscretions occurred. Half the *ton* engaged in dalliances.

Father nodded and pinched the bridge of his nose. "Ruined the poor man and his family. Last I heard, to keep a roof above his two sisters' and invalid mother's heads, Forester married another of Prinny's cast-offs."

Bother, blast, and damnation! Surely this is a terrible nightmare, and I'll awaken any moment.

Father returned to his chair behind the cumbersome mahogany

partners' desk. Frowning, he read the letter from the prince again. He sighed and, apparently defeated, slouched against the leather. He gazed at her, his eyes dark with regret.

"Ivonne, I'm afraid we're at *point non plus*." His voice caught as he spoke. "You'll have to pick a suitor to bring up to scratch. If you don't, I will."

She gasped and clutched Mother's clammy hand.

"The wedding is two months from this Friday." Father tapped the paper, his voice gaining strength. "Prinny expects to meet the groom within a fortnight."

11

That same day, across Town

Eyes narrowed, Chance stared at Samuel Tobbins. Assistant to Franklin Belamont, Chance's solicitor, Tobbins wiped his forehead with his limp handkerchief for the fourth time. The diminutive fellow perspired to such a degree, Chance half expected him to slosh when he walked.

"I assure you, your file hasn't been misplaced." The man flitted about the office like a disoriented moth, searching for the missing folder.

Arms crossed, Chance arched a brow.

"Where are they?" Tobbins bent to peer beneath a haphazard pile of papers atop an otherwise organized desk. Clicking his tongue, he scampered to another stack of files and began flipping through them. "Where in the world are they?"

"You mean to tell me you don't believe *any* of my correspondence or papers are here?" Chance gestured round the tidy office. "You think, perhaps, they've been forwarded to Suttoncliffe? The entire six years' worth?"

This was what came of having the same solicitor as Father and Thad.

"I'm sorry, Mr. Faulkenhurst, but yes." Nodding his balding head, Tobbins pushed his spectacles up his reedy nose. "I'm afraid that must be the case, for I cannot find a single document of yours."

He wrung his hands together, his watery hazel eyes huge and worried. "I expect Mr. Belamont's return from Rochester any day now, certainly not upward of a week. He can set you straight on the matter, I'm sure."

Tobbins riffled through another pile of papers on a shelf behind the solicitor's desk.

"Aha," he exclaimed holding up a letter and practically dancing with glee. One would have thought he'd found a large banknote from his enthusiastic reaction. "Here's a letter for you."

He scuttled to where Chance sat. With the aplomb of a royal courtier, he presented the missive.

After breaking the seal, Chance scanned the short correspondence.

Exasperated by Chance's failure to speedily sign the marriage agreement—for God's sake, what did Lambert expect? Chance had been in India—his lordship had foisted his daughter off on another poor sot.

Chance examined the letter's date. April.

All his worry had been for naught.

He refolded the paper and slid it into his coat pocket. A wry grin crept across his face.

One monumental obstacle out of the way.

"Good news, sir?" Tobbins waited, an expectant look on his face.

"Exceedingly good news."

Chance shifted in the uncomfortable, smallish chair, far more appropriate for waiting in the hall than a lengthy meeting in a solicitor's office. His missing fingers picked today to ache unbearably. Every twinge reminded him of last night and the pleasure of playing the piano with Ivy.

And kissing and caressing her.

That kiss. God help him, but he'd been hard put to keep from ravishing her right there in the drawing room while her parents and brother slept above. Her response had been a precious and unexpected gift. He'd never lost control that completely or quickly. Ivy was like nectar to his parched soul, balm to his wounded spirit.

Then she'd wept, and the vile truth hit him with the impact of a cannonball. He'd tasted her tears, the salt bitter on his lips. More rancorous was the despair that seized his heart, destroying the fragile remnant of hope buried there.

She couldn't overlook his disfigurement.

Anger and hurt had overwhelmed his good sense, and he'd been cruel.

Last night had been a calamity, and except for learning the proposed marriage agreement with Mrs. Washburn was cancelled, little about this day had gone right either. He sighed and stood.

"The moment Belamont returns, please tell him I require an immediate appointment."

"I shall, sir, you can be certain." His relief tangible, Tobbins attempted a smile and opened the office door.

"I'm staying at Viscount Wimpleton's residence. Please send word to me there." Chance slapped his hat on his head. He didn't have a card to offer with the Wimpletons' address on it. "Do you know the place?"

"Oh, yes, of course." Tobbins continued to bob his head, reminding Chance of a nervous quail. "Berkeley Square in Mayfair."

With a curt nod, Chance made his escape. Lost in thought, he set a brisk pace for several blocks. He crossed the street, dodging a landau stuffed with giggling misses. He recognized two of the fivesome, the Dundercroft sisters. He'd made their acquaintance last night.

Poised beneath her lacy parasol, the younger smiled and waved to him.

The elder swatted her sister's hand and, after sending him a glare of reproach, scolded her sister soundly.

It seemed one of the Misses Dundercroft had taken distinct exception to him and the other a definite fancy. He executed a mocking half-bow and allowed a droll smile to tilt his mouth.

A young Corinthian astride a magnificent Arabian trotted by.

Chance needed to purchase a horse—a serviceable, though not expensive, stepper. Perchance Allen could be imposed upon to accompany him to Tattersall's tomorrow.

And perhaps he had an acquaintance who, for a nominal fee, could investigate Robinson and locate his place of business in London for Chance as well. He must at least attempt to regain his lost funds. He blew out a long puff of air. He had about as much chance of that as a jellyfish surviving in the Great Thar Desert.

Rounding a corner, he strode in the direction of St. James Street. He'd sold his lieutenant's commission an hour ago and, after depositing the nominal amount in the bank, had continued on to his solicitor's. Chance had wanted to be on his way to Suttoncliffe the day after tomorrow. By Sunday at the latest, but Belamont's absence complicated matters.

Perhaps Chance wouldn't remain in Town after all. He'd waited this long to speak with the man. Another week seemed insignificant. Besides, his curiosity was aroused. Were his papers and correspondences at Suttoncliffe Hall?

If not, where the devil were they?

He flicked his pocket watch open. Quarter to five. He was late, but White's was only a couple of blocks farther along this street, and Allen would linger. After all these years apart, their friendship hadn't waned. Nevertheless, Chance increased his pace.

The morning and afternoon hadn't gone as anticipated.

First, he'd overslept. No surprise there.

After seeing Ivy partially dishabille, a seductress in that clingy purple gown and robe, he'd given in to the urge to kiss her senseless—something he had yearned to do for years. He didn't regret kissing her. Never had a woman's lips tasted sweeter, made all the more so by his unprofessed love for her.

Love he didn't have the right to proclaim.

Had her tears been born of pity and disgust?

Last night, that notion fueled the anger he'd kept repressed regarding the war, his injuries, his lost fortune, and his father's meddling. His stride slowed. He'd believed Ivy different than the other women who scorned him because of his disfigurements. Her joy upon seeing him in the arbor had given him momentary hope. Her responses to his kisses had fueled his corkbrained optimism further.

Lying awake in the plush, oversized bed, the most comfortable place he'd rested in six years, his thoughts repeatedly turned to her asleep in her room. Why had she come below stairs in the first place? She'd seemed as eager to see him as he'd been to see her. She had enjoyed their kiss too.

Now they were estranged, and he had only himself to blame.

Chance couldn't bear to have her angry with him. If she refused to speak to him ever again, he wouldn't blame her. He'd been an ass of the worst sort. He must make amends and apologize to her before he left for Suttoncliffe.

Actually, his time in England might very well be limited altogether.

Something Sethwick's viscountess had said at the ball last night piqued Chance's interest. Her late father had built a shipping conglomeration, which she now owned. Stapleton Shipping and Supplies had offices around the world, including Boston, Massachusetts. Chance was of a mind to inquire if any positions were available in the American offices.

Seeing Ivy again had made him realize why he'd left England the first time; aside from needing a fortune to entice her father that is.

To have the object of his affection this close, yet always unattainable was unbearable. The bowels of Hades boasted lavish comfort in comparison to the torment. He wasn't confident he wouldn't blurt his feelings to her at some point.

Her repugnance toward his injury was painful enough to tolerate, but that she wasn't ever allowed to accept his love, even more so. Lord

Wimpleton had made it clear that Chance wasn't worthy of his daughter.

No, that was unfair.

Increasing his pace, Chance switched his cane to his other hand then immediately transferred the staff back again. Blast, so easy to forget he wasn't whole anymore.

Wimpleton hadn't refused his proposal outright. The viscount had told him to return when he had something to offer. Chance had failed in that respect.

If Ivy had even hinted last night that she returned his regard with the same fervency he felt toward her, he would ignore his circumstances and ask her to marry him. She was of age, and Wimpleton didn't seem the sort to disown his daughter for marrying without permission. But was she the sort of woman to openly defy her father?

Her response to Chance in the drawing room gave him little confidence Ivy was smitten enough to cause a scandal. Besides, she'd lived a life of luxury and privilege. While not a spoilt *tonnish* damsel, she would find the meager existence he could provide more than difficult. She deserved the finest life had to offer, and he couldn't give her that.

He wasn't the sort to tap into her marriage settlement to make ends meet, either. Those funds belonged to her, to do with as she wished. So, he found himself precisely where he'd begun six years ago.

In love and without a means of providing for her.

Only a fool believed love was enough to make a go of it.

Oh, but he would play the fool a thousand times over for one chance to make Ivy his. He'd gamble his life for that opportunity and worry about how to care for her afterward. He would bury his pride and accept any employment offer that came his way.

Chance smiled as a ragged urchin raced down the street, a scraggly black dog at his bare heels.

He didn't understand Ivy's lack of suitable beaus. He might not be able to claim her, but, as long as he had a breath in his body, she'd never settle for the likes of that piss maker, Kirkpatrick.

Ever.

White's came into view. The Duke of Argyll and Lord Worcester sat in the bow window, no doubt making ludicrous wagers on everything from where a bird dropping might land on the pavement to whether a passerby might sneeze or fart.

Chance supposed those with deep pockets didn't think twice about wasting funds. He couldn't recall the last time he'd wagered on anything, unless he counted the investment fiasco with Robinson. Men with pockets to let, such as he, didn't toss coin about like cracked corn to chickens.

He entered the exclusive establishment, seeking Allen and the others who'd been apprised of Luxmoore's calamity. Sorrow for his long-time friend gripped him.

Where were they?

He perused the interior, spying the group at a table in a secluded corner. Heads bent near, as if they didn't want their conversation overheard, only Harcourt, Sethwick, and Allen conferred at the table. Two chairs sat empty, Lord Wimpleton evidently having departed already.

Chance closed the distance with long strides, suddenly famished and eager to see his friends. By God, he'd missed them these past years. Smiling, he opened his mouth in greeting.

Allen's words stopped him cold.

"Prinny's adamant. Thanks to Kirkpatrick's meddling, my sister must produce a groom within a fortnight and wed within two months."

Bloody hell.

12

Seated on the arbor bench, Ivonne kicked at a small pebble. It pinged against the lattice then rolled beneath some foliage. After the devastating announcement in Father's study, she'd flown straight here, to her sanctuary.

Damnation.

Pick a suitor to marry. Just like that. As if she selected a new bonnet or a pair of slippers instead of a husband. How could the Regent make such an absurd demand? Interfering fat toad. This wasn't the Dark Ages, for pity's sake.

Produce a betrothed and invite me to the wedding or ... or ... off with your head.

Suffocating waves of dread choked Ivonne. She closed her eyes, fearing she would swoon.

Dear God. She must pick a man to wed, or Father would pick for her. This was real, not some horrid nightmare she'd awaken from. What was she to do? She couldn't marry any of the men interested in her. She just couldn't.

She stifled a panicked sob. Pressing her fists to her eyes, she refused to let the tears come. Crying, what a wretched waste of time and energy.

Think, Ivonne. There must be another alternative.

Did her parents understand the dismal selection available?

Ivonne mentally catalogued her choices: two decrepit old scallywags who smelt of camphor and four fortune-seeking rakehells, each of whom possessed a title and likely carried the clap. And—she shuddered, sickened at the thought—wealthy, fetid Captain Kirkpatrick.

Never him. Not while the sun rises.

Arms folded, she sagged further into the bench's carved back. Sorry lot, each and every one. The corpulent prince could starve himself before she ever agreed to marry any of them.

Several black ants maneuvered past her slipper carrying a dead bee.

She couldn't believe her parents would force her to marry to satisfy the Regent's whim. They'd more mettle than that.

Why acquiesce so easily? It wasn't like them at all.

Shoulders hunched, she sighed. This wasn't simply about her. The Sovereign, much like an intractable child, had a malicious streak when opposed. A chill swept her. She hadn't a fool's doubt he would destroy her family, if not financially then socially. They'd be ostracized. She fiddled with the lace along her gown's neckline. Did Prinny have the power to strip Father of his viscountcy?

What would become of her family then?

A pair of beautiful grayish-blue eyes invaded her musings. If only Falcon were a beau, her decision would be oh-so-easy.

"I ought to propose to Falcon. Wouldn't that set the prince and his cronies on their ears?" She scuffed her shoes on the leaf-littered ground. A black-capped coal tit chirped nearby, as if in agreement.

Ivonne suddenly straightened. The idea wasn't that farfetched. In fact, the notion possessed a great deal of merit. Shoving aside her hurt and irritation about Falcon's behavior last night, she took a mental inventory.

His lineage was impeccable, and his honor equally so. He didn't possess a fortune or a title, but then, how many second sons did? Her marriage settlement, if managed wisely, would allow them a lifetime of relative ease. Nothing lavish, but modest comfort, which suited her fine, truth to tell.

They were compatible, already good friends, and he'd enjoyed their intimate encounter. At least she thought he had. That meant he found her somewhat appealing, didn't it?

She bit her lip. Unless last night destroyed any chance of him wanting her.

He'd been brutal—more angry and hurtful than she'd ever known him to be.

Her heart gave a painful twinge. Well then, she'd have to change his mind. She had wanted to marry him for as long as she could remember. Only she hadn't anticipated being the party to initiate the proposal. It just wasn't done in the finer circles.

The coal tit hopped onto a branch and cocked its head, staring at her with tiny ebony eyes. Ivonne chuckled. "What's wrong with a woman proposing to a man, I ask you, my petite friend? Female birds select their mates all the time."

Did she dare?

Why not?

What did she have to lose?

Nothing.

And she had everything to gain if Falcon should agree.

It wasn't likely he courted anyone else, as yet. He'd only been in England a few days.

Ivonne would rather risk humiliation by setting her cap for him than settle on one of the other men interested in her, or rather, interested in her marriage portion. If Falcon refused her, it didn't much matter who she married. She would be miserable, thanks to the prince's meddling.

With Falcon, she could be happy. Ivonne had never been more certain of anything. And she could make him happy, too, given the chance.

She had bribed Burke, the new under footman, to take a note round to Emmy this morning. Ivonne prayed for a prompt response from her cousin. Originally, she intended to use her cousin's talents to prove to the pretentious *ton* that she could attract a great catch if Ivonne chose to. She hadn't been of a mind to lure suitors before last night's events. In fact, she'd done her best to repel them.

However, as of a few moments ago, her efforts centered on a single purpose—winning Falcon. She hadn't any time to lose if, in the next fortnight, she was to convince him to marry her. She wasn't sure how to go about wooing a man, but Emmy would know.

Her outlook much brighter, Ivonne smiled and glanced around the arbor. Last night she thought her life doomed when Falcon uttered those fateful words in the arbor. The Regent's dictate might have made it possible for her to have the one thing that mattered most.

Falcon.

Humming a jaunty tune, she strolled the footpath to the house. Head down, she plotted her tactics. She imagined and analyzed every possible situation. Mother must be informed of the need of an immediate shopping excursion, and a new hair style, perfume ... everything.

Yes, this dowdy bird was determined to shed her dull plumage and leg-shackle herself to a divine husband. One god-like former soldier who'd soon forget he had ever looked upon her as an annoying little sister.

Assembling a mental shopping list, Ivonne plowed full on into a firm male body. She stumbled, her lame leg giving way, and lost her balance. Strong arms encircled her and held her tight to a wide navy-clad chest.

Falcon. She recognized his cologne and the breadth of his shoulders. The urge to snuggle closer to him, wrap her arms around his neck and kiss his jaw overwhelmed her. Instead, she breathed in his scent, savoring his unique aroma.

Now was as good a time as any to set the snare.

Tipping her head upward, she offered what she hoped was an enticing smile. "I was just thinking of you."

Surprise tempered with wariness flitted within his eyes. He stepped back, his hands grasping her upper arms. "Were you now?"

Was he still angry?

"Yes, actually." She nodded and peeked at him, and then, self-consciousness shrouding her, averted her gaze. "I was remembering last night."

Ivonne wanted to say *our kiss*, but she lost her nerve.

Peering at him through half-closed eyes made it deuced difficult to see anything clearly. How women managed to look sultry while doing so, she couldn't imagine. She wasn't about to bat her eyelashes like Miss Rossington did. Ivonne feared she'd appear to be having an apoplexy.

Bother. She had much to learn about womanly wiles and little time to acquire the skills necessary to obtain her husband of choice.

Cautious, Falcon eyed her, a hint of amusement creasing the corners of his blue eyes. "Last night?"

"Yes ... er ..." At her ineptitude, dual paths of heat flamed across her cheeks.

He crooked a brow, his mouth sliding into one of his lopsided, boyish grins, though he offered her no succor. He wasn't going to make this easy, was he?

Drawing a deep breath, Ivonne tried again.

"I enjoyed our time together last night. That is..." She fumbled to a stop.

He bent nearer and whispered, "Which part?"

The seductive cadence of his voice sent tiny delicious shivers skittering across her bare arms. She stared at his lips. She wanted him to kiss her again. Desperately.

A half-smile curving his lips, he regarded her steadily.

An exciting spark heated her womanly places. She'd wager her best bonnet he knew exactly what direction her thoughts had taken.

He focused on her mouth. "Yes, that kissing bit was rather nice, wasn't it?"

"Yes," she breathed.

His gaze glided over her, taking her measure from slippers to hair, lingering the merest jot too long on her bosom to be considered polite. "You are lovely."

Three simple words sent her senses into a riotous dither. Warmth scorched her cheeks again, and her tongue refused to form an appropriate response. Had he forgotten his irritation of last evening, or had he decided to put it aside? It mattered not to her. This was the charming Falcon she remembered. The one she loved.

Tucking her hand into the bend of his elbow, he steered her in the terrace's direction. Her knees threatened to give out at his touch. What a ninny.

Compose yourself, Ivonne.

His forearm flexed beneath her fingers. "I sought you out to apologize for my behavior last night."

"There's no need—"

"Yes, there is." Falcon guided her to a scrolled metal bench in full view of the house's French windows. "Please, sit and indulge me for a moment."

Sinking onto the seat, she cast a surreptitious look at the manor. Dawson probably had her face pressed flat against the upper windowpanes while Mother peeked around the drawing room curtains and watched their every move. The last rays of the sun caressed the structure with their warm glow, making it impossible to discern if anyone did, indeed, spy upon them.

Hands folded in her lap, Ivonne faced him. Did he prefer demure, biddable women? She had no idea. She'd only been his friend until now. Before she bungled this wooing business beyond repair, she must meet with Emmy and discover what men desired.

Falcon sat upon the bench, a respectable distance between them this time. His buff doe-skins revealed long, muscled legs.

She covertly studied his groin, ignoring the tell-tale warmth suffusing her face once more. The bulge his pantaloons couldn't hide seemed similar to those of other men. Everything appeared as it should, at least to her inexperienced assessment.

He fidgeted with his watch fob, running the fingers of his intact hand along the fine silver chain. "Last night, I took advantage of you—"

"No, I—"

He put one finger on her lips. "Shh, let me finish."

She swallowed and clenched her fists to keep from tracing his finger with her tongue, or taking the entire thing into her mouth and sucking on it.

Where are these wanton ideas coming from?

He tossed a glance over his shoulder as if he, too, believed someone observed them. His sculptured mouth twitched. "I think we're being watched."

Ivonne giggled and leaned closer. "I'm sure of it. Too bad we don't dare give them something to gape at."

Staring straight ahead, he didn't respond. "I shouldn't have kissed you. I had no right. But more on point, I beg your forgiveness for accusing you of satisfying your curiosity with me, and then saying those other deplorable things."

He finished the last with a rush of words, as if he'd dreaded saying them.

Ivonne cocked her head, studying his profile. His remorse appeared genuine. Her pulse gave a little leap of hope. This made what she was about to suggest all the more feasible.

"Falcon." Jaw flexed, she pulled in a lengthy gulp of air and delved for courage. She pinched her fingers together, striving for calmness. "I have something to ask you."

"There you two are. Mother said I'd find you out here somewhere."

Allen? Ivonne twisted to look behind her. He strode the distance to the bench. The curtain twitched in the drawing room. Mother?

Ivonne and Falcon sat in plain view.

Had Mother sent Allen after them? Whatever for?

"I received some news that will be of great interest to you, Falcon." Ankles crossed, Allen rested his left hip against the balustrade. A peculiar expression settled on his face. His gaze swung between her and Falcon. "Am I interrupting something?"

Yes, dear brother, you are. A proposal.

"No, not at all." Falcon shook his head.

Allen flashed Ivonne one of his devastating smiles. "Mother asked me to remind you it's time to dress for the Vanbroke's musicale."

Ivonne furrowed her forehead and laced her fingers. "After last night, I expected we'd cry off attending."

"No." Allen firmed his lips and straightened. "Father insists the entire family put in an appearance to curb the gossipmongers' wagging tongues."

Too late for that, she feared. She turned her attention to Falcon. Rising, she straightened her gown. "Are you joining us? Safety in numbers, you know."

She tried to make the question seem casual, not as if her very future depended upon him being by her side from this point forward. Curling her toes in her slippers, she struggled to calm her nerves. If she stuck to him like fuzz on a peach, she'd send a clear message to everyone.

She'd made her choice. He just didn't know it.

"No, I'm afraid not." Falcon slid Allen a significant look.

Allen's eyebrows formed a puzzled vee, yet he remained silent.

Returning his fob to its pocket, Falcon stood. "I've been invited to dine with the Sethwicks this evening."

His gaze lingered on Ivonne's face, as if trying to memorize her features. Or gauge her reaction?

She swallowed, suddenly not wanting to hear what he was about to say.

He stared at her intently. "Lady Sethwick has a position open in her American shipping offices that I'm interested in."

13

Back rigid, Chance held his breath, waiting for Ivy's reaction. A muscle ticked annoyingly at the corner of his eye, revealing his agitation. Much weighed on whether she wanted him to stay. Moments ago, sitting beside her, he'd been tempted to throw good sense to the wind and ask her to be his bride, propriety be hanged.

A soft gasp escaped her. "America?"

She darted Allen an anxious glance before returning her attention to Chance. Her eyes, an unusual pewter shade in the dusky light, widened in astonishment and glistened suspiciously.

Tears?

He revered her with his gaze.

Bronze highlights shimmered in her hair, and her skin, pale as pearls, glowed in the sun's fading rays.

He longed to tell her of her beauty with more than words. To take her in his arms and worship her with his lips and body, to whisper the words of adoration he didn't dare share.

"America?" she rasped again, her lips trembling. Shaking her head, she clapped a hand to her mouth, her curls and peridot earrings bouncing from the frenzied movement. Without another word, she whirled away and hastened to the house.

For the first time, Chance noticed her lopsided gait.

Allen chuckled softly and sent him a sidelong glance. "I'd say that answers the question of where her affections lie, my friend."

Chance had initiated a very candid conversation with Allen after overhearing the remark at White's about Prinny's ludicrous decree. The Wimpleton heir had been delighted when Chance revealed his love for Ivy. Allen promised to throw all his support behind Chance's attempt to win her hand.

If Lord Wimpleton once more denied Chance's request to marry her, wisdom dictated he have an alternate plan. He'd chosen America as that option.

"Yes, my unflappable sister is in a dither at the notion of you sailing off across the Atlantic to the wilds of America." He slapped Chance on the back.

Chance flinched, smothering a foul oath. "Bugger it. Have care for my injured arm, will you?"

"Sorry 'bout that." Allen grinned sheepishly. He jabbed his thumb in the direction Ivy had disappeared. "That wasn't the reaction of a disinterested woman. No, I'd say she's already smitten."

A cocky grin tilting his mouth, he stepped away and took Chance's measure. "I suppose you'll do for a brother-in-law."

Chance allowed himself a cautious smile. "Not so fast. There's your father to convince. He must be made to see that I'm the best choice Ivy has for happiness."

"You haven't seen the competition." Allen laughed and scratched his nose. "Trust me. Father, and Mother, especially, will be groveling at your feet in gratitude. They want my sister to be happy, which is why they haven't pushed her to marry before now."

He rested a hip on the bannister and gazed at the brilliant sunset.

"Truth be told, I'm rather surprised how easily Father conceded to Prinny's demand. I have no more desire to incur the Regent's wrath than anyone else, but Father didn't attempt to stall his royal rotundness."

Allen pulled on his earlobe, his countenance bewildered. "Wholly out of character for my sire, I assure you."

He swung his gaze to Chance, speculation in its green depths.

"It's almost as if he knew of your interest in my sister."

Chance gave a low laugh. "He did. I asked for her hand years ago. The viscount told me to make a request again when she was older, and I had something to offer her."

Allen's mouth fell open. He gaped at Chance.

"Devil it, you didn't. *He didn't.*" Allen turned to stare at the house. "That sly fox. He knows exactly what he's about."

His mouth skewed into an appreciative smirk, he shook his head. "He knows Ivonne's taken with you and won't accept another. Father's forcing your hand."

Chance wished he agreed with Allen's assessment of the situation. Truth be told, his friend's explanation seemed far too simple and fortuitous.

"Perhaps. However, I have my doubts." Straightening his waistcoat,

Chance shifted toward the manor as well.

"I've been absent six years. People will find it peculiar that immediately upon my return to England, Ivy and I are betrothed. You know they'll ask why there wasn't a single hint or mention of an arrangement between us in all this time."

The sun sank lower on the pastel horizon. A cricket's buzzing chirrup rang nearby. He needed to be on his way soon, or he would be tardy for dinner. Not the way to impress a potential employer.

"How do you and your parents intend to explain other men courting your sister in my absence?" He rubbed his sore arm and then snorted. "Brows will raise and whispers will be tossed about, *if* I can somehow manage to get Wimpleton's approval."

"Oh, you'll get it all right," Allen assured him. "And don't worry about the courting. None of those sots ever paid her their formal addresses. A few unworthy curs sought her hand, but Father made it clear they should turn their attentions elsewhere."

A delighted chuckle escaped his friend.

"I'm willing to bet my best mare that Father regretted refusing you the moment he realized where my sister's affections lay. Mother probably deduced the truth and gave him a piece of her mind in the process. Women seem much more perceptive to that sort of thing."

Allen folded his arms, a pleased grin exposing his teeth.

"This is perfect, Falcon, don't you see? You claimed Ivonne was promised to another. Who else would know that except her affianced? Now that you're once again on British soil, we'll circulate the tale that an agreement was reached before you hied off to India."

"Why didn't we marry before I left?" Chance eyed him doubtfully. "No one with an iota of sense would believe such fustian nonsense."

Allen shrugged. "Ivy was what? Fifteen when you left?"

"Almost sixteen."

"Definitely too young." Allen clasped both hands to his chest and, *sotto voce*, declared, "To leave her Mother's bosom and trot off to another continent at such a tender age? Unfathomable."

"You forget, Allen, I don't have anything to offer her. No title, no fortune, no lands. Not even an annual income."

Only the deepest, purest love a man ever had for a woman.

Would that be enough? For her, perhaps, but her father's approval mattered a great deal to Chance as well.

Allen faced him, all signs of silliness gone. His attention sank to Chance's mangled hand. "You love her. The rest shouldn't, and doesn't, matter."

A far-off glint entered his eyes. "I learned that the hard way."

Was love enough? Chance wasn't certain. A title, even attached to a blackguard or rogue, meant much to many of *le bon ton*. Perhaps the viscount numbered among those. Chance didn't know the man well enough to make that determination.

"Besides," Allen stretched his arms overhead. "I have news that might turn providence's favor your way. A few questions to the right chaps at Brooks's and White's, and I learned Robinson has a reputable establishment on Lombard Street."

"He's still conducting business?" Chance's gaze leaped to Allen, and he couldn't contain his surprise. "I thought him a thieving scapegrace long since gone."

A dove landed on the lawn. Watching them with its tiny black-button eyes, the bird poked around beneath a shrub.

"Apparently not." Allen brushed a speck of lint off his coat. "He's reputed to be honest and diligent. Several gentlemen I spoke to have engaged in financial endeavors with him."

He gave Chance a cocky grin. "Very lucrative dealings, I might add."

Ivonne tore to her room, barely making the threshold before the torrent of tears overflowed. She'd feared she would cast up her accounts or swoon when Falcon offhandedly mentioned his interest in leaving England. Collapsing on her bed, she sobbed until her throat and head ached.

Shoving her soggy pillow aside, she rolled over and heaved a gusty sigh.

America.

Falcon's announcement ripped her chest wide open, yanked out her fractured heart, and smashed it beneath the hooves of a thousand horses. Even breathing was a painful reminder of the annihilation of her pathetic dream.

She quirked her lips in self-castigation. When had she become so histrionic? Her gaze fell on a large basket sitting atop the chamber's small, square table. A crisp white sheet of paper peeked from between several wrapped bundles.

She frowned. What was that, and when had it arrived?

Emelia!

Ivonne leaped from the bed, swiping at her damp face with her fingers. She snatched the paper, taking a cursory glance at the basket's contents. After breaking the wax seal with her fingernail, she read the missive.

Her shoulders slumped in disappointment. A tight knot of defeat curled in her middle. Emmy wouldn't help. She'd sent along several fashion magazines, the name of an exclusive modiste, and a basket full of cosmetics, fripperies, and fallalls.

My darling Ivonne,

You've no need for my expertise. You are supremely lovely in your innocence, and any man who fails to recognize that truth isn't worthy of you. I sent along some new cosmetics ...

Ivonne wadded the note into a tiny ball. She tossed it in the fireplace as she dragged herself to the washstand. Eyes closed and fighting tears, she wiped her face with cool water from the pitcher. After changing into her nightgown, she climbed between the sheets. She lay staring at the canopy, her thoughts cavorting about in her mind.

No help from Emmy.

Falcon plans to leave England.

I must produce a groom in two weeks.

All is lost.

Dawson tiptoed into the chamber, her thin face etched with worry.

Her astute gaze took in the basket, crumpled paper, and garments heaped upon the floor. "Can I get you anything?"

"Would you please tell Mother I'm indisposed?" Ivonne turned onto her side, tucking a hand beneath her pillow.

"Of course. I'll bring you some mint tea and toast too."

Dawson padded from the room, no doubt already aware of the reason for Ivonne's distress. Servants knew every tidbit, though how they came by the tattle was baffling, if not downright eerie at times.

Several moments later, two raps sounded at the door. Mother glided into the chamber without waiting for Ivonne to bid her enter.

"Darling, you're not well?" As she took in Ivonne's appearance, her mother's face creased with concern. "You're pale as the moon. Is it your stomach? A headache? Your leg?"

"No, none of those ail me." Ivonne shut her eyes lest her mother see the anguish that no doubt resided there.

Mother laid her cool hand on Ivonne's brow. "No fever, but you look entirely done in."

Ivonne released a shaky breath and opened her eyes.

"You've been crying." Her mother's brow furrowed into a frown. She sat upon the edge of the bed and smoothed Ivonne's hair. "I'm terribly sorry, my dear. This betrothal business has been too much for you."

After tucking the counterpane around Ivonne's shoulders, Mother kissed Ivonne's forehead. "I'll send our regrets to the Vanbrokes at once."

"No, Mother. You and Father should go. Perhaps your presence will help alleviate some of the chatter." Ivonne didn't believe it for a minute.

When the *ton* sank its talons into a juicy bit of gossip, no hope for redemption remained. Vultures on carrion, they delighted in everything foul and putrid.

Her mother shook her head.

"No, what's done is done. I don't give a rat's behind what anyone thinks." She patted Ivonne's shoulder. "And I don't mind telling you, after you left the study, I gave your Father a piece of my mind about this ridiculous marriage hullabaloo."

"I'm sorry you and Father quarreled." Ivonne sniffed as fresh tears threatened. "It's rather a mess, isn't it?"

Her mother opened her mouth then snapped it closed. She stared at Ivonne for a lengthy moment, uncertainty marring her expression.

"Have you considered ...? What I mean to say is, Ivonne is there the slightest possibility, that Mr. Faulkenhurst—"

"He's meeting with Lord and Lady Sethwick tonight regarding a position in America." Harder words Ivonne never spoke.

"Oh. I see." Mother wilted upon hearing the news. Nevertheless, she painted a brilliant smile onto her face. "We'll hatch a plan, darling. There's a little time, yet."

She didn't sound convinced by half. "Here, give me a hug, and then I must inform your father of our change in plans for this evening."

Ivonne pushed herself into a sitting position and shoved her hair out of her eyes.

"I'll check on you before I retire, dear." Mother embraced her, her familiar iris and jasmine perfume oddly comforting. With another reassuring smile, she slipped from the bedchamber.

The moment her mother exited the room, Ivonne collapsed against the pillows.

What was she to do? Falcon contemplated a move to America. Across the Atlantic. A lifetime away from her. She bit her lower lip and fiddled with the ribbon at her neckline.

The answer was simple.

She'd stow away on the ship.

14

"How much?" Chance ran a hand through his hair in disbelief. Surely he'd heard wrong. There was some mistake. There had to be.

Fortune didn't smile on him. But perhaps God's favor finally had. He almost touched his jaw to make sure he wasn't gaping open-mouthed like a gasping mackerel.

"How much did you say?"

"Four hundred ninety-seven thousand pounds ... at last count." Mr. Belamont smiled kindly, his eyes twinkling. "It's rather a shock, I gather?"

"Yes, rather," Chance managed to utter, sounding almost normal. He was a wealthy man.

A very wealthy man. A virtual nabob.

In one wondrous moment he'd gone from nearly penniless soldier to prosperous investor. Most importantly, he now had the means to care for Ivy, which meant Viscount Wimpleton would welcome his request to marry her. Only last evening Chance had expressed his concerns to Allen regarding the matter, and today, that worry no longer existed.

"I kept your documents locked in a private cabinet Tobbins doesn't have access to. Given the amount of your fortune, I thought that wisest." Belamont slanted his silvery head toward the closed door. "He's efficient, but the man babbles when he's taken a nip or is nervous."

"Yes, I experienced that the other day." Chance attempted to calm his thundering pulse.

"All the information regarding Mr. Robinson's business ventures on your behalf are detailed here." Belamont pushed the documents across his desk for Chance's inspection. He pointed to the pages lined with neat columns of numbers. "It appears he invested heavily in silk and spices. Most wise."

Rubbing his injured hand, Chance stared at the ledger, noting row after row of scrupulous records. He met the solicitor's amused gaze. "I don't understand how you came to have this information."

Belamont relaxed into his chair, his hands folded across his slight paunch. "Robinson told me you gave him my name. When he couldn't reach you in India, he forwarded your correspondences to me."

Chance fingered the edge of the desk. Discovering one was wealthy did rather set one's nerves on edge. Not that he had any complaints, mind you. "I'd forgotten I'd told him you were my solicitor."

Overnight, everything fell into place in such a miraculous way; he couldn't believe his good fortune.

"I suggest you call on him today. You might as well deal directly with one another from this point onward." Sitting upright, Mr. Belamont withdrew a key from inside his coat. He unlocked a drawer then rummaged around a bit. "Where did I put that bank note?"

A triumphant smile lit his face. "Ah, here it is."

He removed the note before dutifully relocking the drawer and placing the key in his pocket. "This is yours. Robinson sent the funds last week, and I didn't have time to deposit the note before I left Town. By the way, Coutts & Company Bank is holding your monies."

Chance accepted the note, giving it a perfunctory glance. Another six thousand pounds plus change. He grinned unabashedly. "I'm not going to even attempt reserved composure. In fact, Belamont, count yourself fortunate that I'm not dancing you about the room."

"You've good reason to celebrate." Belamont released a gravelly chuckle. He swept his hand in a mocking bow. "Dance away, Faulkenhurst."

After folding the note, Chance tucked it into his pocket. He stood and gathered his possessions. Sobering, he faced the solicitor and extended his hand.

"Thank you for your diligence and honesty."

Mr. Belamont came around his desk. He gripped Chance's palm in a firm handshake. "It's been my pleasure to be of service. Tell me, if you don't mind, what's the first thing you're going to do with your newfound fortune?"

Chance clapped his beaver hat on his head and grinned. "Buy a wedding ring."

Half an hour later, his mind still partially numb from pleasant shock, Chance inspected the rings the jeweler displayed for him. Primarily glittering diamonds, rubies, sapphires, and emeralds, he dismissed most with a cursory glance. Ivy deserved something unique, like her. He pictured glistening ivory-tinted pearls, the exact color of her skin as she lay naked atop their bed.

"Do you have anything less ostentatious? Something with pearls, perhaps? My intended prefers simplicity." At least he hoped to make her his intended before the day ended.

Ivy, his bride.

Indescribable elation sluiced through him.

"Yes, sir." The jeweler rummaged in the glass case.

"Ah, here we are." With great reverence, he produced a pearl and opal cluster ring. "This is a black opal, though if you'll notice, there's a strong blue color play."

Chance lifted the ring, holding it to the light streaming in from the storefront window. A mazarine blue opal lay nestled amongst double rows of creamy seed pearls. Exquisite. "Have you any matching pieces?"

"Why, yes, there are." An excited glint entered the jeweler's eyes. He produced a grand parure set complete with earrings, necklace, pin, bracelet, and a delicate tiara.

"I'll take the entire set."

Ivy would be resplendent wearing them on their wedding day. For the first time, Chance harbored a genuine belief she'd be his bride.

God truly must be smiling down on him.

"Very good. Your lady is very fortunate indeed."

Chance shook his head. "No, I'm the one who's been blessed."

After locking the display case and securing the key inside his coat pocket, the jeweler gathered the gems. "Let me wrap them for you. I'll be but a moment."

"Thank you." Chance flipped his watch open. Less than an hour until his appointment with Lord Wimpleton. His stomach seized with unfamiliar nerves.

Steady on, old man.

He grinned. What a difference a single day could make in determining one's future. Belamont's missive early this morning, followed by a call to the solicitor, and then an appointment with Robinson had set a whole new course for Chance's life.

Now, the only tasks that remained were to win Lord Wimpleton's approval and to propose to Ivy.

"Miss Ivonne, you need to wake up."

Dawson's singsong greeting yanked Ivonne from a rather wonderful dream about a wedding. Her wedding.

"Your Father requests your presence below stairs," the maid said, followed by the sounds of her laying out Ivonne's morning tea.

Two days in a row? Seriously?

Ivonne flopped onto her back, her eyes firmly shut as she tried to recall the man standing beside her at the altar of St. George's Parish Church.

No use, bother and blast.

His face flitted away on the fringes of her memory. And bother again.

The one man she would ever accept as a groom decided to toddle off to the confounded colonies.

Her throat closed as a sudden rush of tears threatened. She clamped her lips together. No, by George, she wasn't casting her lot in that easily. She could at least ask Falcon to consider marrying her.

Then there'd be no doubt in her mind, lingering year upon incessant year. No always wondering if the outcome of her life might have been different if she'd only plucked up a feather's worth of courage and asked him if he would be her husband.

A cup rattled in a saucer near Ivonne's head. She opened one eye and sniffed.

Hot chocolate. Dawson's attempt at bribery.

"I brought you a cocoa topped with Devonshire cream." Dawson lowered the painted floral saucer to eye level. Thick rivulets of melted cream dripped over the teacup's rim. "You'd best take a sip. I was a mite too enthusiastic with the cream. I know you have a preference for it."

Dawson extended the cup and saucer, a hopeful expression on her face.

Poor dear.

She'd fussed and clucked so much last evening, Ivonne had finally snapped at the maid to leave her be. Immediately chagrined by her churlish behavior, Ivonne longed to apologize, but Dawson had taken her at her word and not returned to the chamber until this morning.

Ivonne sat up. She fluffed the pillows behind her back before accepting the hot chocolate. "Thank you, Dawson."

She took a sip and smiled. "Delicious."

The maid beamed, and after giving Ivonne a pat on the shoulder, set about selecting something appropriate for her to wear.

A full hour later, attired in a pink and white calico morning gown, she caught a glimpse of herself in a hallway mirror. At her request, Dawson had trimmed her hair before twisting the thick mass into a complex Grecian knot. Several curls framed Ivonne's face, softening her features.

She'd experimented with the new cosmetics Emmy sent too. Well-pleased with the effect, she smiled. The paints enhanced her features, although no one could tell she wore any. Just how many other ladies of her acquaintance availed themselves of the same devices and feigned natural beauty?

Once again, Ivonne stood outside Father's study, except today she had determined to take charge of her future. With a brisk knock, she thrust her chin upward a notch and pressed the latch, entering without waiting for permission.

She tripped to an abrupt stop.

Falcon, his legs crossed, lolled in an armchair across from her parents on the sofa.

Allen, one arm resting on the mantel, stood before the fireplace. His countenance remained unreadable, although a smile hovered about his mouth.

Why was Falcon here, closeted with her family? A quick perusal of their faces revealed nothing.

Allen strode to her and, after kissing her cheek, chucked her under the chin. "Courage, minx."

He turned to the others, now standing as well.

"I'm off to Tattersall's. Rumor has it Blackeridge has some prime bit of blood up for auction. I'll keep an eye out for a matched team for you, Falcon." With a smart salute, Allen departed the room.

"Darling, do have a seat." Her mother indicated the settee, as she moved toward the entrance. She paused and bussed Ivonne's cheek. Then, with a fervent hug, whispered, "All will be well, dearest."

What in the world?

Mother, too, made her escape, leaving Ivonne standing befuddled in the center of the study. Why did she need courage, and what would be well? First casting her father a questioning glance, she allowed her gaze to feast on Falcon.

No man should be that beautiful.

The black of his cutaway coat and the royal blue of his striped waistcoat made his eyes more vivid. How could his eyelashes be so dark with hair that fair?

His gaze leisurely roamed her length. Hot little pricks of awareness popped out along the visual path his gaze traveled.

Gads.

Her senses came alive with strange little prickles as they were wont to do when he looked at her that way. If his eyes alone had the power to arouse her this much, imagine what his touch would do. She'd be sliding off her chair if he kept gazing at her so seductively.

She cleared her throat and focused on her father as she advanced further into the room. "Whatever is going on?"

"I think I'll let Faulkenhurst explain." He smiled and winked. After a quick embrace, Father strode from the room, leaving the door ajar.

Staring at the entry, Ivonne shook her head. "Is everyone dicked in the nob this morning?"

Falcon chuckled, that delicious rumble that sent her pulse skittering out of control. "No, they know we have something of importance to discuss and wished to give us some privacy."

Lord, no.

He's leaving for America. She wasn't prepared. It was way too soon.

Her legs now the consistency of warm pudding, she wobbled to the sofa. Scrutinizing his dear face, she plopped ungracefully onto the cushion. She swallowed, fisting her hands in her skirt's folds. She couldn't bear his going away again.

"You're sailing to America. I hadn't thought you'd leave quite this soon." She tried to smile, but her lips refused to turn upward.

Falcon sat beside her. "Ivy, I'm—"

Palm outward, Ivonne raised her arm and cut him off. Her hand quivered so badly, she lowered it to her lap. She must propose this very minute, before he had a chance to say another word.

"Please, I have something to ask you, and if I don't ask now, I'll never have the courage again." She closed her eyes and sucked in a steadying breath. Squaring her shoulders, she opened her eyes and stared directly into the azure depths of his. "I don't suppose you'd consider ...? That is, would you be opposed to ...?"

Quivering from nervousness, Ivonne could barely make her tongue work. She tried again despite her shaky voice. "I wanted to know if you would ...?"

Dash it all, this wasn't how she'd imagined the proposal would go. She lowered her eyelashes as the heat of humiliation crept steadily from her bosom to her cheeks. They likely glowed like candied apples as they did when she was embarrassed. Nonetheless, she must do this.

She peeped at him through her eyelashes.

A bemused expression on his face, Falcon stared at her. "Go on."

"Will you marry me?" she blurted in a breathy rush.

"Yes."

"I know I'm not ..." Her gaze jumped to meet his, and her heart hammered so hard, she could scarcely breathe. "Yes?"

The word emerged as a strangled squeak. She dared a tiny smile.

"You said yes? You'll marry me? Really?"

Falcon smiled, his perfect white teeth a stark contrast against his tanned face. He cupped her cheek with his good hand.

"Ivy, your father granted me permission to propose to you just moments ago."

Ivonne's mouth dropped open. "Oh."

Placing a finger beneath her chin, Falcon closed her mouth. His lips hitched upward into one of his irresistible smiles. "It seems he's been waiting for me to return to England and ask for your hand. I asked to marry you once before, and he refused."

"You did? *He did?*"

Father had turned Falcon away? How could he?

All these years she'd yearned for his love, and he'd already asked her father to marry her. Just wait until she had a moment alone with her sire. She'd give him a colorful earful he wouldn't soon forget.

"He wanted me to come back when you were older and I had the means to take care of you. However, your father realized you loved me, had been pining for me all these years."

Ivy angled her head proudly. "I wasn't pining."

"No?" Falcon quirked a brow.

She lifted a shoulder. "I just never entertained any notion of marrying anyone else."

Eyeing the door, she suddenly stiffened, tucking her chin to her chest. "Father turned you away because you weren't wealthy? I never thought him so shallow."

"He wanted to make sure I loved you for you, and not your marriage settlement. He told me, just now, that when he realized I truly loved you and you loved me, he'd been waiting for me to return and ask for you again."

Chance ran a finger along her jaw.

"He loves you very much and only wants to see you happy."

He took her hand in his calloused one.

"I came here today seeking his permission to wed you. Your father summoned you so I could propose. Only you, minx," Falcon tapped the end of her nose, "beat me to it."

He'd been about to propose to her? Her heart soaring on wings of joy, she managed a tremulous smile.

Scooting nearer, he gathered her in his arms. "Though you were too young and I knew we'd have to wait, I've wanted to make you my bride since you were fifteen."

"Truly?" She blinked back tears of elation.

"I swear." His golden head descended until only an inch separated their lips. "I love you, Ivy. Will you be my bride?"

His mouth grazed hers, a tantalizing promise.

"Yes, Falcon, I shall." With a sigh, she sealed her promise with love's binding kiss.

Epilogue

London, England
Late June, 1818

Standing before the rector, Ivonne smiled into Falcon's loved-filled eyes.

They were married. She'd dreamed that this day might come. Seated in the front pew, resplendent in a plum cutaway coat and matching breeches trimmed with diamonds and rubies, the Prince Regent beamed his approval.

Falcon's family, as well as hers and Miss Kingsley, of course, completed the witnesses. Dozens of guests awaited them at home where an extravagant wedding breakfast had been prepared.

"I love you, Mrs. Faulkenhurst." Falcon caressed her palm with his thumb.

A delicious tremor shook her. What his touch did to her.

"And I love you."

"What say you we make our escape?" He grasped her hand and

hurried her past the small crowd of laughing well-wishers to the waiting carriage.

Ivonne giggled when he tickled her ribs while lifting her into the conveyance.

"Ah, my wife is ticklish." After jumping into the vehicle, he promptly lowered the window coverings.

Settling her on his lap, he proceeded to nuzzle her neck and caress her ribs.

A new bout of giggles ended on a blissful sigh when Falcon claimed her lips in a scorching kiss. She leaned into him, surrendering to her desire, daring to meet his tongue with her own as she slipped her hands beneath his shirt. Hard muscles and warm flesh met her exploring fingers. She'd never tire of touching him.

Several tantalizing moments passed before Ivonne angled away from him. He needed to know she understood theirs wouldn't be the typical wedding night. But how to say so delicately was a bit of a pickle. It wouldn't do to offend Falcon on their wedding day.

"Falcon?"

"Why the serious face?" Bending his neck, he nibbled along her collarbone. He ventured ever lower, releasing her breasts from their confines. He gently cupped the mounds, raining kisses across the sensitive flesh.

God, she would die if he didn't take a nipple in his mouth.

As if he heard her thoughts, he encircled an aching tip with his warm lips. He suckled, grazing the end with his teeth.

A stab of intense pleasure flickered between her legs. She gasped and clutched his head, making him stop. She couldn't think straight when he kissed her so.

"This is important," she gasped, barely recognizing the husky voice as her own. "Please listen."

He raised his head, peering into her eyes.

"All right." He brushed a stray curl from her face. "What is it you are determined to tell me, wife? I have other things I'd rather be doing than chatting."

He stared pointedly at her breasts before sweeping a finger across the top of the mounds. He dipped lower, softly scraping a fingernail across a turgid nipple.

She gasped again, unprepared for the hot desire flooding her. She seized his wandering finger and eyed him, afraid to say anything to disrupt his happiness.

"Come on, love. Out with it." He gave her a playful prod in the ribs.

Ivonne rested against his hard chest.

"You know I love you? No matter what?" She angled her head to peek at him.

His gorgeous mouth slid into one of his stunning smiles. "I know. And I love you. Tell me, what has you worried?"

"I don't mind that we cannot have children." She touched the scar on his cheek.

Falcon stilled and made an inarticulate sound in his throat. His eyes rounded, and his jaw sagged. He stared at her with such intensity, she squirmed on his lap and dropped her gaze to her hands.

He tilted her chin upward with a finger until their eyes met. "Pray tell me, why do you think we cannot have children?"

"Well, because you ..." Ivonne gazed at him warily. Her focus sank to his cravat as she whispered, "You lost your manhood in India."

He threw back his head, exposing the strong column of his throat and laughed, a rich unrestrained guffaw.

"Well, I certainly do not think it's a laughing matter," she huffed, nonplussed by his reaction.

His chest shaking from amusement, Falcon wiped at his eyes.

"Darling, let me assure you, my manhood is in perfect working order." He gripped her hips, holding her firmly to his lap, and shifted his hips upward.

Something hard flexed against her bottom.

"Oh. Oh! Is that your ...?"

"Indeed." He waggled his eyebrows, a wolfish grin on his mouth.

"It works properly?"

He pressed his rigid length against her buttocks once more. "Most assuredly, madam."

Melting into his arms, Ivonne sighed and raised her lips in invitation.

"Then everything is absolutely perfect."

Dearest Reader,

    I'm truly delighted you chose to read *A Bride for a Rogue* and hope it captivated you enough to take a peek at the other books in the series.

    Ivonne and Chance's story was inspired by a scene in *A Kiss for a Rogue*, the first book in my Honorable Rogues™ series. My wounded hero needed a special heroine, and he found that in kindhearted Ivonne.

    Please consider telling other readers why you enjoyed this book by reviewing it. Not only do I truly want to hear your thoughts, reviews are crucial for an author to succeed. **Even if you only leave a line or two, I'd very much appreciate it.**

    So, with that I'll leave you.

    Here's wishing you many happy hours of reading, more happily ever afters than you can possibly enjoy in a lifetime, and abundant blessings to you and your loved-ones.

A Rogue's Scandalous Wish

Dedication

I lost a beloved grandmother, a step-grandfather,
and foster brother in two separate house fires.
I humbly dedicate this book to burn victims everywhere.
Bless you!

Acknowledgements

I must give a shout out to Victoria Vane for arranging the photo shoot that allowed me to purchase the amazing cover model image, and also to Darlene Albert for the fabulous cover. Neither can I ignore my faithful beta readers and ARC reviewers. Thank you!

xoxo

1

Wimpleton's Ball, London, England
Late May 1818

One, two, three, four ... No, I think there are actually five.
Yawning behind her partially open fan, Philomena peeked through the leaves of the enormous cage-shaped potted ficus and counted the wiry hairs sprouting from Lady Clutterbuck's chin. The chinwag and her cronies gossiped a short distance away, their unending litany contributing to the onset of Philomena's nagging headache.

She relaxed a fraction. No sign of Mr. Wrightly, a repugnant would-be suitor, and the reason she'd dove behind the plant when she spied him looking for her earlier.

Pressing two fingertips between her eyes to ease the thrumming there, she located the mantle clock and breathed out a soft sigh. Not yet ten o'clock. She allowed a droll smile. Giles wouldn't consider leaving before the supper dance.

No indeed.

Your brother is determined to find you a husband before Season's end, Philomena Martha Elizabeth Pomfrett. Whether you like it or not.

And she most emphatically did not.

Despite her lack of interest, or the cost to his already fragile health, dear Giles dutifully escorted her to event after event, evening after evening. And she obediently—well, more aptly, reluctantly—husband-hunted.

Content to become a spinster, the mercenary process conflicted with her principles and put her out of sorts, but Giles's time ran short so, for his sake, she pressed onward. Fear of her prospective husband's reaction to her scars created a permanent knot in her belly, and she swallowed against the dryness in her mouth.

Enough.

She shoved the worry aside. She'd deal with that obstacle when the time came. First she had to acquire a spouse, and her prospects weren't altogether promising.

"Oh, would you look at that delicious specimen of manhood." The lascivious tone of Lady Clutterbuck's cohort was entirely inappropriate for an aged, married peeress. "Utterly Scrumptious. Do you know who *he* is?"

The dame actually licked her lips, and thrust her bosoms skyward. Considering her breasts' monstrous size, they barely lifted above her ample waist, and a mere moment later, breathing heavily, she sagged into her former sack-shaped posture.

What unfortunate gentleman had found himself the target of the peeress's lewd attention *this* evening?

"Bradford, Viscount Kingsley. He's just come into his title. One hopes he proves himself worthy of the honor and avoids associating with inferiors and underlings." Lady Clutterbuck's strident voice plowed into Philomena with the force of a winter gale. The dame jutted her superior nose into the air. "That's become so common of late with all the mushrooms and nabobs thinking to force their way into Polite Society. Deep pockets are no substitute for good breeding, I say."

Bradford? Here?

Philomena craned her neck to see around the blasted plant.

Where?

Breath held, she deftly parted the foliage and bent forward.

There, at the ballroom's entrance in his formal evening attire, looking every bit the gentleman of refinement with his lovely auburn-headed sister, Olivia, on one arm and the distinguished Duchess of Daventry on the other. Unable to deny the giddiness seeing him again brought, fleeting excitement filled Philomena.

He swept the room with his brilliant, blue-eyed—slightly bored—gaze, and she jerked backward, kicking the container as she tumbled into the wall.

He can't see you, ninny.

The gossips snapped curious, somewhat distracted glances in her direction.

Drat it all.

She dropped into a crouch with only her forehead visible above the blue and white porcelain, and in a moment, they put their graying heads together and launched into another round of *on dit*. For the first time,

Philomena gave thanks that rumors dominated their narrow, peevish minds.

Peering between the ficus's woven branches, she bit her lip as her stomach toppled over itself. She wasn't ready to see Bradford. Face tanned, his raven hair glistening in the candlelight, he threw back his head and laughed at something the duchess said.

How could he have grown even more beautiful? Deucedly unfair to womanhood.

Still squatting, she pivoted right, and then shuffled left. Where was Giles? He'd promised her a beverage several minutes ago. He was nowhere to be seen, at least not from this awkward position.

Most likely, he'd gotten snared in a conversation with another hard-of-hearing matron. That's what came of exploiting their distant connection to the Dowager Marchioness Middleton in order to introduce Philomena to Polite Society.

Not one of the ladies in the dame's favored circle boasted a birthday less than five and seventy years ago, and inevitably, a matron or two or three, imposed upon him to fetch a ratafia, escort her to the card room, retrieve a wrap, or some other trivial matter. Kindhearted, Giles had never been able to politely make his excuses, so he amiably did as they bid.

Half the time, the old birds didn't need what they requested. They just enjoyed a handsome young man's attention for a few moments.

Biting her lower lip, Philomena braved another glance to the ballroom's entrance. Bradford had disappeared into the crowd as well.

Good. She could make her escape.

A cramp seized her calf as she moved to rise. Curses. Closing her eyes, she gripped the pot's edge, waiting for the spasm to pass. Pray God no one came upon her hugging the pottery. Rather hard to explain her sudden rapt interest in dirt and greeneries.

Easing upright, she surreptitiously examined those nearest her. No one had noticed her. Pretty much a testament to her entire dismal Season. An incomparable, she was not.

Ah, here came Giles now, bearing a glass of ratafia in one hand and punch in the other. His limp had become more pronounced, and his countenance more wan, than it had been scarcely twenty minutes ago. Nonetheless, despite the ravages of ill-health, his striking visage turned many a fair maid's head as he ambled toward her hiding place.

Why did he insist on putting them through this every night?

He wants to make certain you are provided for when ...

She blinked away the familiar prickle of tears and the accompanying rush of anger. His delicate heart could fail at any moment. The injustice galled. He should be strong and healthy, seeking a spouse himself, not gravely weakened by a prolonged fever and resigned to an early death.

How she wished there'd been no need for him to enlist, wished he hadn't been stationed in the West Indies, hadn't been wounded, had received proper treatment. Hadn't contracted Scarlet Fever.

If wishes were horses, beggars would ride.

Forcing composure, Philomena schooled her features into pleasant lines. She would bear her grief with quiet dignity.

His forehead furrowed, Giles peered about in search of her.

Eager to intercept him, and grateful to be spared overhearing more of Lady Clutterbuck's malicious claptrap, Philomena skirted the pot and, after edging along the wall a few feet, stepped out into the open.

Perhaps he would consider joining her in a game of loo or whist. His resting a spell at the card tables would also spare her another partnerless set or two. Blasted hard to acquire a husband when she spent most dances tapping her toes or pretending absorption in cornices, portraits, and elaborately painted ceiling panels.

"There you are." Passing her the ratafia, Giles grinned and winked, his gray-green eyes, so like hers, glinting with mirth. He dipped his honey-blond head near her ear. "Hiding again, little sister?"

He knew her too well.

She shook her head before taking a sip of the overly-sweet beverage. "No, I'm just avoiding—"

"Is that Kingsley?" Gaze as steely and cold as his tone, Giles canted his head to a cluster of guests not more than thirty feet away.

Philomena had thought Bradford attractive across the wide room, but this devilish, rake was garnering moon-eyed sighs and giggles from the younger misses and calculating, seductive glances from the faster, mature set. He hadn't seen her yet, and she wheeled around, presenting her back. The air clamped in her lungs so fiercely, her head spun dizzily, and her glass slipped from her hand. "Oh, dear God."

Her ragged gasp alerted Giles, and he seized her drink, preventing an embarrassing mishap or calling Bradford's attention to her.

Scorn sharpened the planes of his thin face as he scowled at Bradford. Quaffing his remaining punch, Giles then tossed back her ratafia before taking both cups in one hand and maneuvering her into the crowd. His gaze, simmering with sympathy, plucked at her self-control.

"Why don't we take a turn about the terrace, Phil? A bit of fresh air might help steady your nerves and allow you a few moments to compose yourself."

So that you don't make an utter cake of yourself.

She refused to peek over her shoulder, stiffening her spine until the taut muscles between her shoulder blades pinched.

Had the women fluttering their eyelashes and sending coquettish smiles Bradford's way any notion how ridiculous they looked? Scant difference lay between their brazen invitations and those of seasoned, dockside harlots. Not that Philomena blamed them. He'd matured into an arresting figure of a man, while she concealed hideous scars, necessitating a gown far from the first peak of fashion.

Jealousy dowsed with pain nipped her heart. Once upon a time, he had reserved that charming, sensual smile for her alone. Well, she'd convinced her naïve, younger self he had.

"It's just there, through those French windows. You go along, and I'll be right out after I find Lady Middleton's misplaced shawl and put these down or find a servant to take them." Giles nodded in the doors' direction and half-lifted the glasses. "Earlier, I noticed a charming path through the gardens we might stroll."

And exhaust himself further? No. A secluded bench was a far better option.

Dragging her musings from Bradford, flashing his enigmatic smile at the tittering females, Philomena gave a short jerk of her head. "Yes, yes, fresh air and a stroll. An excellent notion."

Escape before the tears she swore she'd stopped shedding for him breached the damn of her resolve and surged down her cheeks. Why did seeing him hurt so awfully after all this time?

She should be over him. Wanted to be over him. Had thought she was until this miserable instant. Joy and anguish at seeing him again wrestled fiercely, each vying for supremacy.

Stupid, fickle heart.

Curling her gloved fingers into fists, and with determination in each step, she deftly navigated through the throng, her focus locked on her refuge—the lantern-lit garden. Perhaps, like a mythical tree nymph, she could disappear into the greeneries for the rest of the evening. Truth be known, no one but Giles would miss her.

Bradford hadn't sent a single letter, not one, the miserable wretch. And neither had he attempted to contact her or Giles after the fire that took Mama's and Papa's lives and nearly hers as well. A blaze that had destroyed their home and that Bradford's fiend of an uncle had started in the sanctuary—accidentally, he claimed, the lying bugger.

Day after day during the months of her convalescence, Philomena had hoped and prayed Bradford would come to see her or at least send word. Her love gave her strength, gave her the will to fight to live, helped her bear the anguish of her healing burns and the horrific loss of her parents and home.

By the time she left her sick-bed, she had relinquished any expectation of hearing from him again. Standing before her aunt's filmy dressing table mirror, Philomena cringed at the havoc the fire had wreaked on her arms and chest. Yet she possessed a measure of gratitude too, that except for a few minor burns on her shoulders and neck, the rest of her body had been spared. Taking her heart and her youthful love, scarred as viciously as her body, she'd tucked them away, determined never to endure pain that torturous again.

Bradford's shallow promises—that he'd love her until the end of time, that as soon as he was old enough, he'd ask for her hand, that he couldn't wait to marry her, that their difference in stations didn't matter—all lies. He hadn't wanted a maimed wife after the fire, and now that he held a title, he could choose a diamond of the first water for his viscountess.

Bitter knowledge to her injured pride and wounded soul.

"You knew you'd probably see him, Phil." Giles steered her further away from the salivating dames and the man who'd trampled her heart. He pressed her elbow. "It's the talk of London, his arriving in England on the cusp of his uncle's death. At least you were spared his company the better part of the Season. And you've suitors aplenty to choose from. Why, just this evening, Mr. Wrightly asked if he might court you."

"He did?"

How ghastly.

Double her age, the thrice-widowed, rich nabob made no secret he sought a young wife to beget an heir on. Coarse, vulgar, and perpetually reeking of rancid lard and sweat, Mr. Wrightly had finally deduced no lady of consequence would consider his suit, so he'd lowered his standards and now directed his attention to Philomena.

Lucky her. As if she were that desperate. Yet. "Please tell me you said no."

"Of course I didn't." Giles affected an insulted mien. "That's for you to decide, but you must make a decision by this Season's end. We haven't the funds to sponsor another."

Neither would he likely live that long.

A quartet of giggling misses, trailed by plain-faced Lady Victoria Southwark, staring longingly at Bradford, plowed across their path, scurrying toward the row of chairs to which he had escorted his sister. Obvious as fur on a frog what they schemed. Empty-headed chits.

"We've nearly used the whole of what Aunt Alice bequeathed us." Tense lines bracketing his mouth, Giles veered his attention from the women.

He wouldn't even permit himself interest in a woman, and sympathy welled at the unfairness of his plight. What a superb husband and father he would have made.

"I know, Giles, and I am trying. Truly."

Philomena compelled her stiff lips to smile. They'd exhausted their connections as well, and if it hadn't been for imposing upon Aunt Alice's distant relation to the Dowager Marchioness of Middleton, no door in London would have opened to them—the insignificant offspring of a second son and his equally unremarkable wife. "There are still a few weeks left in the Season. All is not yet lost."

Giles accompanied her toward the open French windows, lines of fatigue already deepening around his bleary eyes. "I'm not worried, Phil. You've caught the attention of several eligible men, and with your beauty and wit, I've no doubt you shall have multiple offers."

Bless him for his optimism, but blinded by brotherly love, he exaggerated her potential. At two and twenty, with a very modest dowry and a torso and arms riddled with scars, she wasn't sought after.

Her beaux consisted of an ancient, almost deaf baronet with a mouthful of rotting teeth, a former sea captain who yet retained a cargo hold's peculiar odor, a pimply-faced youth in line for an earldom, whose mother had towed him away by his ear upon finding him declaring himself to Philomena at a musicale last week, a banker so tight in the pocket he'd worn the exact same clothing every time she'd encountered him and was wont to stuff his pockets with food when he thought no one looked, a fourth son, without a farthing to his name and a propensity to ogle every bosom within ten feet, and now—*God bless my remarkable good fortune*—the widower, Mr. Wrightly.

Yes, they made a dandy selection to pick from. Why, Philomena was all aflutter, trying to determine which of the extraordinary gentlemen to set her cap for. However could she possibly choose between them?

But choose she must.

To ease Giles's fretting, she'd given her word she would marry, in spite of not wishing to ever enter that state, and they truly had exhausted most of their meager funds. Despite making economies, they'd only enough money to pay the rent and their expenses through July. To keep them from the poor house, and prevent him from seeking employment, she must wed. He was too weak, and sure as the rich guzzled champagne, acquiring a menial position would mean a speedier end for him.

If any one of her suitors didn't set her stomach to roiling worse than a pitching deck during a tempest, she would've said her vows tomorrow.

Squaring her shoulders, Philomena offered him what she hoped was a brave smile.

What needs done, gets done.

Hopefully, none of her admirers lurked outside, for she'd no wish to encounter them alone. She hadn't curbed her tendency to speak her mind, an attribute not favored by males, and she wasn't in a position to spurn anyone's attentions just yet.

Almost to the exit, she touched his arm. "I'll meet you outside, Giles, as soon as you are able. Who knows, I might stumble upon yet another potential husband upon the terrace."

And Lady Clutterbuck might cease gossiping, and snowflakes won't melt in hell.

Haggard lines creased Giles's eyes, and he gave her a firm nudge. "Miss Kingsley is looking this way. Hurry, Phil, go before she recognizes us."

2

"Make it something quite spectacular, will you? Something scandalous to keep their forked tongues flapping for a good long while." Bradford winked and grinned at his sister and her soon-to-be-husband before spinning on his heel. Allen Wimpleton had just proposed to Olivia, and he wouldn't stay and intrude upon his sister's special moment.

Not exactly proper brotherly advice, Kingsley, especially for a viscount.

He'd never much adhered to, nor much cared for, the *haute ton's* version of propriety. Hadn't he just proven that by escaping outdoors? The dozen or so introductions he had endured, mostly to wide-eyed, blushing misses, had quite put him off, and he'd absconded to the garden a half hour after arriving without dancing once or even greeting Lord and Lady Wimpleton. Quite beyond the pale, even for him.

Bradford mentally shrugged. So what?

After glimpsing a woman reminding him of a lost love, joy and shock had momentarily stunned him before reality cruelly whispered the truth. Blanketed in a cloak of disappointment, he'd sought a few moments alone and come upon his sister and her beau.

Perhaps Wimpleton and Olivia would indulge in a wholly inappropriate kiss in full view of the guests mingling on the terrace. Bradford heartily hoped so. He would if he were them. If a dame or two had a fit of the vapors as result, so much the better. At least this ball would be memorable, and the hullabaloo added a degree of interest to an otherwise wholly predictable, and altogether boring, evening.

Whistling to the strains of a waltz filtering through the open French windows, he strode the curved flagstone footpath deeper into the manicured gardens, lit here and there by lanterns atop wrought iron posts.

The giggles, rustles, and muffled groans emanating from the shrubberies he passed hinted at activities much more outrageous than the sweethearts' *tete-a-tete* he'd just witnessed. Olivia and Allen adored each other, and if they wanted to express their love publicly, so be it. Stuff the *Beau Monde's* pompous posturing and endless hypocritical rules.

A throaty laugh floated from a bush several feet away.

Brow raised, Bradford hustled by the shuddering greenery lest he find himself privy to a rather intimate display.

Awkward, that.

On second thought, perchance a modicum of wisdom ought to be observed regarding engaging in public affection. How those tumbling about in the foliage with the abandon of frisky field mice or amorous squirrels expected their mussed hair or wrinkled and stained clothing to go undetected confounded him. Unless they'd stripped stark naked before coupling.

Bare arses bobbing amongst leaves?

He chuckled softly. Wouldn't that raise a few eyebrows? Probably lecherous ogling, too.

Life was meant to be fun and enjoyed, and by Jove, he fully intended to do just that. Better to have a damned jolly time of it, make the most of every moment—as long as he didn't hurt others as he went about his larks. In any event, his wicked wit and hunger for excitement made it impossible to do otherwise. However, his recently acquired title put a confounded damper on things, a cumbersome yoke of responsibility and duty he'd never expected—nor wanted.

Though now that he bore a title, he still didn't know how many days he might have left on this earth, or what twists or obstacles destiny might hurl his way. His new status gave testament to that. His uncle, the former viscount, and cousins—the heir and the spare—had drowned in a boating accident mere months after Father succumbed to apoplexy, thrusting the viscountcy upon an unenthusiastic Bradford.

Death had brushed her icy fingertips across his soul not so very long ago as well, and though he'd escaped with his life, two of the sugar mill workers had not. Mother had died far too young, too, and Philomena—his sweet Phil—had been on the cusp of womanhood when tragedy struck and stole her from him.

His earlier levity fled.

Twice in less than fifteen minutes, she'd stampeded into his thoughts. Shouldn't he be beyond such melancholy reflections by now? He'd known many women since her death, some astonishingly beautiful, witty, and intelligent, yet his heart remained numb and unengaged.

Quite simply, Philomena had been exquisite—the others, forgettable.

Perchance that was his lot, to love only once.

Blast, but he craved a cheroot, the singular bad habit he'd acquired from his sire. One he'd nearly succeeded in putting aside, after witnessing his father's labored breathing at the end of his life, except for moments such as these, when desperation for the familiar calmative overcame Bradford.

Cursed weakness.

Doubly-cursed memories.

Slowing his pace, he sought a private corner to indulge. If he recalled correctly—he hadn't been to the Wimpleton's in over three years—an almost concealed arbor lay nestled in the far corner of the grounds. Few guests had ventured this far from the mansion, and he welcomed the solitude, finding London much too crowded, confining, and noisy after three years living in the Caribbean.

Blessed wonder neither he nor Olivia had contracted Yellow Fever, or one of the other foul illnesses prevalent in the tropics—precisely why, in addition to opposing slavery, he'd sold the blasted plantation and booked passage to England as soon as they'd laid Father to rest.

A sweet fragrance wafted past.

Honeysuckle.

Warm and subtly erotic, the scent triggered youthful recollections of love lost. Again. Wistfulness he'd not experienced in a long while seized him. He'd have married Philomena had she lived. At six and twenty, he'd yet to find another woman who made him feel even a fraction of what he'd felt for her as a fumbling youth.

Ah, there stood the arbor, at the end of the path where the glow of two lanterns penetrated the shadows. Bradford quickened his pace, canvassing the area.

Alone.

Perfect, he'd take a puff or two, just enough to satisfy his craving, and then return to the ball. A ravishing brunette had caught his eye earlier. Even after all these years, he couldn't bring himself to direct his attentions to fair-haired women. It seemed a betrayal of Philomena's memory. If he could finagle an introduction, he was of a mind to ask the dark-haired beauty to save a dance for him. It shouldn't be at all difficult to arrange. He was prime stock on the Marriage Mart these days.

As Mr. Kingsley, he'd been an agreeable companion, comfortable in the pocket, a nice fellow to have about. Suitable, but not hotly pursued. As Viscount Kingsley, however, he could scarcely make a public appearance without forward Mamas thrusting their eligible daughters in his path. However, he'd no intention of acquiring a viscountess just yet. Adjusting to his new position, as well as acclimating to England again, was quite enough to take on at once. He wasn't a damned martyr, for God's sake. He'd have to be addled to take on a bride at present.

He felt rather like one of the savory dishes his hostess had laid out for supper. Not at all pleasant to be eyed like a tasty morsel, or lusted after by ladies of the *ton* more brazen than a Covent Garden strumpet.

Earlier, a seductive-eyed, full-bosomed peeress had given him a lecherous wink and licked her full lower lip suggestively. Her bold invitation left him cold. Or, perhaps her unfortunate eyebrows, melding into a single furry line across her forehead that wriggled and writhed when she spoke had prompted his escape to the gardens where he'd discovered Allen and Olivia.

He ought to have been outraged upon interrupting their tryst, but relief that they'd quickly made amends had spurred genuine happiness for them. At least one Kingsley would have a youthful promise fulfilled. His hopes for love had died with Philomena.

At the bower's entrance, a movement overhead caught Bradford's attention. He gave a crooked smile as several shooting stars streaked across the midnight-blue sky. Closing his eyes, he wished Olivia and Allen a lifetime of happiness.

And lots of babies. He quite looked forward to being an outrageous uncle.

Sentimental sot.

He cracked an eye open. Two more flashes whooshed above, their feathery tails leaving a reminder of the universe's vastness and his insignificance.

Such an opportunity shouldn't be wasted, even if it was superstitious drivel.

Wasn't every day the sky lit up like fireworks over Vauxhall Gardens. His eyelids drifted shut once more.

I want to find the passion true love promises again—

"—to experience true love's kiss," a beguiling feminine voice whispered.

His eye popped open.

A woman surveyed the heavens, the moon illuminating her upturned face and flaxen hair as she rested one shoulder against the other entrance's post. In her white gown, a wide, whitish ribbon encircling her curls, and her features faintly blurry in the half light, she appeared ethereal. Angelic.

"You made a wish too." Bradford stepped forward.

Giving a startled squeak, she whirled to face him and tripped on something—a root or uneven stone, perhaps. Unbalanced, she flailed her arms, dropping her fan.

He sprang forward and caught the tempting armful around her trim back. Generous breasts pressed his chest, leaving two molten spots, and her fragrant hair teased his nose. Inhaling the flowery essence blending with the honeysuckle-laden air, he tightened his embrace. She fit into the hollow of his arms as snugly as a hand fits a custom-made glove, her plentiful curves promising passion.

Who was she?

"Good God, are you insane?" She scrambled free of his embrace then gave his chest a forceful shove. "You scared the stuffing out of me and ten years off my life, you ill-mannered lout. You might damn-well warn someone before you prowl up behind them unawares."

Though he couldn't see her features clearly, he didn't doubt the sharp-tongued angel glowered at him as she bent to retrieve her fan.

"What are you doing gadding about out here alone?" She jabbed the accessory toward the path. "Shouldn't you be inside dancing, or seducing, or doing whatever handsome, privileged men do at these affairs?"

What was *she* doing lurking in the bower alone?

"How do you know I'm handsome? I could be a pock-scarred, toothless troll." He couldn't identify her in the shadowy enclosure. Had they been introduced tonight? "It's too dark to make out my features. I know, because I'm doing my utmost to see your face. If it's anything like your voice, I can expect utter loveliness."

"Of all the flowery hogwash—" She poked her head out the entrance, her champagne-colored hair shiny in the lantern light, and after looking both ways, she retreated deep into the bower.

Was she expecting someone? Not unusual. Many lovers took advantage of gatherings to indulge in an assignation. Disappointment that she waited for someone prodded him, nonetheless.

"I beg your pardon," she said. "That was unpardonably rude."

Transparent, honest, and quick to apologize. How refreshing. Perhaps she truly was an angel.

"I've never been able to bridle my waspish tongue, I'm afraid." Her husky, self-conscious laugh had him imagining all sorts of things she might do with her tongue.

Bradford edged nearer. Something niggled in the back of his mind. They'd met before. He'd bet on it. Probably before Father had hied him and Olivia off to the sweltering, disease-riddled ends of the earth.

Three years wasted on a doddering old fool's pursuit.

Ah, well. Naught could be done to alter the past. He much preferred the present and the intriguing sprite hovering in the arbor. He typically avoided blondes, but this woman with her light hair drew him. "No apology necessary. I confess, I was so disconcerted by your wish mirroring mine, I didn't think to alert you to my presence."

"You did give me a tremendous start." Releasing a musical laugh, she flipped her fan open and waved it before her, not coyly but fervently, as if overheated. "I confess. I'm mortified you overheard my wish. You must think me a ninny, talking to myself."

He was forgiven. Just like that. No pouting or fussing. Definitely an angelic being.

"Not a bit of it." After all, his wish had been as silly. "I dare say, we are at our most honest when we speak to ourselves, are we not?"

"Hmm, I suppose."

In the nebulous lighting, he couldn't read her expression.

She wore an unusual gown. Not the typical capped sleeve with a wide expanse of bosom exposed. Her sleeves fastened tightly around her wrists, and the neckline covered her collarbone.

Perhaps she was bent on creating a new fashion or didn't give a whit about current trends. Or, unlike a number of ladies present at the ball, wearing dampened gowns and bodices that all but exposed their nipples, she claimed exceptional modesty.

In any event, the gown overlaid with some sort of golden overskirt shimmered in the filtered light and clung to her form, reaffirming what he'd discovered when he'd held her in his arms. She possessed a goddess's supple figure; just the sort of woman he favored in his bed.

Digging into his memory's bowels, he couldn't produce a whit of recollection regarding where he'd met this treasure or what her name might be. Having spent the last years abroad, tending a declining sugar plantation—a loathsome task since he abhorred slavery—while Olivia nursed their sickly father, Bradford, a self-confessed, dismally poor correspondent, had lost contact with his school chums and those previously in the Kingsleys' social circle.

"I know it's devilishly boorish of me, and utterly improper, but please allow me to introduce myself, though I feel certain we've met before."

"I know who you are, Viscount." Snapping her fan closed, she peered out the entrance again, the lanterns' light bathing her face. She gave him a sideways look. Not coyness exactly, more guarded uncertainty, and she definitely expected someone. "All of London is abuzz about the return of the Kingsleys and your good fortune in acquiring a title and wealth."

"Not sure my uncle and cousins would see it that way as they all drowned." He swatted distractedly at a tiny insect flitting about his head. Nothing compared to the hordes of blood-sucking, bird-sized tropical mosquitoes.

"You have my condolences." Her stiffly offered commiserations rang falsely.

Curious.

"I'm convinced my uncle would have eaten his Wellingtons with his few remaining teeth, rather than entertain the notion I would ever inherit the viscountcy." Bradford had never entertained the idea either. "The entailment gave him no choice, however."

Pity, that.

Herbert Kingsley had been an unethical, avaricious curmudgeon obsessed with peerage purity and wholly contemptuous of commoners. He barely tolerated peers' kin, deeming all but those holding the highest ranking beneath his touch.

Considering that even in his prime, the miserly chap couldn't boast more than four inches beyond five feet tall, and he'd shrunk to a wizened shell of a man by the time he met his fate amongst the fishes, the notion that anyone was beneath him tickled Bradford's irregular sense of humor.

"You weren't close to your uncle? I'd heard—" She cocked her head, and a moonbeam illuminated the lower portion of her face, revealing a pert chin and Cupid's bow lips, the lower clamped between her small, white teeth.

What color were her eyes? Blue as was typical of many blondes? And what did she know of his uncle? For more than half a decade, Herbert had sequestered himself at Bromham Hall, and except for infrequent and unsolicited encounters with his heir, Horace, a cocksure weakling of dubious moral character, Bradford seldom had news of the sot his father had once called brother.

"He didn't hold you in his confidence? I thought the Kingsleys an intimate, closed-mouth family, wary of outsiders." The angel cast a harried glance to the entrance before edging nearer to Bradford.

Had he interrupted a lover's assignation? Annoyance jabbed at Bradford's jealousy, doing its utmost to garner a reaction from him. He quashed the impulse. What she did in secluded, moonlit vestibules wasn't his concern.

Then why did it trouble him so much?

"Indeed, not. I hadn't spoken to him since ..." Since the fire that stole Philomena ... No. He wasn't trudging down that lengthy and ghoulish trail. He scratched his jaw just below his ear. "Well, in very long while. You might say we were at permanent odds. What had you heard?"

She stood before him now, so close he could touch her—brush her silky cheek with his thumb or cheek. The graceful curve of her mouth—

lips molded for kissing—snared his attention. Her enticing perfume enveloped him once more, demanding he recall where he'd seen—*and smelled?*—her before.

Blast and damn, why couldn't he remember?

"At odds?" She peered up at him, her gaze unpretentious. "Why?"

Did confusion dance across her features? The pale light filtering through the lattice might have caused the illusion.

He brushed her jaw, the flesh warm and silky, with his knuckles. "You oughtn't to be out here alone. What if an unscrupulous chap came upon you?"

"How do I know you aren't just such a man?" She didn't pull away, though her breaths came quick and shallow, and she swallowed before wetting her lips. Not the reaction of a woman meeting her lover. "Even now, you might harbor dishonorable designs."

His pulse leaped. Oh, he had an idea or two, but he wouldn't call the musings dishonorable, more along the order of improper, but absolutely delicious, sensual imaginings. Not altogether wise, contemplating kissing a nameless woman in an obscure arbor housed in the gardens of his soon-to-be-brother-in-law.

The moisture glistening on her plump and pink lower lip, enticed temptingly.

But, then again, who was he to turn down such an unexpected and precious gem? He was about to see one of the fantasies of a moment ago realized.

Bradford lowered his head a couple of inches, and her sooty eyelashes swooped downward, fanning her cheeks. Hovering over her parted lips, her breath sweet and slightly fruity as if she'd eaten berries, he booted caution aside.

What could one kiss hurt? He had no intention of taking the moment as far as those in the bushes outside. Perhaps if he kissed her, he would finally recall how he knew her.

No, fool. If you'd ever kissed this woman before, you'd not have forgotten.

True. This woman would leave her mark on a man's soul. Savoring the moment, he trailed his tongue along the seam of her lips, wanting her to experience the same enchantment encompassing him. How easily he could become snared in this temptress's grasp. He nipped the corner of her mouth.

She gasped and gripped his forearms, swaying slightly before relaxing into his chest and offering her parted lips.

Gathering her into his arms, he pressed his mouth to hers. Lust exploded, flooding through his veins and roaring in his ears. Tendrils of want wended around his senses, and he pulled her closer, deepening their kiss and cupping her lush buttocks.

"Pray tell, what the hell do you think you are doing mauling my sister, Kingsley?"

3

For the second time in ten minutes, Philomena gave a startled yelp and lost her balance—only this time, mortification licked her cheeks, and the muscled arms already encircling her kept her steady. Averting her gaze, she slipped from Bradford's embrace. Putting a respectable distance between them, she retreated to the bower's corner where she could observe her brother and the man she had once loved without revealing her flustered state.

Or before Bradford finally recognized her.

She unfurled her fan open to cool the blast of warmth suffusing her.

What did it matter if he discovered her identity? He would know soon enough. It changed nothing, and she certainly wasn't going to make a scene about the kiss. Absurd, this hurt constricting her chest because he still hadn't realized who she was.

He had truly forgotten her.

She had known him the instant he entered the Wimpleton's gilded ballroom. But then, to be fair, a hundred blazing candles lit the room, and here, only silvery moonbeams filtered through the rose-covered arbor.

Nonetheless, she would have recognized him anywhere. The way he moved, the timbre of his voice, the angle of his head, his animal grace ... his scent.

His essence had long ago been etched into her memory—her soul—and could no more be erased or obliterated than she could change her eye color. In her youthful naiveté, she'd thought the same true of him, but he *had* forgotten her, and the knowledge sent a fresh surge of betrayal to her heart.

In the bower's seclusion, he'd taken her in his arms, but he had also given her the opportunity to resist, to pull away, and she hadn't. She'd lifted her mouth in anticipation, wanting the kiss she'd been denied as a constantly chaperoned miss during his visits.

Hadn't she wished for that very thing a mere moment before?

No, she'd wished for *true* love's kiss, and Bradford had proven he didn't love her.

Utterly foolish, however, indulging in an actual kiss. It only served as reminder of that which she would never have. Besides, Giles had been most clear he regarded his former friend as his greatest foe, and her presence at the ball was for one purpose only.

To snare a husband as swiftly as possible—God forgive her and Bradford was beyond her reach now.

Nevertheless, she wouldn't regret her impulsive action. When he'd slipped into the arbor, time propelled her back seven years, to the innocent girl, too young and protected to do more than hold hands and make secret, fervent vows of undying love. A shallow, youthful love—at least on his part—incapable of enduring hardship and separation.

Her wish, cast upon a series of stars pelting across the heavens, had been to experience true love's kiss before she surrendered herself to a match of convenience and bore the fumbling and groping of a husband whose touch she only tolerated, or worse, repulsed her.

A delicate shudder skittered across her shoulders.

How shall I bear it?

Giles.

She would do it for him, because he'd sacrificed so much for her.

Risking his life, he'd saved her that terrifying night, pulling her from her bed and carrying her from the inferno as their home disintegrated around them. He'd sought out their peculiar, reclusive aunt with her healing gift and retained the best physician he could afford to tend to Philomena's burns. With no other options for immediate employment, he'd enlisted, sending the majority of his paltry wages home to pay for her medical fees.

Neither she nor her brother had suspected that Aunt Alice had secreted the monies away, along with the dotty woman's life-savings, and when their childless aunt died six months ago, she'd left them a tidy sum. Not enough to live on for a lengthy period, but enough, if they were frugal, to provide Philomena the Season Giles insisted upon.

She hadn't wanted to spend their funds on something so frivolous, but he'd quietly confessed that the physician had said his heart grew weaker, and Giles had but months to live. The now familiar pain of losing him blossomed in her chest.

Her brother's courage and selflessness mustn't be for naught, and if her finding a husband brought him peace of mind and extended his life a single day, she would willingly make the sacrifice.

She'd all but given up on him joining her in the garden, he had taken so long. His happening along as she clung to Bradford, savoring his firm lips upon hers, was pure coincidence—or perhaps, it had been providential, because she wasn't positive she would have been able to stop him if he'd wanted more than an ardent kiss.

No, she wasn't sure *she* would have been able to stop. Her girlish daydreams and fantasies fell short of the mark of his devastating, glorious kiss, and once she'd tasted his mouth, coherent thought had fled swifter than a startled bird to wing.

"Well, Kingsley?" Chest heaving and struggling for breath, Giles shuffled farther into the enclosure. "What say you?"

Had he been running, fearful for Philomena's safety when she wasn't on the veranda as agreed? Dash it all. She oughtn't to have ventured this far, but Mr. Wrightly had appeared, likely in search of her so he could present his address, and to avoid him, she'd fled into the garden's protection. She wasn't ready to refuse him just yet, nor could she force herself to accept him either.

A pleasant twinkle in his eye, Bradford inclined his head, not the least nonplussed. "I humbly beg your pardon. I was overtaken with the magic of the moonlight and the beauty of the woman I found staring at the same shooting stars as I."

"Save your flowery poppycock for someone who appreciates such claptrap." Giles seized a nearby post, and Philomena bit her lip to keep from crying out.

He detested others knowing how weak he became when he exerted himself. He would especially not want Bradford to know. They'd been the best of chums before the fire, swimming, hunting, and riding together whenever Bradford's family came down to the country to visit the viscount.

She crossed to Giles's side. Slipping her arm through his, she winced at the tremors shaking his frail frame.

"Extremely poor judgement on my part, brother dear. Let's go home, shall we? I'm quite done in."

"I fear you have me at a disadvantage." Even in the alcove's dimness, Bradford's teeth flashed brightly. "You know who I am, but I haven't the same privilege."

Giles's breath left him in a long, shuddery hiss, his eyes gone dark and cold as a wintry forest at midnight. When he spoke, the icy disdain in his voice raised the hairs on her nape. "You mean to tell me you don't know who you kissed just now? Who you've so carelessly compromised?"

"Surely a single, chaste kiss doesn't qualify?" Philomena didn't like the turn the conversation had taken, and although she hadn't any experience with kissing, she was positive the tongue tangling, explosion of sensation she'd just experienced had been a far cry from chaste. She tugged at her brother's arm. "Come, let's take our leave. No one but we three need ever know of my foolishness."

That she'd yielded to temptation, too sweet to resist, at the expense of guarding her heart and reputation. *Fool.*

"There was more than innocent kissing going on." Giles jerked his chin toward Bradford. "I saw Kingsley pawing you."

Whether anger or difficulty drawing his breath caused Giles's husky voice, Philomena couldn't determine, but her alarm spiraled. He mustn't become agitated. It stressed his heart too much. "The fault is not entirely his. I shouldn't have been out here alone, and should have returned to the house at once when he entered the bower."

And I kissed him too.

She couldn't bring herself to confess that to Giles. He'd done everything a loving brother could to help her heal as well as forget Bradford's betrayal and abandonment, and she'd cast caution and good sense aside with the ease of a laundress tossing out dirty wash water.

Bradford shook his head, his keen gaze fluctuating between her and Giles. "I confess, I don't, but from your reaction, I fear I should. I thought I should as well, but I've been away from England these three years past, and have never been adept at remembering names."

"Have we changed so very much?" Pulling himself upright, a skeletal shell of the virile man he'd once been, Giles gave a short, harsh laugh.

Yes, he had.

He jerked his head toward Bradford. "Phil, he doesn't even remember us. *You.* The cawker just meant to take advantage of a woman he found alone."

"It wasn't like that at all. Please, you mustn't upset yourself." Philomena yanked on his thin arm. "Let me take you home. I'll prepare a hot toddy to help you sleep, Giles, and—"

"Giles?" Bradford went rigid, and then took a half-step forward before halting abruptly. He shook his head as if dazed, and even in the shadowy light, his probing gaze raked her. "Phil? Philomena Pomfrett?

No, it's not possible. You're dead."

Raw pain and stunned disbelief radiated from his eyes, and his confused expression gave him a helpless, boyish appearance. He shook his head and scraped a hand through his hair, more vulnerable than Philomena had ever seen him.

"Dead? You imbecile, does she look dead?" After shaking off Philomena's restraining hand, Giles stomped the few feet to Bradford. Giles's unreserved wrath spewed forth like a river breaching a dyke, and his face contorted into a snarl as he jabbed Bradford in the chest. "She did almost die and has the scars to prove the hell she endured. Made worse because the man she adored abandoned her."

"I'd been told you died in the fire." His face folding into distraught lines, Bradford held out one hand in entreaty. "Please, you must believe me. I didn't know."

Her breath snagged as compassion welled within her chest. Had he suffered too?

"It doesn't matter. It's in the past. Water over a dam cannot be retrieved." Far too late for recriminations, at this juncture. She touched Giles's forearm, reluctant to reveal that he ailed, but anxious to calm him. Muted voices and a dove's sleepy coo trickled into the garden nook along with a violin's faint strains. "We risk someone coming upon us and overhearing, and that would ruin everything. My suitors mustn't know of this indiscretion."

"Suitors?" Surprise registered on Bradford's face before his features closed. "You've more than one?"

Why so astonished? She wasn't altogether repulsive to gaze upon; at least not clothed. He needn't know her beaux bordered on the dregs of humanity. Piqued, she arched a brow. "Indeed, several as a matter of fact."

Unless her indiscretion became known.

Dear Lord, she'd be ruined. Just like that. All because of the irresistible temptation of true love's kiss. And then what would she and Giles do?

Stupid, rash girl.

Unyielding, his breathing shallow and rapid, Giles glowered at Bradford and flexed his hand as if he wanted to pummel him. He mustn't become more agitated.

"Giles, please. Your heart." She pressed her fingertips together, her heart racing with apprehension.

He would have none of it, however. "Let me guess. Your ruddy uncle told you she died, didn't he, Kingsley? Why am I not surprised? Did it ever occur to you that the manipulative old bugger lied? He reviled us from the moment the bishop appointed Father vicar. Most especially, the cur objected to you spending time with a family he held in such low regard. Did you even attempt to find me, to learn the truth, to see how I fared? After all, you thought I'd lost my entire family and my home."

Philomena flinched as if slapped, an ache burgeoning in her chest. She'd never considered the depth of Giles's hurt and anger, that his dearest friend had never sent his condolences or tried to see him. Absorbed in her physical and emotional pain, she'd been oblivious to his misery, and dear Giles wouldn't burden her with his suffering.

How selfish could she have been?

A cloud drifted across the moon, plunging the arbor into darkness, and her earlier joy along with it.

"My friend, please accept my deepest, most heartfelt apologies, but I thought you dead as well." Closing his eyes for a moment, Bradford rubbed his right temple.

Even in the dim light, she could see the strain pinching his mouth, and she yearned to smooth the tension away with her lips.

"I was beside myself when I heard the news," he said, "and by the time I could bear coming down to Bromhamshire, weeks later, nothing remained of the vicarage and church except the garden wall and the charred bell tower. My uncle claimed all had perished in the fire. In all these years, I haven't returned. Not once."

"Am I supposed to feel sympathy for you?" Giles attempted a laugh, which ended on a wheezing cough. Something was wrong. His breathing rattled and rasped with each labored breath.

"No, but I want you to know I mourned mightily." He sought Philomena's eyes for a brief moment, and she couldn't help but feel he meant the words for her, almost as a request for forgiveness.

Her earlier anger at his callousness faded, replaced by searing regret. They would have been happy together, and now, that bliss was lost to her. He would find some exquisite, unmarred bit of loveliness to wed, and she would settle on whichever man she could most stomach for the rest of her life.

"Perhaps some sixth sense alerted me, and that's why Philomena enchanted me when I saw her just now." He flicked a hand in her direction, though his attention never faltered from Giles.

"My sister is not some fast wench you can dally with." Hand shaking, Giles stripped off a glove then whacked Bradford's face, the slap echoing in the enclosure. "I demand satisfaction."

"Giles, no!" This was a damned fine turn of events. All because she hadn't the backbone to stand up to Mr. Wrightly.

Bradford cupped his cheek. "The devil you do. Are you dicked in the knob? You can barely stand upright."

Philomena pushed her way between the men and pursed her mouth. "You're being utterly absurd. Please, let's leave, before this situation becomes any more ludicrous."

"It's my responsibility to protect you, Philomena. I may not have long left on this Earth, and I may be as weak as a suckling runt, but by God, I shall see you properly married and set up in your own home before I cock up my toes."

Her eyes misted. He championed her, even sick as a cushion.

Giles swayed and stumbled forward, bumping into the arbor and sending a shower of leaves and petals cascading down upon them.

"Giles!" Something was definitely wrong.

Was there a physician in attendance? Perhaps their hosts could recommend one to her. He needed immediate attention.

"What's this?" Bradford swiftly steadied him. "Are you ill, Pomfrett?"

Giles yanked free and laughed, the rasping bitter and hollow. "No. I'm not ill. I'm dying."

Stunned silence reigned for a pregnant moment.

"My God, you cannot be. You're only ... what? Seven and twenty?"

Forehead puckered, Bradford sent Philomena a beseeching glance. "Consumption?"

Sagging against the lattice, Giles half-closed his eyes. "No. Scarlet Fever. Untreated. Damaged heart. I won't see another Christmastide."

"I'm truly saddened beyond words." Neck bent, Bradford inhaled a hefty breath and rubbed his nape as if overcome with emotion. "Are you sure? I could arrange to have another physician examine you, if you would allow it."

"Won't change anything," Giles said with a rueful slant of his mouth. "I'm as good as gone."

Philomena stifled her agonized protest at his declaration and turned her head away to swipe at the confounded tears that insisted on seeping from her eyes despite her best efforts. "Enough of this wretched talk. I won't hear it. We're going home. Now. And I'm sending for a physician, no matter what you say, Giles."

Surely someone with the manor could recommend a competent fellow whose fees she might afford.

Slouching further into the brace's support, he shut his eyes and shook his head. "No. Either Kingsley meets me on the field or ..."

Thank God, he had another option besides a confounded duel. Relief weakened her knees, but she managed a tremulous smile. "Or what?"

He slowly opened his eyes, and the bleak despair warring with desperation sliced straight to her soul. "Or he marries you. It's his choice which he does on the morrow."

4

Bradford snapped his head up, his jaw drooping. He didn't see that coming, and he should have. "The devil I shall. Your illness has you talking nonsense, Pomfrett. I'm in agreement with Philomena—"

A bolder moonbeam lit Philomena's stunned countenance, and she hastily averted her face.

"She's Miss Pomfrett to you." Pomfrett pulled his spine straight and faced him, although he swayed like a tree during a storm's onslaught.

Bradford couldn't help but admire Pomfrett's devotion to his sister, though somewhat misplaced. Demanding satisfaction or marriage ... Over a kiss. An eager, willing kiss, at that.

It wasn't as if he'd been caught with his hand up her skirt. Typical *tonnish* overreaction, except Pomfrett hadn't been raised amongst the upper ten thousand, and Bradford had never known him to be the dramatic sort. Guilt stabbed him. If Wimpleton hadn't already offered Olivia marriage, Bradford would have demanded he do right by his sister too.

That made him the worst sort of hypocrite.

"I'll have my satisfaction. You will—" Shaking a finger at him, Pomfrett suddenly choked on a gasp then clawed at his chest.

"Oh, my God, no!" Philomena lurched forward, trying to catch her brother as he slumped. "What's wrong?"

The terror in her voice congealed Bradford's blood. Pomfrett spoke truthfully; he wasn't long for this world.

Bradford reached him first, managing to prevent her brother from plowing into the pavers. Illness had ravaged his sparse frame, and Pomfrett weighed little more than a woman.

"Philomena, hurry to the house and request Wimpleton send for a physician."

"No, no." Pomfrett shook his head. "I just need to sit. I know better than to become overwrought." He tapped his chest feebly. "The ol' ticker doesn't like it. Blood doesn't flow like it ought."

Philomena came round to Pomfrett's other side and, after wrapping her arm about his waist, helped Bradford lead her brother to the bench at the rear of the enclosure. Bradford might have carried him to the house but feared wounding Pomfrett's pride.

Once he'd taken a seat, Philomena set to loosening her brother's neckcloth. Bent over him, she brushed his pale hair off his forehead and presented Bradford a delightful view of her rounded backside.

"Please let Bradford send for a doctor. I would feel ever so much better."

Did she realize she'd addressed him by his given name? He'd never thought to hear his name on her pretty lips again, and pleasure coiled around his ribs.

God, he'd missed her musical voice, the graceful length of her creamy neck, the way she wrinkled her nose and cocked her head when deep in thought—her sultry laugh which could cause the most staid person to smile.

"There's nothing to be done, Phil. I shall be fine. Just give me a few minutes." Pomfrett patted her cheek before resting his head against the arbor's wall. "The leech would want to bleed me in any event, and I'm not forfeiting another drop of blood to cure my ill humors. Leaves me nauseated and weak every time."

Gracefully sinking onto the seat beside him, she took his hand. "I agree. Senseless practice, but perhaps he can prescribe something to calm you and help you sleep."

"Laudanum? I think not. Leaves me wooly-headed, and I cannot abide the bittersweet odor. Gags me, it does." Pomfrett grunted or cleared his throat. Hard to tell which. "I'd rather have a glass of fine Scotch."

Something he likely hadn't indulged in for a very long while. Bradford made a mental note to ask Wimpleton where he might procure a bottle or two of top-notch whisky.

Standing to the side, Bradford slanted his head. That Philomena and her brother held one another in the deepest affection was clear. What would he do if he were dying and Olivia had no means of support, no family to rely on? Wouldn't he be just as frantic to see her provided for before he passed?

At two and twenty, some dolts might consider Philomena past her prime, on the shelf even, and Pomfrett had said she bore scars from the fire, hence her unique gown. If known, that made her an undesirable to most of the shallow coves seeking wives, further reducing her chance of acquiring a respectable match.

Just how badly had she been burned?

His stomach clenched into a gnarled mass that threatened to burst. The pain she'd borne ... God, it didn't bear pondering. The thought left a sour taste in his mouth and a leaden lump in his throat. That his Phil should be reduced to accepting the hand of someone unworthy of her made him gnash his teeth.

Life proved savage to a woman without means or protection. London's East End teemed with harlots, many from respectable backgrounds, who had been left with no recourse to avoid starvation other than to lift their skirts for coin. Such a life guaranteed disease and an early death.

Philomena would not suffer such a fate.

Tilting his head skyward, he drew in a long breath and searched the fragments of firmament visible between the arbor and greenery. Stars flashed and winked a millennium away, but none careened across the expanse.

The Almighty wasn't doling out any more wishes tonight.

"So, what's it to be, Kingsley? Pistols or the parson's mousetrap?"

The air left his lungs in a whoosh, Pomfrett's feeble rasp and failed attempt at humor unceremoniously plummeting Bradford back to Earth.

Philomena made an impolite noise, somewhere between a snort and growl, and plunked her hands on her hips.

Bradford hid a grin.

"Do stop, Giles! He shan't do either. Leave off with that silliness, or I shall become quite cross with you." Worry rather than censure tinged her words. Her eyebrows swooping upward, she sent Bradford an apologetic smile.

Such an expressive face. She'd always been so readable, her candid, wide-eyed gaze giving away her every thought. And outspoken too. She didn't mince words, didn't dance around pretext or use coy innuendoes. If she thought something, she usually said it.

"This once, I'll bear your displeasure, my dear." His mouth compressed into a stern line, Pomfrett stared at Bradford expectantly. "Well, what shall it be?"

No force in heaven or hell could compel Bradford to meet the dying man on the field of honor, especially not over a single kiss, and Pomfrett damn well knew it.

Nevertheless, what a way to re-enter Polite Society. Scarcely a week back in England and Bradford had been challenged to duel, not that he gave a ballock what others might make of it. An hour ago, he might have cared a mite for Olivia's sake, but she was neatly betrothed now, so ... Cock a snook at them all.

Marriage hadn't crossed his mind either, at least not for a good while, though his pesky title now obligated him to find a wife and beget an heir someday. He rubbed the bridge of his nose. What he wouldn't give for a cheroot and a swallow—a bottle—of brandy.

Meshing his lips, he scuffed his shoe across the flagstone, the blood rushing in his ears.

Only one thing to do, fiend seize it, and he would only consider it because Philomena was the woman. She made the sacrifice worthwhile.

He plowed his fingers through his hair and tried not to sneer the word, for her sake.

"Marriage."

"I beg your pardon? Have you taken leave of your senses?" Philomena gasped and lurched to her feet, outrage fairly billowing from her in tense waves. She flapped her hand back and forth, gesturing between them. "We cannot marry. Most ridiculous thing I ever heard." She touched her eyebrow and squinted her eyes as if her head hurt. "Completely preposterous," she muttered, glaring at him. "I shall not marry you."

Arms folded, Bradford crooked one side of his mouth upward, not the least surprised by her vehement denial though, her fervency did rather bite. "See there, Pomfrett. She won't have me. That's the end of it, then."

Her refusal rubbed the wrong way—chafed his arse, truth to tell—even if Bradford hadn't been thrilled about a forced union. Philomena had always been his choice for a wife, and now that she'd miraculously risen from the dead, the idea held merit. Great appeal, in truth.

Just not at this precise moment or under these circumstances.

Hell, who did he think he fooled?

He'd marry her tonight if she'd have him.

Bloody good thing his uncle already lay rotting, or Bradford would have choked the life from the worthless cull for lying about her death. And Pomfrett's. The manipulating cur had suspected Bradford intended to offer for her, and even though he was only fourth in line for the title, wanted to ensure a lowly vicar's daughter didn't become Viscountess Kingsley. Why else would he have gone to such extremes to keep the truth from him?

Any sympathy Bradford had entertained about his uncle's drowning fled on the cool breeze wafting into the enclosure.

Pomfrett pressed a hand to his forehead. "Phil, though I'm not keen on the idea of you marrying this bounder, you must admit, he's far superior to the others."

Indeed? How many others?

"And how is coercing him into marrying me better exactly?" She flung Bradford a brusque look.

Offering a puny grin, Pomfrett quipped, "He has all his teeth, and he smells rather nice."

Her determined chin jutted up as she leveled him a withering look. "The Season is not yet over. I may still attract the attention of someone else."

"Who can offer you a title, a fortune, and who you already know?" Bradford shook his head. They'd gotten on well before, and the misunderstanding about her death aside, he saw no reason they shouldn't again. "I don't think so. Phil, be sensible."

"I am being sensible. I am not the naïve young girl I once was, and a title and fortune hold no allure for me. As for knowing you, youthful infatuation does not make a solid basis for a successful marriage, and I'd be a gullible fool for thinking otherwise." She flicked a bit of something off her skirt. "The adults we've become know nothing of the other."

Pomfrett valiantly pulled himself upright and faced her. "It would ease my mind greatly if you married Kingsley, and I would be spared further outings. They do rather test my stamina, and I'm finding it increasingly difficult to manage. And Phil, the doctor advised rest, even taking the waters at Bath. That I cannot do until I see you wed."

To admit to his weakness must have come at a tremendous cost to Pomfrett's pride.

"I know, Giles," Philomena whispered, folding her hands in her lap and tucking her chin to her chest, her voice thickened by tears. "I'm sorry to be a burden."

Pomfrett gathered her into his arms and kissed her temple. "Stuff and nonsense. I never said you were a burden. I know you had deep feelings for Kingsley at one time, and that cannot be said of any of your others suitors. I've more of a desire to see you happy long after I'm gone then marched down the aisle with someone you can never care for."

"I know you only have my best interests at heart." Acute consternation turned her pretty mouth down, and she fiddled with her fan's handle. Shoulders slumping, she released a long-suffering sigh. "I just wasn't prepared to wed so unexpectedly."

Bradford certainly understood that. Since learning that she lived a few moments ago, his thoughts clanged around his skull, helter-skelter, making it deuced impossible to form a coherent thought.

Married.

He gave a sardonic shake of his head. He'd been worried about Olivia's reception this evening and what would happen when she encountered Wimpleton again. Egads, now it seemed he, too, was destined to marry his first love, only unlike Olivia and Wimpleton's joyous match, his bride might choose him as the least undesirable of her suitors.

Rather humbling.

Bradford eased to the entrance, not only to give them privacy, but to check on the prattle growing ever louder. Others approached, and he'd rather have this conversation kept amongst the Pomfretts and himself. He folded his arms and crossed his ankles, leaning a shoulder against a supporting brace. Of its own accord, his gaze trailed to Philomena before he drew it back to rest on the signet ring circling his little finger. He couldn't see the Kingsley crest or motto engraved there, but he'd heard it his entire life.

Misericordia et Fortitudo. Compassion and courage.

Philomena possessed both in abundance. He could ask for no finer viscountess, and even if her dress covered a myriad of unsightly scars, she was his choice.

"I propose we wait three weeks to wed. Olivia and I are currently staying with our aunt, the Duchess of Daventry, as my uncle let the Mayfair house." *Anything to gain a farthing or two.* "I need time to find us accommodations, since I've never been partial to the place and have no interest in living there. Three weeks allows time to have the banns read, and also eliminates gossip fodder."

"I suppose that's more acceptable, and," Philomena extracted a kerchief from her bodice, "it's not quite so rushed." She dabbed at her eyes. Not ecstatic at the notion, by any means.

"No." Pomfrett shook his head. "It is not acceptable."

"But, Giles ..." She slowly lowered her hand, confusion and chagrin warring in her eyes.

He waved her off with a curt flip of his wrist. "I must insist you wed

Philomena tomorrow by special license. If I die within the next three weeks—" A strangled cry escaped Philomena, and Pomfrett patted her knee before continuing. "Mourning protocol would require her to wait at least a year to wed. That I cannot—shall not—allow. She has no funds to live on and nowhere to go."

Her cheeks dashed scarlet, she majestically lifted her head. "That's none of his lordship's affair. I should manage somehow."

Ah, here came the formality. He'd been Bradford till now.

"How, pray tell?" Frustration and desperation hardened Pomfrett's voice. "I've thought this through, from every possible position. If I die before you are wed, you are destitute, Phil." He clasped her hands in both of his. "You know what that could mean. I won't have it, I tell you."

His voice broke on the last word.

Tears tracked down her high cheekbones, and it was all Bradford could do not to gather her in his arms and promise her anything she desired to dry her eyes and bring a smile to her beautiful face once more.

To allow Philomena and Pomfrett time to marshal their composure, Bradford dipped his head on the pretense of sniffing a fully-bloomed peach rose. He inhaled too deeply and sneezed.

"Even if I can procure an appointment with the Archbishop of Canterbury on the morrow, I still need time to find lodgings for us." One suitable for his exquisite bride, though Aunt Muriel would offer to let them stay on with her, he'd warrant. Neither her son nor her daughter lived nearby, and, although she'd lick a blacksmith's anvil before admitting it, she was lonely. "And you can bet your brass buttons the rumor mills will churn furiously if we wed so hastily when I've only been back in England a week."

The tattlemongers would have a glorious time of it in any event.

"He's right, Giles. You can take to your bed while we wait, and I'm sure, as my future husband, Bradford wouldn't deny you the best possible medical care." Philomena flashed Bradford a fleeting glance, a challenge in the angle of her head. Probably sparking in her eyes, too. "Why, you might make a full recovery. Three weeks isn't so very long."

By far the oddest proposal and acceptance he'd ever heard of. Perhaps she hoped to buy time with the delay. For what? Another suitor? Pomfrett to change his mind? His health to improve?

Time to get to know her future husband, dolt?

"Three weeks ... *is* too long." A violent bout of coughing seized Pomfrett. One hand covering his mouth, he fumbled about in his coat pocket, his shoulders shaking.

Philomena passed him her handkerchief, her face as pale as the lace-edged cloth. "Here. Use mine."

A few moments passed before he stopped hacking and pulled the kerchief from his mouth. He quickly crumpled the strip into a wad, but not before Bradford saw the scarlet splotches. Her attention remained fixed on her brother's hand holding the telltale stained handkerchief.

She'd seen the blotches too.

The anguished, pleading gaze she turned on Bradford tore his heart from his chest. "Can you ... I know you wanted to wait, but would you please consider seeing the Archbishop tomorrow about the license? To at least have it on hand?"

"I—"

Two half-foxed young bucks stumbled into the enclosure.

"Say, wot's this? A lovers' tryst?" A stout fellow with a neck so short his chins appeared to rest upon his thick shoulders snickered and elbowed his cohort. Tilting his head, he took a lengthy swallow from his flask. An equally long belch followed, sending him into another fit of chortling. He clomped forward, flask extended toward his friend. "Care for a nip?"

"No, and don't be daft, Henderson. That's Pomfrett and his sister." The fop's gaze scraped Philomena head to toe before narrowing to slits upon spying Bradford. The drunken coxcomb slid her a sly smile. "Or perhaps, something *is* afoot."

Bradford straightened, forcing the cull to crane his neck to meet his eyes.

"Nothing of the sort. The Pomfretts and I are old friends, and I am the most fortunate of men that Miss Pomfrett has just agreed to become my viscountess, honoring a promise made many years ago."

"You don't say?" The portly chap slapped the other on the back. "I won that bet, Underhill. Told you she had her sights set higher than a fourth son, I did. And you said no one of upper worth would have her. Calls for a celebration, it does."

Philomena bristled and impaled Underhill with her narrowed eyes.

Maggot.

Bradford itched to plant the boor a facer. He wasn't fit to wipe her slippers on.

Henderson quaffed another long swallow from his flask. The stench of strong spirits emanated from him, and Bradford's nostrils twitched. Seems the bosky chap had been celebrating a great deal this evening.

Underhill scowled at his chum before striking a superior pose and elevating his nose. "Rather poor form, encouraging a gentleman's attentions when you're already promised to another, Miss Pomfrett. I admit to being quite put upon. The *ton* doesn't tolerate such fast and fickle behavior."

Bradford clenched his fists. Only uneasiness about Philomena's reaction kept him from bloodying Underhill's nose.

"The only thing fast and fickle in this arbor is you, Mr. Underhill. You flit from silly girl to silly girl quicker than a bee after nectar, always with the intent of relieving her of her dowry and virginity, and not necessarily in that order. I am not such an empty-headed ninnyhammer and never once encouraged your attentions." Philomena stood and gave the fop a frosty stare, clutching her fan as if she'd like to give him a good poke.

The Philomena of old would have.

Another chilly breeze blew past, sending the greenery to quivering, and she hugged herself, shivering. Though mild for a May evening, the temperature had dipped in the last half hour, a not-so-subtle reminder that spring hadn't yet lost winter's sting.

"If you were already spoken for, why did your brother go about practically begging men to take you off his hands?" Underhill's reedy voice exploded into the stunned silence.

"That's outside of enough, you lying, ill-begotten swine." Giles lurched to his feet, his sister immediately scooting to his side and restraining him. "Apologize to my sister—"

Damn it to hell.

Seizing Underhill's lapels, Bradford jerked him off the ground. He gave a sharp shake, satisfaction thrumming through him. Underhill provided just the outlet he needed for his pent-up emotions. "You will apologize to the future Viscountess Kingsley and her brother, and then take your sorry arse and leave. Is that understood?"

Bullies like Underhill seldom stood up to bolder men.

Underhill gulped audibly, his toady eyes bulging. His mouth worked, but no lucid sound emerged for a few seconds. At last, he managed a strangled, "Yes. Quite. My lord."

"Viscountess Kingsley? Thought I heard my cousin tittering something about a Viscountess Kingsley. Cannot 'member what, 'xactly." Henderson scratched his chins and squinted at Bradford. "Victoria does prattle on 'bout the queerest things. Spent a quarter of an hour discussin' various shades of yellow embroidery thread last time I saw the gel. She had seventeen. I try m' best to ignore her."

Babbling must be a family trait.

Bradford lowered Underhill until his feet settled on the pavers. Keeping one hand firmly round his arm, Bradford propelled the bufflehead toward Philomena and Giles, each looking ready to topple head over bum.

"Please accept my deepest, most earnest apology, Miss Pomfrett, Pomfrett." Underhill's grudging mutter, steeped in insincerity, clearly conveyed the opposite.

Not bloody good enough. Not by half. Bradford jerked Underhill's upper arm. "And?"

Underhill's brows crashed together in an irate glower. "I was completely out of order and unaccountably rude."

"And?" Bradford intended to wring every drop of remorse from the cur for insulting Philomena.

Underhill shot Bradford a venom-laced glare. "I humbly beg your forgiveness."

"And?"

As he swung to face Bradford, Underhill's face contorted into a snarl. "What the bloody hell else am I supposed to say?"

Bradford chuckled, quite enjoying taking this uppity cawker down a peg.

"That you're a foul-mouthed, thoughtless chucklehead who's undeserving of a woman as magnificent as Miss Pomfrett, and that she even deigns to be in the same room with a twiddlepoop such as you is an honor beyond measure."

"Chucklehead. Twiddlepoop." Henderson released a girlish giggle, his flask at the ready once more. He hiccupped. "'Pon my rep, tha'ssh funny."

"Stubble it, Henderson." Huffing his displeasure, Underhill wheeled round to face Philomena again. "I'm a thoughtless—"

"Giles?" Philomena's husky voice rose in alarm. "Bradford!"

Bradford lunged too late.

Pomfrett hit the ground with a portentous thud.

5

Fate proved most fickle, bestowing a welcome blessing after extracting an excruciating toll. Philomena could find no other explanation for her and Giles staying in the Duchess of Daventry's luxurious home while he battled for his life.

The duchess's wholly unexpected generosity and kindness knew no bounds. Immediately upon spying Bradford carrying Giles's limp form into Wimpleton's manor, she'd sailed to the entrance, called for her coach, and insisted Giles be transported to her much closer house rather than the humble—more aptly, tumbledown—cottage Philomena and Giles rented on London's outskirts. The colorful dame had also sent for her personal physician and insisted on paying Doctor Singleton's fee as well.

"You're my guests, Miss Pomfrett. I won't hear another word about paying Singleton. That crusty, old barnacle ought to tend your brother for free considering how frequently I've needed his services of late." She'd winked, a mischievous youthful glint in her eyes, despite the wrinkles etching her once handsome face. "Aging is not for the faint of heart."

"I'm sure that is true," Philomena murmured politely, uncertain what else to say.

"Besides, I quite anticipate seeing my nephew at sixes and sevens with you underfoot. That cocksure boy could do with a good rattling. I remember how eagerly he anticipated visits to Bromhamshire, my dear, and I know it wasn't anticipation of seeing his cantankerous uncle or wastrel cousins at Bromham Hall that had him gallivanting to the country at every opportunity."

With a painful pang to the region near her heart, Philomena remembered too. Blinking back tears, she forced her lips to turn up. She couldn't retrace her steps and relive the past few years. Her only choice was to move forward, wherever that obscure path might lead her. "I'm not positive his lordship's affections are what they once were, Your Grace."

"Hmph. More fool he then." The duchess's expression grew solemn, though kindness brimmed in her eyes. "My dear, if things shouldn't work out between you and my nephew, I would be honored if you would consider becoming my companion. My son's wife prefers that I not visit often, and once Olivia marries ... well, this drafty old house gets lonely. And I dearly want to visit my daughter in Spain but have hesitated to take the journey by myself."

Glad tears blurred Philomena's eyes. An answer to one prayer. "Your offer is very generous, Your Grace, and one I gratefully accept."

"Excellent. You've made me very happy, though in truth, I hope that boy comes to his senses." After kissing Philomena's cheek, her grace had set off to the kitchen to ensure a hearty broth was prepared in the event Giles awoke.

Now, whether he lived or died, Philomena wasn't compelled to wed.

Profoundly relieved, the closest thing to peace she'd experienced in long while engulfed her. She smoothed the rich satin counterpane across his chest again, then—holding her breath—tentatively rested her palm upon his gaunt chest. Yes, he still breathed, though shallow and weak, his lips blue tinged and his pallor as white as the sheets he lay upon.

Ten days he'd lain here, rarely rousing. Ten trying, yet wonderful, days as Giles struggled for his life, and she and Bradford became reacquainted. Fate's capriciousness again, bringing Philomena's only love back into her life just as she faced losing her brother.

She'd fallen in love with Bradford all over again. More accurately, she'd never stopped loving him, but in recent days, she had dared to allow the emotion she'd deliberately buried so long ago, to reemerge—perhaps foolishly, and she would regret her lapse later. Her love had grown and bloomed into something wondrous and magical, way beyond a young girl's adoration into the permanent binding of her soul to his.

How could it not? Loving him came as easily as the sun rising or rain falling.

There would be no other man for her. Ever.

He, on the other hand, had given no indication, not the merest hint, whether he returned her affection, and the uncertainty kept her lips sealed. Especially, since there'd been no further mention of them wedding either—not that she'd hold him to the absurd bargain Giles had negotiated, rather demanded, in the bower.

Nonetheless, that knowledge, added to her despair about Giles, had become an almost unbearable ache. She was at once, her happiest and gloomiest, a jumble of conflicting emotions.

Giles stirred, mumbling something incoherent before stilling once more. Only a trace remained of the purplish, egg-sized bump on his forehead and the ugly scrape along his left cheek from his tumble. With each new dawn, she praised God that he still lived.

A regretful half-smile tipped her mouth as she examined the chamber.

He'd never slept in finer bedding, yet he couldn't appreciate the quality of the luxurious ivory and gold coverlet or the opulent room. That couldn't be said of the Kingsleys' rotund, orange-striped tabby. Socrates, his nose tucked beneath a white-tipped paw, lay curled against Giles's legs, snoozing contentedly.

Sitting beside Giles, she lifted his limp hand and closed her eyes in silent prayer. *Please God.* She pressed the back to her cheek then kissed the cool flesh.

"You must get better, Giles. You're all I have. I know it's selfish of me, and would extend your suffering, but I cannot bear losing you. I'm not ready to be alone yet. It's too soon."

I shall never be ready. How can I let him go?

A tender touch to her shoulder made her eyelids fly open.

"You have me, Philomena."

Bradford had slipped into the chamber, leaving the door ajar. His taut-fitting emerald jacket emphasized the breadth of his wide shoulders, and his ivory pantaloons accentuated his ridiculously long, muscular legs. An emerald stickpin winked from the folds of his cravat, and sooty stubble shadowed his strong jaw. Was he one of those men who needed to shave twice daily? She longed to rub her cheek against the roughness and inhale his unique, manly scent.

Her heart turned over, or perhaps the peculiar fluttering centered in her stomach—so difficult to tell which, when her breath snagged and her pulse stumbled momentarily.

He'd never looked more striking, and a flash of awareness dampened her palms.

The youthful Bradford had been such a charming scamp. The mature man, a dangerously rakish rogue. Both had captivated her heart, although the latter proved the more formidable.

He'd always been deft of foot and used to creep into the vicarage's gardens too. He relished surprising her with a new ribbon, a handful of posies, a book, or even on occasion, *La Bell Assembleé* or *Ackermann's Repository* he'd filched from his mother.

How Philomena had delighted in perusing Ackermann's fashion plates and reading the latest *on dit*. And gleaning every useful morsel that might help her be a wife worthy of him when the day finally came. Moisture pooled in her eyes as much for the loss of their innocent, uncomplicated love as for her brother.

"Do I have you, even though Giles meant to coerce you into wedding me?" She searched Bradford's face. How she adored him.

Compassion deepened his eyes to midnight blue. His handsome mouth tilted sympathetically, and he squeezed her shoulder, leaving his sturdy hand there, the possessive gesture infusing her with his strength. "You always have and always shall."

Unbidden warmth welled in her chest, spiraling outward, the heat spreading into her veins, giving her hope. Did he mean it? Could he truly care for her still?

Had time diminished her feelings for him?

No, but unlike a besotted schoolgirl blinded by giddiness, a woman clearly recognized love's poignancy and fallibility, and the risk it took to surrender oneself to the emotion. To love with abandon meant relinquishing part of your soul to another, trusting unreservedly. The pain she'd endured when she thought Bradford had betrayed her had been a thousand times worse than her burn-ravaged flesh, and she never wanted to endure that agony again.

She wouldn't survive.

To hide the maelstrom of regret assailing her, Philomena busied herself tucking Giles's hand under the bedding, atop his chest. After smoothing the covers once more, she plucked the faded gingham skirt of the well-worn dress Bradford had retrieved from her cottage this morning.

"Thank you for this. I'm rather self-conscious about others seeing my scars, else I would have gratefully accepted Olivia's sweet offer to borrow a gown."

Which would have been several inches too long, and probably too snug around as well. Olivia sported a tall, lithesome figure, whereas Philomena was of average height and much rounder curves shaped her form.

"Understandable." His attention dipped to her chest for a fraction, no doubt curious what, precisely, the gown hid. Except the appreciative gleam in his eyes gave her pause. Mayhap he speculated about something other than the scars, and for the first time since the flames had ravaged her flesh, womanly awareness puckered her breasts.

His penetrating gaze again swooped downward again. Could he see the pebble-hard tips? "Do they bother you?"

My nipples?

"Do they hurt?"

Not hurt exactly, more of an ache.

Jaw slack, and in an unaccustomed dither, Philomena struggled for an appropriate answer. How did one respond to a gentleman discussing your bosoms?

A set down and a sharp slap, that's how. She couldn't muster the vexation for either, or more on point, didn't want to. His impertinence should outrage her, and that it didn't revealed just how deeply, and absolutely he'd captured her. Again.

"I beg your pardon." His gaze snared hers before he rolled his head, his sheepish expression that of a rascally child who knew he'd overstepped the bounds. "That was much too forward. I but worried the scars yet caused you discomfort."

"Oh."

See, nincompoop. He wasn't talking about your breasts at all.

Thank goodness she hadn't scolded him. His intent had been solicitousness. Then why did she feel mildly disappointed he hadn't been ogling her? She raised a shoulder and fingered a loose thread at her wrist. "They itch at times, and I dislike how they feel when I touch them. I don't think I shall ever become accustomed."

She wouldn't. Would he or any other man? How could she expect them to?

That was one reason she'd been reluctant to encourage her

undesirable suitors, despite her promise to Giles. Nevertheless, she retained the smallest iota of hope that a man would yearn to wed her and not be disgusted by her scars. If only that man could be Bradford.

"I imagine it would take time." No hint of distaste registered on his face or in his deep voice, only sympathy. "Are there many?"

"Several. You do know the viscount started the fire?" Focusing on a Blue John vase atop the fireplace mantel beyond his shoulder, she relived the horror. The scorching heat and acrid smoke. The agony and the terror. She veered Bradford a sideways glance. "Giles told me he confronted him. Your uncle claimed he accidentally dropped a candle near the altar when he kneeled to pray."

"That damn—" Nostrils flaring and jaw taut, Bradford smothered the vulgar curse.

He needn't on her behalf, for she had condemned Herbert Kingsley to every kind of hell imaginable, particularly in those first horrendous weeks. She hadn't forgiven him entirely either, perhaps never would be able to. Every glimpse of herself unclothed in a mirror reminded her of her parents' needless deaths, Giles's suffering, and the loss of Bradford's love. She rolled a shoulder in an attempt at graciousness. "Perhaps he truly had sought God's guidance."

"What utter rot." Bradford took a deep breath. "Forgive me, but my uncle hadn't set foot in a church for decades, and if that spawn of Satan prayed, it wasn't to God Almighty, I assure you."

"I supposed as much." Nodding, she blinked drowsily.

Sleep had eluded her these past weeks. Anxiety for Giles, apprehension about their finances, and dread of an inevitable marriage robbed her of slumber nightly. Though she needn't worry about the latter two anymore, Giles's condition still kept her tossing and turning. She yawned behind her hand, weary to her bones' marrow. "I've always wondered why he hated us so."

"That we'll never know." Bradford cupped her nape and rubbed her knotted neck muscles, the long strokes and gentle kneading bringing much-needed relief. "How does Giles fare? Any improvement?"

"No." She shook her head. "Though, he's no worse either."

Bradford made a short sound in the back of his throat. "I had hoped for better news, for your sake."

For the life of her, she couldn't form a single protest at his impudence, or the impropriety of his caresses, but instead, closed her eyes and bowed her neck, breathing out a silent sigh. She'd missed his touch, and like a long-parched plant, soaked the sensation into every arid pore.

"That's it. Relax. You deserve a modicum of respite. You're half asleep on your feet." He brushed her hair aside—tied back with a ribbon rather than knotted properly atop her head—

before setting both hands to massaging her neck and shoulders.

Could he feel the few irregular, hardened ridges through her dress's thin fabric? The worst scars, the ribbons of unsightly, rigid flesh, marred her front and her upper arms. She sighed as errant flickers pulsed in places she had no business noticing with her dying brother lying beside her, and she shifted, edging away from Bradford.

Socrates raised his head and, citrine orbs barely open, eyed her disdainfully for disturbing his nap before yawning and resuming his slumber.

"When was Doctor Singleton last here?" Bradford's voice, velvety and warm, hinted that touching her had affected him too.

Examining the bedside clock, she frowned.

Three o'clock already? Where had the day gone?

Her stomach rumbled and contracted. She'd forgotten to eat from the tray a servant had brought up hours ago. "He was here just after twelve, and said he would return this evening with different medication."

Bradford pulled an armchair up beside the bed and, after flipping his tails out of the way, took a seat. He rummaged in his pocket, and his mouth edged upward as he removed a velvet case.

When she didn't reach for it, he set the box on her thigh. "Here."

"What is it?" A jolt of awareness spiraled outward. Philomena eyed the maroon square guardedly.

"A betrothal ring. It belonged to my grandmother, and Aunt Muriel was adamant you should have it." He gave her another lopsided grin and arched a raven brow. "One does not tell the duchess no."

Definitely not. Philomena's mouth twitched into a nascent smile. "Yes, I gathered that, but she is a dear, if somewhat formidable."

"If you don't like the style, we can purchase another." He patted his coat, his signet ring flashing in the candlelight. "I have the special license, too, and I have arranged for a cleric to perform the ceremony." A grin lit his eyes, the same deep azure of the horizon at sunset. "I even found a suitable house to rent until we can find something permanent to purchase. It's small but will suffice for now."

He had a license as well? Her heart somersaulted. And found a place for them to live? Happiness embraced her. He meant to honor what he said in the arbor? Giddiness capered atop her ribs. She couldn't have known. He hadn't spoken of it.

He hadn't mentioned love either.

Doubt poked its beastly head up, quashing her internal celebration.

Did Bradford want to marry her, or did guilt and obligation compel him?

Her joy plunged to her scuffed half-boots, and lay there wallowing pathetically. He mustn't marry her out of duty or a misplaced sense of honor and forgo his chance at love. She must tell him, make him understand that it was all right if he didn't wed her. She would be fine.

Turning, she faced him square on.

"Bradford, you don't have to marry me. I know I'm not your first choice, and now that Giles is ..." She blinked away the fresh sting of tears and swallowed past the lump clogging her throat. "Well, not meeting anyone on the field of honor anytime soon, there's really no need to bother to see this through to the end. I do thank you for the noble gesture, nonetheless."

Though curiosity screeched in umbrage at being denied a glimpse of the ring, she placed the unopened jewelry box in his palm. Better not to know, for all that stood between her disintegrating into a weeping ninny was an eyelash's width of pride.

Bradford stared at the case for a long moment before lifting his thick-lashed eyes to hers, and her heart gave a painful flip. Love shouldn't be simultaneously agonizing and glorious.

Unblinking, he looked at her.

She could get lost in those beautiful pools. He'd always had the most vivid eyes, and his lashes caused many a lady to jealously gnash her teeth.

"Philomena, I know we haven't seen each other in almost seven years, and much has happened in our lives to change us. But, these last days, I thought ... had begun to believe ..." He pointed his attention ceilingward and puffed out a short breath. "Isn't there even a spark of what we once had?"

"I ... I don't know. Yes. Maybe. Probably."

Liar. You know blasted well there is.

Pressing her fingertips to her temples, she strove to order her scattered thoughts. "It's more complicated than that. I'm not sure we can simply resume where we left off."

She could, but could he?

Did he love her?

"I truly did not know you lived." He took her hand and entwined their fingers like he used to. So natural and comfortable. "I was almost grateful Father decided to drag us off to the Caribbean, because it meant escaping England and the memories of you. They haunted me, tortured me, nearly driving me mad."

"You truly grieved for me?" Searching his striking face, the planes harsh with remembered sorrow, her resolve slipped.

Shutting his eyes, he compressed his lips and gave a terse nod. "For months. Years." His deep voice rumbled, and he opened his eyes, a glint of moisture confirming his words. Pressing her hand to his firm lips, he murmured against her palm, "I wanted to die."

Needing to comfort him, Philomena brushed a lone droplet from the corner of his eye and offered a tremulous smile as she caressed his cheek.

"Hurts bloody awful, doesn't it?"

"Most excruciating thing I've ever endured." Bradford bent nearer, until inches separated their mouths, the smoldering smile on his lips only slightly less heated than the scorching luster in his eye.

Sliding her hand to the back of his head, Philomena smiled. She spread her fingers in his silky hair and pulled him closer. "Me too."

His lips settled on hers, and she wrapped her arms around his neck, clinging to him. This kiss, each nibble and touch of their tongues, spoke of sorrow and forgiveness and pledged healing and hope. Their mouths meshed, she scooted onto his firm lap and gave herself over to the experience, reveling in the momentary joy.

A pillow softly smacked her.

6

After wresting her mouth from Bradford's, Philomena leapt to her feet. "Giles, you're awake!"

"A man cannot even die in peace. He must rouse to defend his sister's honor."

Heat swept up the angles of her cheeks at being caught kissing Bradford again, but she returned Giles's feeble grin.

"How long have I been out?"

Philomena grasped his hand, her mouth quivering. "Ten days. I feared you'd never waken."

Giles's turbid gaze locked on Bradford. His focus sank lower, to the jewelry box still clasped in Bradford's hand. "You said you had retained a cleric?"

Hands on her hips and lips pursed, Philomena angled her head. "Just how much of our conversation did you eavesdrop on? And why didn't you tell me ... us," she spared Bradford a swift glance, "you were awake?"

"One cannot eavesdrop on a conversation taking place over one's deathbed." Giles's lips bent into a tired smile. "As for not telling you I'd awoken, I found the conversation most fascinating, and truthfully, it took too much effort to open my eyes or speak."

"I do hope you don't intend to call me out again." Bradford winked and patted Giles's shoulder.

"If I weren't so relieved, Giles Joseph Pomfrett, I would ring you a peal, you sneak." Philomena smiled through her tears and kissed his cheek. She'd never thought to hear his voice or see the playful gleam in his eye again.

Dark circles ringing his bleary eyes, he struggled into a sitting position, his gaze wavering between her and Bradford. "You still love each other?"

"I ..." She sent Bradford a helpless glance. Why must that be one of the first things Giles asked upon waking?

"I love her. I always have." Bradford's voice entwined around her heart. "Even more so these past few days as we've become reacquainted—not that we needed to. We resumed right where we left off, didn't we, Phil?"

She took the hand he extended, the answering warmth in his eyes turning her knees to custard. "Yes, and I do love him. But I think you suspected that, brother dearest."

The tiniest twinkle glinted in Giles's eyes. "I but hoped and played the hand as if you did. I nearly danced a jig when I came upon Kingsley kissing you in the arbor. Quite opportune, I must say."

"That was well done of you, Giles." Bradford brushed a tendril from Philomena's cheek that had escaped her ribbon when they kissed. "And that's why I asked Reverend Archer to pay a call at four o'clock to discuss the ceremony. Quite by chance, I met the man of God at a dinner party when I first returned to London, and when I came upon him today after obtaining the marriage license, I asked him to officiate."

"Yes, that was fortuitous." Moments ago, she'd been moping about because there'd been no mention of marriage, and now she was aflutter at the suddenness of Bradford's arrangements.

He gave Philomena an apologetic smile. "Forgive me for not discussing this with you, but the Archbishop just returned to London last evening, and I honestly didn't expect to encounter Reverend Archer today. Things just fell into place, and I snatched the opportunity while it was available."

"Phil, Kingsley has the license, and you love each other. Why not simply marry when the rector arrives?" Giles's question sent her pulse stampeding uncomfortably.

Four o'clock today?

She would have preferred a bit more notice to prepare.

"I cannot be married in this old rag. I must change, and arrange my hair." Glancing downward, Philomena grasped her dress and grimaced. Chagrined, she darted Bradford a hesitant glance and sighed. "You must think me vain and silly."

He cupped her chin. "What's wrong with wanting our wedding to be as special as we can make it?"

"I cannot suitably express my gratitude or what a balm to my soul it is to know Philomena is provided for after I'm gone." Giles extended a trembling hand, which Bradford promptly clasped. "I can rest peacefully now."

Philomena's heart gave a queer leap. His words rang with a resignation and finality she'd not heard before. "Giles, don't talk like that. You may still grow stronger."

"Bradford." A scratching at the door preceded the Duchess of Daventry sailing into the room, followed by Olivia and a twitchy little man of the cloth. "Reverend Archer requests a word with you."

"You're early, Reverend." Bradford beamed, nonetheless.

"Yes, your lordship, if you please." The reverend ducked his head and wrung his hands, moisture edging his upper lip. "Perhaps we could step into the corridor?"

Olivia sped to Philomena's side and, after embracing her, hugged Bradford. "I'm so happy for you both. Brady has often teased me about my doldrums over Allen, but do believe me when I tell you, Philomena, he was much changed after the fire." Bestowing a bright smile on Giles, Olivia touched his shoulder. "And I'm so grateful you've roused, Mr. Pomfrett. I will pray for your continued recovery."

The strain of so many gathered in Giles's sick room concerned Philomena. She would wait until the doctor examined him before she allowed the dash of hope that had taken root to grow and bloom. Too soon for celebrating, just yet. Nonetheless, his awakening in time for the ceremony was a profound blessing.

Her grace regarded the cleric with thinly disguised curiosity but turned her attention to Giles. "I'm so pleased to see you awake, Mr. Pomfrett. You shall have the pleasure of witnessing your sister's nuptials, though I do believe we should make the ceremony as short as possible so as to not exhaust you."

"Er, well, Your Grace, there is a small matter I need to discuss with his lordship first." The cleric's nervous gaze darted here and there, and perspiration ran in thick rivets down his beet-red face. As quickly as he sopped the moisture with his soggy kerchief, more appeared.

Goodness, he appeared unwell or on the brink of apoplexy.

"Have your say, good sir, so that we might be about marrying." Bradford encircled Philomena's waist with one arm. "I've waited nearly seven years to marry this minx, and don't want to wait another day."

"You are going to have to wait, my lord." Reverend Archer clasped his hands, his head bobbing like a pigeon.

Bradford stiffened and leveled him an acerbic stare. "And why is that?"

Every eye in the room fixed on the clergyman.

He licked his lips and tugged on his ear. "Someone has come forth with an objection to the marriage."

Her ocean-blue eyes rounded, Olivia grasped Philomena's hand. "I am so sorry, Philomena."

Henderson and Underhill had wasted no time in spreading the news of Bradford's betrothal claim, it seemed. And someone, though God only knew who, didn't want Bradford and her to wed. Well, actually, she could think of several hungry-eyed women who wouldn't be pleased, but none had legal reason to protest the joining.

She pressed two fingers between her eyebrows where a steady cadence thrummed.

"Who dares?" Her grace narrowed her eyes to incensed slits and shook her finger in the reverend's face, causing the man to blanch and stumble backward. "I'll see they are banned from every respectable assembly. They won't be able to nibble Sally Lunn's cake with anyone of refinement by the time I'm finished. They'll be buying their vegetables from the slop yard."

Bradford maintained a visage of calm, though anger tempered his speech. "What's this about? Unless they are here to state their objection during the ceremony, they can caterwaul and complain from the rooftops and it will do no good."

"Your uncle entered into a contract with Lord Southwark, agreeing his daughter would be the next Viscountess Kingsley." After taking a deep breath, the cleric hurried on, running his words together. "The-late-viscount-accepted-the marriage-settlement-and-the–terms-stipulated-the joining-occur-before-Parliament's-dissolution."

Her grace released a snort worthy of an incensed bull. "Figures. Raynott Southwark's a covetous, ambitious fribble. And that bland-eyed daughter of his has more hair than wit." The duchess made a circular gesture near her temple. "She's not all there in the attic. Simple-minded, the unfortunate dear."

The poor girl was a slow top, but this had nothing to do with Bradford and Philomena's wedding.

"Easily remedied." Bradford flashed a reassuring smile, completely unaffected by the reverend's announcement. "I shall return the settlement since my cousins are deceased. However, as my future brother-in-law's health is extremely delicate, we'll proceed with the nuptials as planned."

Philomena released her pent-up breath. A simple misunderstanding brought about by the prior viscount's untimely death. In truth, she wouldn't object to a short courting period, a few weeks delay to further reacquaint herself with the man she had pledged to marry, but Giles's health made that impossible.

"Yes, it is my brother's express wish that Bradford and I marry as quickly as possible." She couldn't bring herself to say because Giles might not live to see the deed done if they delayed.

"I'm dying, Reverend, and would see my sister wed before I leave this world." Giles wearily shut his eyes, and poignant silence reigned for a long moment.

"I understand, and you have my utmost sympathy, but the matter isn't so easily rectified." The reverend fussed with his collar, his face glowing. How was it possible for a human to turn the same hue as a parrot's plumage? "The contract doesn't specify or identify *which* viscount Lady Victoria is to marry."

Philomena exchanged a baffled glance with Olivia. Why did the man persist? He obviously knew Bradford wasn't party to any of these legalities, and what difference did it make whether the agreement identified the viscount? Everyone knew it couldn't be Bradford. He'd been out of the country until just over a fortnight ago and was last in line to inherit, to boot.

"Speak clearly, man. What are you saying, exactly?" Bradford's countenance settled into sharply hewn angles. Though not easily riled, his patience appeared at an end.

The cleric gulped and sucked in a large breath. "Simply put, the contract states that Viscount Kingsley will join with the Lady Victoria

Southwark within one week of Parliament's recessing."

"Preposterous and unenforceable."

Bradford shook his head and flipped open the jewelry box. He removed the garnet circled in seed pearls and held it up. The crimson jewel glittered in the candlelight, a vivid flash of hope amongst darkness and despair. "I mean to marry Philomena."

"But, my lord—"

"Nothing this side of the Good Lord descending from heaven and trussing me like a turkey will stop me." Undeterred, he slid the ring onto her slender finger. "And even then, He and I would have a fierce go round."

"Blasphemous." Reverend Archer sputtered, shaking his finger at Bradford. "You should do penance for such profane irreverence."

"Nonsense. I have no intention of martyring myself by marrying a chit I've never met to preserve family honor I didn't taint."

Uncle Herbert could bugger on in his grave, and Southwark could work his wiles somewhere else. No erroneous sense of duty compelled Bradford to toddle down the aisle with an insipid stranger. Not now that his beloved Phil had been returned to him.

"It's quite exquisite." Philomena fingered the slightly loose ring, wonder and disbelief, wreathing her face.

He'd been drowning in similar sentiment since discovering she lived and wasn't about to let her escape him this time.

Another emotion lingered on her features as well. He looked closely. Yes, there about her eyes. Discomfit? Uncertainty? About what?

Women of Philomena's ilk were rare and irreplaceable, and she was so entangled in his being that, for the first time in a great while, he felt whole once more. Marry her first, then worry how they'd get on, for if he lost her again, he'd become a shell of a man with nothing to live for.

Besides, they loved each other, and this past week and a half had been the happiest he'd experienced in the past seven years. Everything about her fascinated and enthralled him, and he held no doubts that his love for her would only grow.

"It belonged to my mother, Bradford and Olivia's grandmother. She was a Prussian princess, you know." A faraway look entered Aunt Muriel's eyes. "Now that's a lovely story. Father rode his stallion right into church, swept her onto the saddle, and kissing her passionately, galloped away. The gossip was deliciously scandalous."

"I'd like to know how Grandpapa managed the kiss, the horse's reins, and the pews all at once. Some feat, that. Were his eyes closed? I always kiss with my eyes closed." Bradford's quip earned him a dark look.

"Do shut-up, Bradford." Aunt Muriel motioned toward the ring, the tiniest hint of censure pulling her mouth downward. "Daventry's bride wanted something more modern—to the tune of five hundred pounds more—my Isobel was gifted a familial ring from her husband, and Olivia has her mother's ring, one similar to the garnet." Vulnerability bathed her expression for an instant. "I understand if you prefer your own, but I thought for today's ceremony ..."

Now cancelled for lack of a clergyman.

Caressing the ring, Philomena shook her head. "Your Grace ..."

"Pooh, none of that nonsense." Aunt Muriel flapped her hand as if trying to swat a pigeon-sized fly. "We're to be family. Aunt Muriel, please."

"Aunt Muriel." Philomena's pretty mouth bent upward. "I am honored beyond measure you would gift me with something so precious."

Aunt Muriel beamed and tutted a bit, before surreptitiously patting the corner of her eye.

Philomena's compassionate gaze met Bradford's.

No, by God, nothing and no one had better attempt to keep him from taking this thoughtful, enchanting woman to wife.

"Sir, perhaps you should view the agreement?" Archer shifted from foot to foot, not quite daring to meet his eyes.

Hand on his hips, Bradford curled his lips contemptuously. "My uncle may have thought himself clever, but that contract is worthless and will not stand legal examination. No one with a modicum of common sense would expect me to honor it."

"Hence why that lackwit, Southwark, thinks you will." Aunt Muriel ran ringed fingers over the drowsy cat, now sprawled on his back, purring. "The man's not given to common sense."

"That may be, sir, but I cannot, in good conscience, perform the ceremony." The cleric half-turned to the door, reminding Bradford of a cockroach scuttling back to its hidey-hole. "You may encounter difficulty in finding someone to marry you until you clarify you are not already betrothed, my lord."

"Humph, sounds suspiciously like a threat to me, you little weasel. Southwark probably greased a scoundrel's fist to spy on my nephew and follow him around with orders to report back when Bradford saw the archbishop." Aunt Muriel stomped to the cowering parson, giving him a crushing glare.

"Is that why I just happened to run into you, Reverend?" Bradford stepped forward a pair of paces, threateningly. Would he burn in hell for shaking a man of God until his teeth clacked?

"Isn't Southwark part of your congregation? Which did he do?" Aunt Muriel prodded the man of God's chest none-too-gently. "Bribe you to not perform the ceremony, or threatened to take his patronage elsewhere, you grasping little toad-eater?"

Archer, quailing under her scowl, recoiled as if shot and bumped into the bed.

Lord, but Bradford admired his spirited aunt.

Socrates flopped onto his stomach and, letting loose a reproachful yowl, swatted the reverend's back end. Archer howled and jumped, grabbing his injured buttock.

Bradford chuckled.

Liked his sister's damn cat, too.

"Undoubtedly he did both, the wretch. Probably hovered about like a bat waiting for Bradford to approach his eminence." Philomena regarded the cleric with the same favor she would a piece of moldy fruit. "Despicable behavior from a man of the cloth."

"How do you live with yourself? As a representative of God's house, you should be above such unscrupulousness." Reprove curled Olivia's mouth and narrowed her gaze.

The color drained from Reverend Archer's face, and he swiped a hand across his beaded brow. With a show of bravado, he thrust his scrawny chest out and lifted his nose. "I am a servant of God, and I resent your scurrilous accusations."

"Scurrilous? Surprised he even knows the word," Giles mumbled, cracking his eyelids open for an instant. "How about charlatan and fraud? Pharisee?"

Archer pursed his thin lips, giving Giles a haughty look. "Have a care, sir. You should be asking for absolution, not tossing names at God's appointed servant." He turned his disapproving, bug-eyed scrutiny on Philomena. "The Church takes a dim view of hasty marriages. Perhaps, if you spent more time on your knees in prayer rather than aspiring to a station above you and making plans to gallivant off on a honeymoon when your brother lies dying—"

"Rubbish and rot!" Aunt Muriel claimed the cleric's elbow and hauled him to the door. With a less then gentle shove, she thrust him over the threshold.

Damn good thing she'd reached Archer before Bradford did. He itched to break the cleric's bulbous nose or ring his skinny neck.

Philomena canted her head, her gaze shooting green daggers. "And what is the Church's view on corrupt, immoral clerics?"

"Mayfield." Aunt Muriel bellowed for the butler. "I'm clearing the premises of vermin. Show Reverend Archer the door." Before the majordomo arrived, she slammed the door in Archer's flabbergasted face then swung round to face the others. "I know a rat when I smell one."

"What now?" Philomena folded her arms and thrummed the fingertips of one hand on her arm. Not precisely fretful, but not unaffected either. Truthfully, she appeared quite agitated.

Aunt Muriel waggled her eyebrows and rubbed her hands together gleefully. "It's very simple. Bradford cries off."

"I do?" Understanding dawned. "Indeed. I do!"

His long gait carried him across the room to his grinning aunt. Giving her an exuberant hug, he laughed in delight. "Oh, the scandal! The cut directs. The *on dit*. Marvelous. We'll be ostracized. I can retire to the country and retain someone respectable to sit in my place in Parliament. What a fortuitous development."

"Bradford's not overly found of the *beau monde* set." Aunt Muriel's droll observation earned her another embrace.

"He rather likes to stir the waters, if you take my meaning." Olivia's eyes danced with amusement. "At times, it proves most offputting, and I wonder that I call him brother at all."

"Don't try to frighten my bride away with your flimflam." Striding to Philomena, he extended his hands. "I've never hidden my disdain for those affecting superior airs."

"I remember." At once, she gracefully rose and grasped his fingers.

Nevertheless, he detected the merest hint of reticence amid the eyes gazing so trustingly back at him. What went on in her head? She had always been one to speak her mind before. But then, she'd suffered greatly, still did for her brother, and misery altered a person. He knew that full well. "Tell me, darling, would you be terribly put out with me if we didn't remain in London?"

A beatific smile swept her features, her nose crinkling adorably in more enthusiasm than he'd seen since their reunion. "Not at all. I'm more suited to country life, in truth. I've seen as many fops, dandies, coxcombs, and supposed ladies acting the part of light skirts than I care to in a lifetime."

"There is still the matter of marriage. If the reverend spoke true, and I believe he did, Southwark has likely made the rounds and intimidated all the clerics who are malleable." Giles tiredly rubbed his beard-stubbled jaw. "We are new to Town as well, and I haven't any idea whom to approach."

"You could elope to Scotland." Shrugging, Olivia gave a tight, apologetic smile. "If all else fails, that is."

"But that means leaving Giles." Philomena sank onto her brother's bed, and after giving him a falsely cheerful smile, clasped his hand. Her expression took on a stubborn set.

There's the old Philomena.

"I cannot go to Scotland, Bradford. I'm sorry."

"Of course we won't. It shall not come to that." Giving a sage nod, he drew his brows together in concentration and paced beside the bed, rubbing his chin. He swiveled in his aunt's direction. "Surely there is an honest cleric in all of London. If not, then a neighboring town."

"I have it." Aunt Muriel snapped her fingers, her expression exuberant. "I know a new vicar ... Alexander Hawksworth. He's the rector of a large parish outside London. Knew his father and mother. Much too handsome for a man of the cloth. His church pews don't stand empty on Sunday mornings, I can tell you. Though, how the man can preach over the tittering, whispering, and indelicate display of bosoms, I'll never know."

Philomena cast Giles a troubled look. His grayish skin and hollow cheeks bespoke a man not long for this world. She exchanged a pained glance with Bradford.

When her brother passed, she would grieve profoundly. They'd be making arrangements for a different type of service in the near future unless God intervened and performed a miracle. Why did this decent man have to suffer an early death while lickspittles like Underhill went about their merry, depraved lives?

Knowing someone you loved would soon die was excruciating. Bradford had gone through this very thing with Father, yet, at least his sire had lived a goodly number of years. If only Bradford could spare her this anguish.

"Do you think he would be willing to perform the ceremony, Your Grace?" Toying with the ends of her hair, Philomena hid a yawn behind her hand. The slight slump of her shoulders and faint bluish shadows beneath her eyes revealed her exhaustion, no doubt the result of sleepless nights.

"Indeed." Aunt Muriel delivered a shrewd smile and secured her fringed shawl more firmly. "He and my son were wont to get into all manner of mischief together at university. Hawksworth isn't cut from the typical cleric's cloth. When his Anglican priest uncle hied off to Gretna Green with a French nun, Hawksworth was expected to fill his uncle's shoes. He did so, rather reluctantly, I might add. I would wager my favorite Maid of Honor tarts, Hawksworth would jump at the chance."

Olivia made for the door. "Well then, Aunt, let's see about penning him a letter. He sounds like such a fascinating fellow. I want to ask Allen if Reverend Hawksworth might officiate at our wedding too."

"How soon can he come?" Giles's hoarse question immediately sobered the atmosphere. Socrates chose that moment to crawl onto his chest and gently bat Giles's face. "Seems even this portly feline worries for me."

Touching her chin, Aunt Muriel pondered for a moment. "If I send the letter with a trusted footman immediately, perhaps tomorrow afternoon? I'm sorry, Mr. Pomfrett, but I cannot be positive Hawksworth will be in residence or able to leave at once. I will make certain he's made aware of the urgency of the situation, however. I can also send word about Town that I seek him. He may be frequenting one of the gentlemen clubs, and I believe he's particularly fond of the theater."

"I'd be very grateful, Your Grace. I worry that I may experience another episode and fall insensate again." Giles turned his head in Philomena's direction. "Promise me, Phil, if I do, you will proceed with the marriage."

Shutting her eyes, Philomena nodded, but her lashes trembled against her cheeks. Poor darling. This ugliness had taken quite a toll on her. He couldn't help but think rushing into matrimony added more strain, even if they were in love.

"A moment, Aunt Muriel, if you please." Bradford cupped his nape, and pulled in a hefty expanse of air. "I hesitate to bring this up now, but I want to know, and I'm sure Philomena and Giles would as well."

"What is it, dear?" Aunt Muriel peered up at him, her expression open and inviting. She'd always been like that, never one to shy from the truth.

"Do you know why my uncle held the Pomfretts in such contempt? He was a self-seeking crotchety boor to all but an elite few, but his animosity toward them seemed beyond his normal spitefulness." He clasped Philomena's hand, needing to touch her, to reaffirm she was truly going to be his wife at long last.

Consternation swept his aunt's features as she slowly nodded. "It's an age old tale of thwarted love. He had a *tendre* for Mary Pomfrett, and when she publically chose a lowly vicar over him, well, it turned Herbert—always privileged and spoiled—into a bitter man."

"So rancorous he would deliberately set a fire to keep me from marrying Philomena? One that killed her parents and scarred her?" Bradford shook his head, unable to procure a speck of empathy or pity for the old viscount's plight. "Pray God forgave his acrimonious soul, for I shan't."

"Yes, even I struggle to believe he stooped to such unsavory methods." She opened the door, Olivia right behind her. "Don't bother to dress for dinner. Philomena, do you intend to join us, or would you prefer a tray in here?"

"A tray, I think, if you do not object." Regarding her brother as he lay sleeping, Philomena's usually smooth brow furrowed. "I'll help feed

Giles, too. Would you send Robins to sit with him for a spell first, though?"

While the maid monitored Giles, Bradford and Philomena had strolled in the quaint courtyard together every afternoon since her arrival, spending a pleasant half an hour reminiscing and renewing their friendship. He'd been hard-pressed to refrain from sweeping her into his arms and kissing her breathless each time, except that instinct warned she needed time to adjust.

"Certainly, my dear. I'll send her at once with fresh linens, too. Come along, Olivia. We've much to plan for your nuptials. I was pondering the menu for the wedding breakfast and ..." Sweeping from the room in a flurry of skirts, she continued to issue orders until the women were out of earshot.

Philomena stood and, after stretching her arms overhead, petted the cat whose contented rumbles increased in volume. "Doctor Singleton should be here shortly. If you don't mind, I should like to seek some air in the garden."

By herself?

Her falsely merry tone didn't fool Bradford. On the cusp of weeping, she sought privacy. Did she fear Giles wouldn't survive until she and Bradford had wed? Didn't she know he didn't give a tittle what the *ton* thought? They would be married straightaway, even if the unthinkable occurred, if Giles died, protocol be hanged.

He scooped the cat into his arms rather than crush Philomena to his chest and banish her fears. "A grand notion. I shall accompany you."

"There's no need," she demurred, her gaze cast to the floor.

Yes. By herself.

A kernel of an idea took root. "Why don't we go to Reverend Hawksworth, with a letter of introduction from Aunt Muriel? We would be gone an hour or two at most."

She touched a knuckle to the corner of an eye. "I ..."

Tears. Admirable, her self-control.

"I must speak with you." Seizing his arm, she dragged him toward the open door.

Trepidation sank her talons deep. Philomena didn't want her brother overhearing whatever she had to say. Giles didn't stir as she towed Bradford along. Had he sunk into oblivion again or had the exhausted sleep of the ailing claimed him?

Closing the door behind them, Philomena canvassed the hallway. She clasped her hands beneath her chin and shut her eyelids, dragging in a ragged breath. Her lashes slowly eased open, her turbulent gaze a *mélange* of anguish and regret. "I'm not positive we should marry at all."

8

Guilt poked Philomena, its sharp little claws digging deep. She must wed, to bring Giles peace, and she did love Bradford. Desperately. But so many things remained unresolved, not the least of which was whether Bradford could abide her scars.

If not, and he found her abhorrent, couldn't bear to touch her, then how would he beget an heir? He should see what he was getting before committing himself to a lifetime of regret. Well, she could insist he never see her naked, however, he didn't seem the sort to fumble under a nightgown in the dark, and she couldn't very well disrobe and let him gawk his fill before they wed.

A door shut along the corridor, and she wheeled around. This conversation wasn't meant for the servants' gossip fodder.

Robins, her arms full of linens, bustled their way, her white cap flopping up and down with her brisk pace. The maid grinned, her cheeks apple-plump and her owl-like gaze swinging between Philomena and Bradford. "Her grace said I was to sit with Mr. Pomfrett, and Peters and I are to change his sheets after he eats."

"Yes, please. I've asked for a tray to be brought up for him later. I'll be in my chamber or the garden should you need me." Philomena couldn't contain her ecstatic smile. "He awoke earlier and spoke."

"That's wonderful, miss." Robins moved to the entrance, and Bradford eased the door open and then stepped out of the way. "Thank you, my lord."

He angled his raven head in acknowledgement but remained silent as the maid disappeared inside, closing the door softly behind her. He extended an arm toward an oriel window. Dust particles danced in the sun rays shining through its floor-to-ceiling mullioned windows. "Let's move there, shall we? More private, I think, yet still respectable. Servants have been known to listen and peek through keyholes."

Their feet swishing softly on the plush Aubusson runner, they silently covered the short distance. Around a bend in the passageway, the recess wasn't visible from any bedchamber door.

Philomena faced Bradford and folded her hands before her. "I know I've shocked you, however, I have some reservations."

Shocked herself, truth to tell. Nonetheless, the unanswered questions and uncertainty had bubbled forth until she couldn't contain them any longer.

"Why? What are you afraid of?" Bradford regarded her silently, concern or curiosity, perhaps both, crinkling the corner of his eyes.

Giles dying.

Hastening into a marriage for the wrong reasons.

You finding my scars disgusting.

Biting her lip, Philomena breathed out a silent sigh. The reasons seemed trifling if spoken aloud, and chagrin taunted her because her love hadn't quashed every doubt. Shouldn't love do that? Plow aside hesitation and trepidation?

He gathered several tendrils of hair curling over her arm and, after rubbing them together, gave a slight tug. "Out with it. Tell me."

When he toyed with her hair, his fingertips caressing the strands, sensual musings of those long fingers elsewhere wreaked havoc with her concentration. Flinging her hair over her shoulder, she willed her romping pulse to behave itself. "I will not leave my brother under any circumstances. Not even for a wedding trip. And there's been no discussion of what happens to him if I marry. What's he to do? His care could be lengthy and costly."

Bradford's beautiful eyes widened, bemusement replacing the seductive glint. "Whether he lives a week, a year, or more, I never expected you to leave your brother. I would do the same if it were Olivia." A shock of hair had fallen onto his forehead, and his mouth lifted into a wry smile "In my eagerness to wed you, I've been remiss in explaining my thoughts, but I assure you, I assumed he would live with us for the remainder of his life, and I fully intend to pay for his needs. He'll be my family, too."

"Oh. I wasn't certain ..." Suddenly chilled, she wrapped her arms across her chest and clasped her shoulder. Giving him a shamefaced smile, she hitched a shoulder. "I confess to a fit of the nerves. I'm cold and my feet are freezing."

His attention sank to her scuffed half-boots.

"In those? Really? I can call for a hot brick and woolen stockings. A lap robe too." Giving her a devilishly provocative grin, he cocked an eyebrow and chucked her chin. "Or ... there are other, much more enjoyable, ways of warming you. We *are* betrothed ..."

At his allusion, a whorl of heat spread languidly through her veins. He'd always been able to do that, ease her fears and calm her with a few sensible words, as well as send her desires soaring. If only she possessed the pluck to snatch Bradford by his large hand and haul him into her bedchamber. She'd fantasized about lying with him for so long, she feared the real act might disappoint.

Rubbish. What she really feared was his reaction upon seeing her naked.

Sensibility reigned.

"No, you goose." *More's the pity*. Not until the vows are spoken. *If they're spoken.*

Philomena leaned against the wall beside the oriel. Careful not to bump the framed portrait of an intense looking fellow with a ruffled collar and neatly trimmed beard, hanging beside her, she tortured the edge of the carpet with her boot.

"What else troubles you? I see it in your eyes, Philomena, the doubt and consternation." Joining her alongside the paneling, he positioned himself so his shoulder supported his weight. He traced her jaw, his eyes gleaming with longing. "I do love you, more with each passing day. More than I believed a human could love another."

"My scars ..." She released a puff of air and examined the cornice edging the ceiling. "They are quite unsightly. I fear after you see them, you'll not desire me anymore, not want to bed me, and that, in time, you'll grow bitter and resentful, that you'll grow to despise me."

Tenderly grasping her chin, he turned her face to his. "Never. Because it's you I love." He tapped her temple then her chest over her heart. "What's in there matters more than all else, though I find you tempting beyond reason, woman."

Cupping her ribs with his hands, he trailed hot kisses from below her ear to her shoulder.

God above.

She clamped onto his shoulders as sensation sluiced to every nerve. If his kisses did this to her, she'd shatter if they joined.

His breathing heavy and irregular, he pulled her tight against him and rocked his pelvis into her. A hard bump probed her belly. "Even if your entire body were scarred, you'd still do this to me. I love you. The rest matters naught."

Sincerity colored his words, but the look in his eyes, complete adoration, convinced her he spoke the truth. He did love her.

Others might not understand how quickly their love had rejuvenated, might hint it wasn't possible and that such unions only happened in fairy tales or silly novels, but Philomena knew what they had was real. And that's all that mattered, not whether anyone else believed it possible. Just as some people fell in love at first sight, others had a love like she and Bradford's. It would never die, not even when they breathed their last breath. Her spirit was tethered to his, and in the afterlife, they'd find one another and spend eternity together.

"I believe you." Philomena clasped her arms behind his back, basking in his love and caresses. She'd be an utter fool to forfeit this ...

him. "And I love you, too."

With a final searing kiss, he leaned away. "Enough, or I won't be able to stop, and I'm positive tupping my future viscountess in full view of Berkeley Square would go down in history as a marked act of depravity." He winked and bobbed his head toward the window. "Although, I'd wager we'd draw quite a titillated audience."

The street outside bustled with activity. She giggled. "No doubt."

Bradford touched his pocket. "The license is good for three months. Why don't we take it one day at a time? I shall even court you, and you let me know when you are ready."

"No, we wanted to wait three weeks originally, but then Giles coughed up blood." She pushed away from the wall and snared his hand. "I don't want to wait that long."

Darting a quick look over the balustrade—no one lurked below listening to their conversation—she gave him what she hoped was an inviting smile. "Come."

Almost running the corridor's length, their hurried steps muffled by the plush carpet, she made straight for her bedchamber, a bemused Bradford unquestioningly allowing her to lug him along. As she reached for her door latch, misgiving again tried to raise its disagreeable head, but Philomena quelled it with a firm box to the ears.

She would know today which path providence had set her on, and it would be of her own making. Releasing Bradford's hand as she unlatched her door, she smiled over her shoulder.

"Lock it, will you?"

Not waiting for him to answer, she made straight for the ornate panel dressing screen with its charming cherub motif. She started slightly when the door's bolt slid home. Well, at least they wouldn't be walked in on. Most discomfiting that would be if her plans went as she hoped.

"What are you about?" He stood just inside the room, one hand on his slim hip and a crooked, sensual smile that suggested he knew precisely what she intended.

"You'll see."

Would he ever.

Flapping her hand at the overstuffed velvet armchair before the marble hearth, she squashed her romping nerves. Foreign to brazen and seductive conduct, she might very well come across as an inept trull with her first paying customer. "Please make yourself comfortable. I shall be but a few moments."

"That's the ugliest piece of furniture I have ever laid eyes upon." He strode to the chair and, after tossing aside a tasseled throw pillow, sat down.

She quite agreed. The burnt orange and moss green decor, as well as the cumbersome, carved furnishings reflected the duchess's bold taste.

Casting every misgiving aside—well, actually, she tromped atop their pointy little smirking heads—Philomena swept behind the screen. Taking a bracing breath, she bent to remove her footwear.

You can do this.

Faint rustling carried to her from beyond the screen. Bradford must have become restless and wandered the room. Perfectly wonderful. How soon before boredom prompted him to take his leave? She couldn't let him go.

Hurry!

Biting her lip, she tried to, but as often happens when one rushes, she possessed ten thumbs, each of which conspired to prevent her from removing her clothing.

"Dash it all," she mumbled into the dress's folds wadded around her head.

"What's that?" His question sounded distant and muffled.

Was he leaving? No, by George.

Yanking the ribbon from her hair, and still wearing her chemise, she bolted from behind the screen, stubbing her toe on the panel's edge.

Curses.

"Bradford—" Tripping to an abrupt stop, jaw slack, she blinked in disbelief.

Bare-chested, the most tempting smattering of black, curly hair visible above the loudly-colored counterpane draped across his lap, he sat propped in her bed. He gave her a smoldering smile that sent tremors to her toes.

"I didn't think it fair that you should be the only one undressed."

She pressed her hands to the worst of her scars peeking above her lacy neckline. "Are you ... *naked?*"

"Indeed, though I'm wholly disappointed you are not. I'll admit, you are quite fetching in that filmy thing." He feigned a pout, which didn't deter his ravenous examination of her from toe to shoulder before returning to the dark tips showing through the chemise's thin fabric. Slowly, appreciation sharpening the lines of his face, he lifted his gaze to hers.

"Did I misunderstand?"

A jot of uncertainty tempered his voice.

"No. I'd hoped we would ..." Heat crept up her neck to her face. She likely glowed like a fire coal. "After I showed you my burns."

"Come here." He beckoned with one hand while patting the bed with the other.

The intensity of his gaze drew her forward until she stood beside the bed, afraid to look into his eyes, to see rejection there.

He touched the damaged flesh, the pads of his fingers tracing the burns, and she closed her eyes, to both relish in his caress and block out any disgust that might flit across his expression or spark in his eyes.

He whisked her chemise over her head, and she gasped against the rush of cold and abrupt vulnerability.

Refusing to open her eyes, she balled her hands and held her breath ... waiting.

"Philomena, look at me."

Bradford nudged her chin, and she stubbornly shook her head.

"Silly, love." He snaked a well-muscled arm around her waist and had her lying beside him before the air left her lungs in a startled squeak.

"These," he spread his hand over the thick, reddish marks crisscrossing her chest above her breasts, "make me adore you more. My heart, my very soul, aches for what you've suffered, but do not ever entertain the slightest notion that I would spurn you because of them."

A tear leaked from the corner of her eye, and she turned her head away from his tender expression. "They are ugly. I am ugly."

Her nakedness didn't embarrass her, but she found her scars

mortifying. How could she expect him to become accustomed to their hideousness?

Bradford pressed his lips to the disfigurements. "I love you just as you are, whether unblemished or scarred. I want to make you my wife," he flattened his hand over her belly, "fill you with my children, and live every day as if it is our last. I'll never leave you again, never. You have to give me a chance to prove my love. Don't reject me, crush our happiness, and forgo our future out of fear. Please, trust me."

Turning onto her side, Philomena searched his face. Placing her hands on either side of his square jaw, she kissed him with all the pent-up longing and adoration she'd held in check. "I do trust you, and I do want to marry you."

He skimmed his hand the length of her rib, sending a myriad of sparks skittering across her. Squeezing a buttock, he kissed her forehead. "No more doubts?"

"Not a one." She pressed her mouth to the juncture of his throat and neck. His manly smell, slightly spicy but with a hint of musk and tobacco, enveloped her. Nuzzling his neck, she sniffed.

A deep rumble reverberated in his chest as he chuckled. "Here I am trying to seduce you, and you're sniffing me."

"Well, you smell wonderful." She grinned, giving him a coy look, and rested her chin on his chest. "It was I who set out to seduce you. Remember?"

A mock expression of horror swept his face. "Say it isn't so. My future viscountess is a seductress? How splendid."

He cupped her breast and captured her lips in a sizzling kiss.

Groaning, she squirmed, trying to get closer, to press her entire body against his skin. She kicked the sheets aside and leaned into his solid thighs and torso. Exploring his rigid muscles with inexperienced fingers, she mimicked the hot thrusting of his tongue. Her head swam with the force of her passion.

Three sharp raps interrupted their kiss.

Stiffening, Philomena tore her mouth from Bradford's, and he turned his head toward the door.

"Oh dear. I did tell Robins I'd be in my chamber," she whispered, shifting to rise. Bloody awkward, being caught abed by the maid.

"Bradford, Philomena, Reverend Hawksworth has arrived."

The duchess.

Philomena clapped her hand over her mouth and clobbered Bradford with a pillow when he chuckled.

"As luck would have it, he was at White's with Wimpleton." Aunt Muriel's voice shook suspiciously. "When you're finished, please meet us in the drawing room. Don't rush on our account. I've invited him to dinner, so you've plenty of time. Enjoy yourselves."

The duchess's delighted laughter echoed in the corridor.

"Good Lord. She knows." Philomena pressed her hands to her scorching face.

"That's that, then. We must wed at once now. I've utterly ruined you." Bradford pounced on her, pressing her back into the bedding and tickling her ribs.

Giggling, she gasped, "Not utterly, yet."

"Oh, trust me, woman." His hot gaze sank to her breasts. "I mean to compromise you beyond redemption."

Epilogue

Bromham Hall, England
August 1819

"Bradford, look!" A series of stars whipped across the night sky. Philomena leapt from the settee, pointing. "Just like the night we were reunited."

She scooped her infant son from his cradle. Hurrying to the French windows—open to let in the evening's cool air—she kissed his downy head.

"See, Giles? Mama and Papa saw stars like this the night your Uncle Giles, smart man that he was, insisted we wed."

Bradford encircled her from behind and dropped a kiss on her crown. "I owe your brother a debt I'll never be able to repay."

"The same is true of me." Lifting the gurgling infant, happily waving his tiny fists, she brushed her face against his soft, sweet-smelling cheek and closed her eyes. "At least he lived long enough to meet his namesake."

"A miracle, that. I didn't think he'd last the night after his collapse at Wimpleton's ball." He tightened his arms a fraction as he bent to bestow a kiss on their son. "His life was short, but at least his last days were peaceful and painless."

"I'm so grateful he didn't suffer."

Resting against Bradford, Philomena gazed at the clear sky, each star so vibrant, it seemed she could snatch it from the heavens. Another star whizzed past.

"See, there's another. Make a wish." Bradford nudged her head with his chin. "Hurry, before it's too late."

"What could I possibly wish for?" She slanted her head to look at him. "I am already blissfully content."

"Anything, my love." He kissed her nose. "It can only be a boon to our happiness."

"Well, then, what I wish is to couple with you, every day, twice on Sundays, until I'm an ancient, shriveled crone." She chuckled at the image.

"That's a scandalous wish for a lady." He turned her in his embrace, and lowered his head. "But one I'm positive will come true, starting this very moment."

Dearest Reader,

I knew the minute I introduced Bradford in *A Kiss for a Rogue* that one day he'd get his own love story.

Readers adored him and kept asking me about him.

It was time to add another book to The Honorable Rogues® series. Naturally Bradford was my first choice for a hero, and so, *A Rogue's Scandalous Wish* came to be.

Philomena's character was tricky for me. A few years ago, I lost three family members in two separate house fires within ten months, and with a brother and brother-in-law who are fire chiefs (and a sister who is a fire captain) the whole issue of a heroine scarred by fire became very personal.

I hope you enjoy the telling of their story!

Please consider telling other readers why you enjoyed this book by reviewing it. Not only do I truly want to hear your thoughts, reviews are crucial for an author to succeed. **Even if you only leave a line or two, I'd very much appreciate it.**

So, with that I'll leave you.

Here's wishing you many happy hours of reading, more happily ever afters than you can possibly enjoy in a lifetime, and abundant blessings to you and your loved-ones.

About the Author

USA Today Bestselling, award-winning author COLLETTE CAMERON® scribbles Scottish and Regency historicals featuring dashing rogues and scoundrels and the intrepid damsels who re-form them. Blessed with an overactive and witty muse that won't stop whispering new romantic romps in her ear, she's lived in Oregon her entire life, though she dreams of living in Scotland part-time. A self-confessed Cadbury chocoholic, you'll always find a dash of inspiration and a pinch of humor in her sweet-to-spicy timeless romances®.

Explore **Collette's worlds** at www.collettecameron.com!

Join her **VIP Reader Club** and **FREE newsletter**. Giggles guaranteed!

FREE BOOK: Join Collette's The Regency Rose® VIP Reader Club to get updates on book releases, cover reveals, contests and giveaways she reserves exclusively for email and newsletter followers. Also, any deals, sales, or special promotions are offered to club members first. She will not share your name or email, nor will she spam you.

http://bit.ly/TheRegencyRoseGift

Manufactured by Amazon.ca
Bolton, ON

34879792R00184